Party Favors

An Erotic Adventure

JAIME CLEVENGER

BELLA
BOOKS

Bella Books, Inc.
P.O. Box 10543
Tallahassee, FL 32302

First Bella Books Edition 2017

Editor: Amanda Jean
Cover Designer: Judith Fellows

ISBN: 978-1-59493-545-9

Other Books by Jaime Clevenger

Bella Books
The Unknown Mile
Call Shotgun
Whiskey and Oak Leaves
Sign on the Line
Sweet, Sweet Wine
Waiting for a Love Song
Moonstone

Spinsters Ink
All Bets Off

Acknowledgments

Thank you to my fearless first-pass readers, Carla and Courtney, for your comments and encouragement. Thank you, Rachel Calish, for the sage advice. You kept me smiling with the many synonyms for you-know-what. Thank you to my editor, Amanda Jean, for catching the important stuff. And most of all, thank you to Corina. You make everything I write better—and sexier.

Dear Reader,

Welcome to your story. Since you are the main character, there are a few things you should know before you begin. I wish I could meet you in person as I am quite smitten with you. That said, in the ensuing pages, I have placed you in some fairly uncomfortable situations. My apologies. Know that I always have your best intentions at heart. Mostly.

To improve your experience on this adventure, resist the urge to read your story straight through as you would a typical novel. Consider each question and then follow your first impulse down the chosen path. In most cases, you will be satisfied by chapter's end. But not always. All events occur simultaneously, and you can have as many do-overs as you need. Go back in time and change your mind. Or look ahead before you commit. I won't tell anyone you're a peeker.

You are about to meet over a dozen women who want to sleep with you. Some of these women are also sleeping with each other. Tread carefully. The following list may help you keep track of names and roles:

Janine–Your Girlfriend (or Soon-To-Be Ex)
Maxine (Max)–Your Best Friend
Alison–Actress
Katherine–Party Host
Carmen–Pilates Instructor
Amélie–French Model
Mckenzie–Cream Puff Server
Lara–Bartender
Becca–DJ Dee at Rumors (dance club)
Courtney–Dancer at Rumors
Margo–Senior Associate at Your Law Firm
Frankie–Margo's Friend/Liz's Partner
Liz–Margo's Friend/Frankie's Partner
Angie–Your Neighbor

Good luck and enjoy,
Jaime

CHAPTER ONE

You've made a mistake. Not the typographical their-versus-there in an email to a boss sort of mistake, but the life-changing kind of mistake that results in a sixty-dollar Batman costume rental.

One week has passed since you told Janine you thought your relationship needed some breathing room. Things had gotten serious too quickly. Surprisingly, she agreed. But a few days later, you couldn't help wondering if you'd made a mistake. Maybe you didn't need any breathing room. Maybe you only needed Janine. When she called to see if you would still meet her at the fancy dress party you'd both been invited to months ago, you immediately said yes. Unfortunately, you misunderstood a *fancy dress party* to mean a costume party.

Now you stand in the marble entryway of a Victorian mansion in the priciest neighborhood of the city. Everyone is dressed in ball gowns and black ties while you are unmistakably Batman. Costumes have never been your thing, but knowing that this particular party was important to Janine, you splurged.

The complete costume includes Batman's hooded mask that the rental store manager insisted on calling a cowl, a sculpted latex chest piece with upper-arm muscles the Hulk would find impressive, black gloves, a black cape, a yellow utility belt, boot covers, and outer briefs with a molded jock cup. You only had to pick out black Lycra tights that hugged your ass—one attribute that you knew Janine liked—to complete the package.

"May I take your coat?" the doorman asks. His black hair is slicked behind his ears and a faint mustache lines his upper lip. The tux is impeccable, and if you were actually Batman, he could have been your butler. A smile briefly passes his lips as he adds, "I mean, cape?"

"No." What was Batman without the bulletproof cape? There'd be too much Lycra. Your perfectly shaped butt was not going to save you from this evening. "No, thank you. I'm not staying."

Janine texted that she was running late. She'll be pissed if you stand her up, but you'll save your pride if you leave. You spin on your heel and reach for the brass door handle, but before you can turn the handle, the door swings open.

Alison Greer walks in. Alone. Her dark green gown hugs her ample chest and its hem drapes against the marble floor. She slips off a shawl, revealing bare shoulders, and only then looks up to meet your eyes. You've imagined this moment countless times. Well, not exactly this moment, but a chance to catch Alison alone. She always has a date—some hot woman who's out of everyone's league except Alison's—or she's in the center of a crowd of friends. And not once have you managed to say anything more than a hello when someone else has introduced you. She's a regular in one of the big theater companies and has snagged leading roles in everything from Shakespeare to *Rent*. Everyone wants to know her. Or at least be seen with her.

Alison stares at you for a long moment and then, before you can slip past her and out the door, she runs a fingertip up Batman's corded abs. Her coy smile stops you in your tracks.

"Hello, Batman. You make one fine superhero…whoever you are under that mask." She pauses. "When did this become a costume party?"

Alison's hand lingers on your chest. Batman's chest. Your breath is caught in your throat and words fail you. Dark amber eyes are locked on yours. You wonder if she knows the power she holds over you. Her smooth skin is a shade lighter than her dark brown curls. Her curves could stop traffic, but it's her dimples that get you. She's cut her hair short since you last saw her; you blame this, and the jade earrings dangling from perfectly shaped earlobes, for why you can't look away. You are close enough to kiss her full lips, and you wonder if Batman would do just that. But you aren't Batman, and that's unfortunate, because if you were, Alison might actually kiss you back.

"We don't know each other, do we?" Alison asks.

You sense a nervous edge to her voice, as if she's worried that she's flirting with an ex. You shake your head quickly.

"May I take your shawl?" the doorman interjects.

You step aside as Alison hands off the shawl, and then someone calls Alison's name. You both turn at the sound. The host of the party, Katherine Flaggerty, stands in the hallway with two glasses of white wine. If money were a sign of age, then Katherine would be ancient. But she's only thirty-seven and youthful at that. No crow's feet dare to mar her tan complexion. Good genetics, or the time she regularly spends at the day spa for facials and massages, are paying off.

Katherine inherited millions from her late mother and then invested in stocks as if she'd had an insider's advantage at every deal. Word is that every company she picks becomes the next hot thing a day later. Aside from the stock market, Katherine has two other well-known passions: fitness and women. You both have memberships at the same gym, and you've had a chance to appreciate her dedication on both the elliptical and the stair climber. Her body is a testament to the personal attention she's given it, and on more than one occasion you've fantasized about giving her muscles some of *your* personal attention. The black gown she's picked for the evening dips low in the back to show off every finely crafted muscle. Her blond hair falls in soft waves to just below the nape of her neck. According to Janine, a stipulation of Katherine's inheritance was that she be married before she received the money. Although no one ever sees the phantom husband, she wears a square ruby on her fourth finger as proof.

Katherine glances first at you and then at Alison. "Are you two together?" Her eyebrows arch.

Alison turns to you rather than answer. Her lips part, and you stare at each other for one moment too long. You've imagined kissing her a thousand times—and much more than kissing. A thrill races down your chest and warms the place between your legs, reminding you of the fantasy. You manage a step back, figuratively and literally, from Alison Greer, hoping that she doesn't guess any of your thoughts, and you meet Katherine's gaze.

"I was just leaving," you say quickly. "Wrong party."

"Of course you can't leave," Katherine says. "Nothing even remotely interesting ever happens at these events, and I'm always wondering why. Clearly I need to change the dress code."

Before you can argue, the door opens again and Janine walks in. She's wearing a red dress with a slit clear up to her thigh, showing off the length of her sculpted legs, and she's been to the salon to add a red streak to her usual light brown locks. Your first thought is whether or not she's wearing underwear. Janine looks you up and down, and then recognition crosses her face. Her nails are manicured and her lipstick is perfect. She cocks her head, and you feel sick as she says your name punctuated by a question mark.

You raise your hand in a timid wave, melting on the inside. Tonight could not have gone more wrong.

"Why are you dressed like that?" Janine asks. Her brusque German accent is even sharper than usual.

"We're not sure, but I've already told her that she has to stay," Katherine answers. She turns to Alison and hands her one of the wine glasses. "I wanted to snatch you up before the rest of the crowd has you cornered. There's someone I want to introduce you to." Katherine slips her arm through Alison's. She glances again at you and sweeps an air finger up from your briefs to your cowl. "That costume is really quite perfect. For something. Come find me later and tell me where you found it." Katherine turns and leads Alison down the tiled marble hallway.

Janine hands her coat to the doorman who now has a wide grin plastered on his face. But he's not laughing at you. Yet. You start for the door.

"Oh, no, you aren't leaving," Janine orders. Her pale skin reddens when she is upset. Or embarrassed. Tonight you've probably managed to make her feel both simultaneously. Her cheeks are scarlet.

You straighten your shoulders and face Janine. Chin up, you think silently. *This can't get any worse.* Behind Janine, you see Alison. She's halfway down the hall, but she's paused to glance over her shoulder and meet your gaze.

Do you:
A) Face up to Janine and stay because you need a glass of champagne and your night can't get any worse (read on)
B) Leave the party with a wave of your cape and an ounce of dignity (go to Chapter Nine, page 146)

Face up to Janine and stay

"You said fancy dress. I thought that was some German way of saying this was a costume party—not a formal dinner party." You hold out your arms in exasperation. The black polyester of your cape swirls and then resettles around your body. "Everyone's in ball gowns and I'm…"

"Who cares what everyone else is wearing?" Janine touches your cheek. The tenderness in her gesture catches you off guard. "I like what you're wearing."

You shrug off her hand. "I'm dressed up as Batman, Janine." Stating the obvious has never felt so painful.

"Clearly it was a simple misunderstanding. I'll tell everyone it's the language barrier."

"You speak fluent English."

"I wasn't talking about me. But everyone can blame the German woman for the little misunderstanding. And since you make a very handsome Batman"—she pauses to adjust the collar of your cape—"no one will mind that you are in costume."

"I look like an idiot."

"Not at all. You look ready to save the city from horrible villains." Janine smiles. "Maybe you could save me first."

"This really isn't funny."

"Maybe Katherine could loan you something else to wear. I'm sure she has a closet full of dresses. Or maybe her husband has a tux lying around."

"Katherine's husband?"

"He travels a lot, but maybe he keeps some clothes here. Or you can borrow one of Katherine's gowns. You two are almost the same size." Janine glances at the doorman and then down the hallway to the crowded ballroom. She turns back to you and touches your chest. Batman's chest. Her index finger trails down to your utility belt and a smile edges her lips. "Still, I'd rather you stay dressed like that. Are you hiding anything in these pockets?" Janine unsnaps one of the pockets on your utility belt and fishes out your cell phone. "I wonder who Batman calls."

Janine is one of Katherine's financial advisors. She doesn't talk shop much, but you know that she's hoping to pick up new clients by rubbing elbows with Katherine's friends tonight. She hands your phone back without checking to see who you've called. Maybe she decided she didn't want to know. You snap the pocket on your utility belt and clear your throat. "Look, I know this party is important for your work. Networking, connections and all of that. You really want to be seen with me like this?"

"I've been thinking about work too much lately. Maybe I should take the night off," Janine says.

The classical music coming from the ballroom is overtaken by the sound of your heartbeat when Janine suddenly steps forward to kiss you. But she stops a half an inch away from your lips. You can smell her faint perfume. Her eyes meet yours. She presses her fingertip to your lips and then pulls away, sighing softly.

"I told myself I wouldn't kiss you," she says. "I thought we were going to break up tonight...and then you do this." Janine starts to laugh. "What am I supposed to do with you now?"

The breath slips out of your chest. That's what Janine does to you. You square your shoulders and straighten up only to glimpse your reflection in the mirrored display cabinet behind the doorman. Batman stares back at you. Even your reflection is silently passing judgment. "This is ridiculous. I can't stay at the party like this." You hold up the edge of your cape. "No one does capes anymore."

Janine smiles. "But they should."

"How about we meet up tomorrow at the café?"

"No. I want you to stay." Janine catches your gloved hand. She squeezes the foam on your fake arm muscles. "I love that you're Batman tonight. Otherwise I would take you too seriously."

The door opens and two straight couples come in. You were silently hoping someone else would show up in costume—humiliation loves company. But the men are in tuxes and the women are in ball gowns. The couples stop to hand off coats to the doorman, pretending not to stare at you.

Janine ignores the audience. "You know what I thought when I first walked in the door? *Damn, Batman is so much more sexy than Superman.*" She keeps her hold on your arm but shifts her body closer. Her breath is warm against your neck. "I've never seen you stand quite like that. Or look more out of reach. So tempting. And the way Alison and Katherine were eyeing you...you didn't seem to mind the attention." Her eyebrow arches.

You long to press into her lips, but when you step forward, her hand presses on your chest. She shakes her head. You touch her shoulder and then run your hand down her side, pausing for a moment at her waist before slipping over her hip. You find the edge of the fabric where the slit opens, and your fingertips play against her thigh. Janine glances down at your hand. It would be easy to hike the cloth up past her hips, and you're wet with the thought of doing exactly that. You know exactly how she likes to be touched, and your body is begging to feel her against you.

Janine doesn't move away from you. Instead, she leans forward until you feel the rise and fall of her chest. She tilts her face up to yours.

"Just because I think you're hot doesn't mean I'm going to let you kiss me," she says.

"Why not?"

"Because *you* wanted to slow things down." Janine takes a step back and glances over at the audience. The doorman's mouth is gaping wide. The two couples are still in the entryway. Staring. Janine looks back at you. "This past week has made me do a lot of thinking. About us." She pauses. "And whether or not we should be together."

"You want to break up?"

"That's not what I'm saying," Janine argues.

You wait for her to continue, but she doesn't. "Tell me what you want." Angry tears press at the corners of your eyes, but you clench your jaw to hold them back. You rub your eyes through the mask, hoping Janine will think it's only frustration.

"I've had a lot of time to think, but it wasn't until I saw you tonight that I realized what I needed," Janine says.

You clear your throat and force a smile. "It's the outfit, isn't it?"

"No. But maybe it helps." She touches your lips with her fingertip. "I hate how much I want to kiss you right now. And I've been thinking—why'd we get together in the first place? You're smart. Funny. But not too funny." She smiles. "We have the best conversations in bed. And you're hot. I even like the way you smell. That cologne you wear sometimes…But is that enough?"

"I could wear more cologne."

"I'm serious. When I first met you, I thought it was perfect. We're practically neighbors. We have some of the same friends. We like the same café. You even have good taste in music…But then I started to worry that maybe we were dating because it was easy. Convenient. Now I don't know if you really want me or if I'm just easy. When you tell me you love me, do you mean it? You say you love a lot of things."

"Ouch."

"I'm not criticizing. I'm being honest. And maybe this sounds crazy, but don't you wonder the same thing sometimes?" She doesn't wait for you to answer. "So, then I thought, what if tonight we aren't exclusive? We said we'd take a week off, and tonight's the last night. We're at Katherine's party. We both know there will be available women. What would happen if we kissed anyone we wanted to kiss? Dance with anyone, go home with anyone…What if anything goes tonight?"

"You're serious?"

"Completely. I want you to be sure that I'm the right one. And I want to be sure about you. Think of tonight as a fun little challenge. Flirt with someone right in front of me." Janine motions to a group of women in the ballroom. Backs are turned to you and they're too far away to hear their conversation, but you can't imagine flirting with any of them. Not now. "Try to make me jealous. I'll let you off the hook because I'll be doing the same thing. Then tomorrow we meet at the café and decide if we want to be exclusive."

"What if one of us meets someone tonight and that changes how we feel about *us* tomorrow?"

"It's possible," she agrees. "And it's also possible that we'll realize how much we like each other."

An hour ago, standing in front of your bathroom mirror as you brushed your teeth, you might have had a perfect rebuttal. Some argument to convince Janine that you don't need her to make you jealous and that you're ready to do anything to be exclusive. Unfortunately, she has a point. You started dating her because it was easy. Convenient. And maybe that's why she dated you. But that can't be the reason that you stay together. Your stomach is balled up tight. If you need to break up, she's giving you the perfect out. But you want to kiss her more than you want to say good-bye.

"Okay, maybe you're right," you say. "Maybe it wouldn't hurt if we both flirted with someone else tonight. But sex?"

"If it happens, it happens. We're both single tonight," Janine replies. "Are you jealous already?"

"Yes."

"Good." She brushes her hand across your cheek. "I know it won't take long for you to make me jealous, too."

"That sounds like a dare."

"It is." Janine smiles. "Go find someone to kiss. I'd wish you luck, but I know you won't need it. I'll see you at the café tomorrow."

The other couples step aside as she passes. You watch her hips sway down the hallway and then catch the doorman watching as well. You're tempted to call him out on ogling your girlfriend, but she isn't yours tonight.

The doorman grins when you look over at him. "There goes trouble," he says.

"Tell me about it." You take a deep breath as Janine disappears into the crowded ballroom. You glance over at the doorman again. He's an inch or two taller than you but otherwise slim and about your build. "Any chance you have a spare uniform?"

"No, but my manager might. She's outside running security." The doorman taps his ear and then speaks into a small microphone under his jacket lapel. He looks up and shakes his head. "Sorry. Out of luck. Anyway, I'd keep the Batman gig up if I were you."

Do you:
A) Gather your Batman bravado and walk into the ballroom (read on to Chapter Two)
B) Go find Katherine and beg for a change of clothes (go to Chapter Four, page 52)

CHAPTER TWO

Gather your Batman bravado and walk into the ballroom

Katherine's ballroom has more square footage than most houses. As you look closer, you discover it's actually two rooms with a collapsing wall in the middle. The middle wall has been opened up to make the one large space. Across the room from where you stand, a robust fire crackles in a huge marble fireplace. The love seats surrounding the fireplace are all filled with guests, none of whom are in costume. A series of round banquet tables set for the dinner are on the left side of the room, and on the right is a bartender's stand. A handful of guests sit clustered around one of the banquet tables, but most everyone else is mingling at the other end of the room by the bartenders.

The walls and most of the ceiling are covered in a glossy dark oak and a chandelier hangs in the center of the room. Below the chandelier is a grand piano and a woman in a long black gown sits at the bench, her hands flowing over the keys. Debussy's "Clair De Lune." You assumed the classical music was a soundtrack piped in through a stereo system, but of course Katherine Flaggerty would pay for a pianist.

A waiter passes with a tray of champagne glasses, and you help yourself to one. You sip slowly, counting on a headache later if you were to follow your impulse and pound the bubbling wine.

The waiter makes it only a few more steps before he's stopped by the two couples you remember seeing in the foyer—the ones who couldn't stop staring at you and Janine. One of the women glances over at you and then quickly turns back to the group's conversation. She seems familiar and you stare a moment, trying to place her. Dark brown hair is pulled up in a bun that shows off her slender neck. A clingy dark orange dress complements her olive complexion, and you can't bring yourself to look away from her perfect curvy figure. The short cut of the dress reveals toned legs that go on forever. Diamonds sparkle on her fingers and ears. Your best friend Max would call her "expensive."

Then it hits you. Pilates. You feel your stomach tighten and glance away, hoping she won't recognize you or realize you've been staring too long. Carmen teaches the Pilates class at your gym. You have to get to the gym fifteen minutes early to save a spot for her class.

The pianist has moved on from Debussy's light and delicate notes to a more serious tone. Handel. The composer is always the easy part to place, you think, straining to remember the name of the piece. Your old piano teacher would be disappointed. Across the room you see Janine chatting with Katherine, and then as you watch them, they both turn and look your way. You swallow and force a smile. Clearly they were talking about you.

As you glance back at Carmen, you wish she could be someone you don't know. Some other hot Latina woman who you didn't already have a crush on. Maybe you could meet Janine's challenge with a stranger. Carmen's eyes flash in your direction and you look away. The three people standing next to Carmen are talking animatedly, but she seems distracted. Finally she says something to the man closest to her and then turns and starts walking straight toward you. You glance around, wondering if perhaps she has a friend near you, but no one is within ten feet of your spot.

"Do we know each other?" Carmen asks. "I didn't want you to think I was staring because of your costume. It isn't that. Or because of what happened in the entryway. It isn't that either. I just couldn't help but think that your voice sounded familiar. That you look familiar…"

So much for the disguise. "Pilates. I take your Tuesday and Thursday night class."

"That's right! I knew I recognized you. You're always in my back row."

"Only because your classes are full. It took me a minute to recognize you too. You look different with your hair up. I mean, you look good. Not just different." Carmen laughs. You're certain that you're blushing, but at least the mask will cover that. "And that dress is fabulous, by the way."

"Well, thank you," Carmen says. "Your costume is fabulous as well."

"Tonight I'm the wrong kind of fabulous."

"At one of Katherine's parties, anything goes."

You think of Janine's words and clench your teeth. Janine is still chatting with Katherine across the room.

Carmen continues, "The mask did make it hard for me to recognize you. It drives me crazy when I can't place someone… Are you friends with Katherine?"

"Acquaintances. My girlfriend is one of her financial advisors."

"Was that who you were talking to in the foyer?"

You nod. "But I probably shouldn't call her my girlfriend. We're trying some time apart."

"I know firsthand that Katherine has very good financial advisors, but that doesn't mean I'd recommend dating any of them. Or anyone on her payroll, for that matter."

"Sounds like that comes from experience."

"My husband is Katherine's lawyer." She points to the man she'd come in with. Then she points to the man standing next to him and adds, "His best friend is on her team of financial advisors. They are both very good at what they do. Making money, making their own rules…and making themselves look good. As it turns out, those qualities aren't necessarily good for long-term relationships." Carmen watches her husband. Something he's said has made the woman standing next to him laugh. After a moment, Carmen seems to remember you. She adds, "The good news is that this is the last time I have to come to a function with my husband."

"Why's that?"

"We sign divorce papers on Monday." Carmen smiles. "God, that feels good to say aloud. So, tonight I intend to make the best of a bad situation."

From Carmen's tone, you wonder if she was the one to decide on the divorce. She certainly isn't disappointed. "I wish I could do the same. But how do you make the best of a bad situation dressed up as Batman?"

Carmen laughs. "I'm dying to ask why you're wearing that."

"It was a misunderstanding. Janine's German and I thought she meant a costume party when she said fancy dress...and I was hoping to win her back tonight. So I decided to go all out. We've been talking about breaking up. Or moving in together."

"And so you decided on Batman?" Carmen covers her mouth, trying hard not laugh at you. Again.

"I know. You can laugh. But check out my biceps."

Carmen squeezes your foam arms. "Impressive. I really can't imagine why your girlfriend would let you slip away."

"Tell me about it." You find yourself laughing along with Carmen. She always has a way of making you relax in class. And she's doing the same thing here but the purely professional vibe is gone. For the first time you'd swear that she's interested in you. Unfortunately her timing is off. You're still distracted with Janine. "Can I ask you something?"

"Of course."

"Janine dared me to kiss whoever I want tonight."

"Interesting dare," Carmen says.

"And she gets to kiss whoever she wants," you add. "We're supposed to try to make each other jealous. But I have a feeling she's going to win this game. And I'm not sure if I should take the dare at all. Maybe it's a trick?"

"Jealousy is a waste of time," Carmen says. "No one is going to win that game. How much do you like her?"

"I thought I liked her a lot. I don't know. Janine has me wondering if maybe we only got together because it was convenient. But we get along great. Sex is good. Why break up?"

"Are you in love?"

You hesitate. "I'm not sure. Maybe? Sometimes I think love is overrated."

"I don't agree," Carmen says. "But then again, I'm the soon-to-be-divorced one who definitely should not be handing out relationship advice."

"Or you're the perfect person."

"Show me your girlfriend," Carmen says.

You point out Janine across the ballroom.

"I recognize her," Carmen says. "You said she's a financial advisor for Katherine? I wonder how closely they work together."

Your throat tightens at Carmen's suggestion. Katherine and Janine look comfortable together. Maybe too comfortable. The champagne cools the burn in the back of your throat and you suck down half the glass. "She looks happy, doesn't she? Clearly she doesn't need me. I thought I needed her, but now I'm wondering if maybe I was only lonely. And bored. And she was convenient." Katherine and Janine are laughing. Janine leans close to say something in Katherine's ear. You feel a jealous pang at the sight of Katherine's hand settling on Janine's hip. The touch is almost too friendly and you think of Carmen's words again. "Damn, I'm already jealous. I should walk over there and tell her she's won the contest."

"No. If Katherine's part of it, you can't be jealous."

"It's hard to control jealousy."

"Well, there is one secret," Carmen says. She leans in and whispers, "Fuck someone else."

You laugh too loudly and have to cover with a cough when someone from Carmen's group glances your direction.

"I'm serious," Carmen says. "One night with someone new and you'll forget about the jealousy."

"That's not exactly fair to whoever I hook up with."

"You'd be surprised how many women only want a hookup. Especially in this crowd." Carmen continues, "But if that's your plan, you better stop moping in the corner. There's a lot of available women here. I could point out a few."

"I'm not moping," you argue. "I'm being elusive."

"In that costume?" Carmen brushes fuzz off the polyester cape and lets her hand linger on your shoulder. "Do you have a type?"

"Not really. Janine, I guess." You glance at the spot where you'd last seen Janine and Katherine. They've both moved, but you find Janine in a new crowd of women. With ease she's joined in on the conversation and soon has everyone laughing. Always the extrovert. You love the fact that Janine can make you laugh. She's waving her arms animatedly and the crowd is hanging on every word. One of Janine's coworkers at the investment firm, Sarah Mackey, hands her a glass of wine. You see a look pass between Janine and Sarah and can only wonder at its meaning. Sarah is in her late twenties, sexy and single. Whether or not she's straight has been up for discussion for the past few months since she joined the firm.

Carmen turns your chin until you're looking right at her. Her touch sends a bolt through you. "I'm afraid you need an intervention. Stop worrying about what she does, who she talks to. Drink champagne and enjoy the party. Don't think about her at all. Don't even look at her. Look at someone new instead."

"Is that your plan as well?"

"That depends on you."

Carmen has your full attention. It isn't the diamond jewelry or the designer dress that fits perfectly. It's something less tangible. Her eyes hold you captive, and the desire to kiss her is mounting. When you raise your glass of champagne, Carmen clinks her drink against yours.

"You've got nice abs, by the way. I can't compliment you in class without it sounding like a come-on, but in that outfit…"

"Now it doesn't sound like a come-on at all." You rub your hand over Batman's six pack. "Wish I could claim them."

"I like the real ones you're hiding under there even more. And since we're on the subject, I'll add that I always enjoy tapping your ass into the correct position."

"I hadn't noticed," you lie.

"Was it that obvious?" Carmen's cheeks flush.

"Only once." You grin. "But then I talked myself into thinking I was crazy. Now I know better. And I'm guilty of a few indiscretions as well. It's possible I've enjoyed more than a few things about my Pilates instructor. After seeing you in that dress, I have to say that the jogging pants you wear in class don't do you justice."

"You really should be paying more attention in class."

The way Carmen leans in makes you ready to admit everything you've noticed about her. Noticed and enjoyed. But she is still your Pilates teacher, and since you plan on attending her class next week, you decide to play it safe. "I pay very close attention."

"Then I'll consider asking you for fashion advice the next time I pick out my workout attire."

"I'd be happy to help."

Carmen smiles. You sip your champagne and wonder at how easy it is to flirt with the same Pilates teacher whose name you've cursed as you sweated through her plank torture. Your champagne glass is only half-empty, but you already feel a warm buzz.

"Katherine does have a lovely house," you say. "Clearly someone she has on her payroll is doing something right."

"It's not anyone on her payroll. It's Katherine. She's an incredibly sharp businesswoman. When she inherited this house, it was a mess. She's redone this place from top to bottom along with the rest of the family business. Since I've known her, she's picked up a villa in Spain, a beach house in St. Martin, a cabin in Aspen...And she has no trouble with cash flow. Sometimes I think she has the perfect life." Carmen sighs. She scans the room as if she's looking for Katherine now. "And she's always a generous host."

"I like that this place still has the original décor. So many of these old mansions have been completely remodeled. People with too much money and no sense of character." You tap your hand against the wood-paneled wall. "This one is vintage."

"You should see the rest of the house. I'd give you a tour if I could, but she locks up the other half of the house when she has these events. Of course I don't blame her for keeping the bedrooms private."

You spot Katherine then. She's near the bartender's table talking with a couple. You glance at Carmen and realize she's also found Katherine and is watching her carefully. "Are you close friends with Katherine?"

"Very close."

"Lovers?"

"What I usually say is that we've known each other for a long time. My husband has been her lawyer for years, and Katherine's made us feel like part of her family." She eyes the group she left. The man she came in with is talking to the other man gesturing animatedly, and the woman is laughing on cue. "I always enjoy seeing this place done up for a party. There's something about this house. It has a special feel. I think that's why Katherine stays here."

Of course Carmen and Katherine are lovers. Somehow you hadn't guessed that earlier, but now the familiarity you've noticed between them in the Pilates class makes sense. But Carmen seems ready to have more than one lover. "I've only seen the ballroom, but I can't say that I'd mind living here."

"My favorite part is the backyard. Katherine's garden is amazing. She has a koi pond with a stream leading down to a gazebo. And there's the pool with the waterfall…"

"I'd love to see it," you say.

Suddenly Katherine is standing next to you. "What would you love to see?" she asks. Katherine meets Carmen's gaze and smiles. "Why am I not surprised that you've found the most interesting guest here?"

"Jealous?" Carmen sips her champagne. "I was just thinking of stealing her for a moment to show off your gardens. I noticed you'd lit up the gazebo."

"And I turned the heaters on," Katherine adds. "It is a lovely night out there. But I'm not sure that I'll let you take her quite yet. I've just heard a secret about our Batman."

"Oh?" Always your first strategy—you stall. You take a slow sip of your champagne. Katherine's eyes are steady on yours. What could Janine have possibly told Katherine?

Katherine continues, "Apparently you play the piano. And according to Janine, you play very well. Since I implicitly trust everything Janine tells me, I'm wondering what I need to do to convince you to play a song or two. Ingrid, the pianist, requested a bathroom break on the hour."

"I'm not—"

"Janine warned me," Katherine interrupts. "She said you wouldn't agree without some arm twisting. But I prefer offering an incentive."

Although you're tempted to ask, Katherine's incentives probably won't be worth humiliating yourself any more than you already have tonight. "I haven't played any classical pieces in a long time. Not since high school."

"Play something else then," Katherine insists. "Two or three songs should be enough for Ingrid to have her break. And when I reward good behavior, I make it worth it."

Good behavior? The look in Katherine's eyes is enough to have you ready to sign up for anything, but you don't like the fact that she seems used to getting whatever she asks for. You glance at Carmen and feel a tug. You're nearly guaranteed a kiss if you accept her invitation to a garden tour.

Do you:
A) Go for a garden tour, hoping to do more than smell the roses (read on)
B) Agree to play the piano (go to Chapter Three, page 31)

Go for a garden tour

Why Janine decided to share your piano hobby with Katherine is a mystery—and one that you don't feel like solving at the moment. But now you need to gracefully decline Katherine's invitation, and saying no to a beautiful woman has never been your strong suit. Still, when you weigh Carmen's offer over sitting down at the piano in costume, the choice is clear.

"As much as I'd love to try out your piano, I don't think tonight's the night."

"Janine tells me you're very talented." Katherine's voice has a distinct purr. "You're certain I can't convince you?"

"I'm sure."

Katherine sighs. "I had to try." She taps her glass of wine against Carmen's champagne glass. "Find me later."

As soon as Katherine walks away, Carmen turns to you and says, "Not many women say no to Katherine. I'm impressed."

You let out the breath you'd been holding. "I have a feeling I'm going to pay for it later."

"Not at all. She'll probably respect you more for turning her down."

"I'm more worried about what Janine will say."

Carmen touches your arm. "I thought we were forgetting about her for a while."

"I might need some help."

Carmen sips her champagne. "Let's go get some air." She points to a narrow doorway behind the dessert buffet table. "There's more than one way to get to the gardens, but we can sneak through the study and no one will notice. I love all the secret passageways in this house."

As you pass the group Carmen came to the party with, Carmen flashes a smile and waves. The smile is clearly fake. Her husband looks at you briefly and then turns his attention back to the woman at his side.

Carmen leads you down a hallway to a dimly lit study. An oil lamp casts a warm glow on an oversized desk. Behind the desk are a pair of French doors, and beyond these is a brick patio with a fountain in the center. The spray of water catches the light of the colorful swinging lanterns overhead. Carmen opens one of the doors and steps outside, waiting for you.

The cool night air is a welcome sensation. Statues dot the corners of the patio and terracotta pots overflowing with flowers rim the border. Carmen points to a path leading down a slope to a gazebo. A stream winds alongside the path and small footbridges pass over the stream every twenty yards or so. As you follow the path you pass a swimming pool. A waterfall backlit in blue spills out of the hot tub on the slope above the pool. Soon the stream opens up to a koi pond. Beside the pond is an enclosed white gazebo with glass windows and a glass door. A string of white lights has the gazebo glowing like a Christmas tree.

Carmen hesitates after she reaches for the door handle. She glances up the hill to the house. From here, the scene in the ballroom is fuzzy. Figures passing by the windows cast long shadows. Faces are blurred.

"Everything okay?"

"I was going to ask you the same thing." Carmen sighs. "Maybe we both needed to get out of that ballroom."

"You saved me from humiliating myself on the piano. And offered something I didn't want to pass up."

"Sometimes I feel like I can't breathe when I'm in the same room as my ex. Almost-ex."

"Was he cheating on you first?" You hope your question won't upset Carmen. "With that other woman that you came with?"

"How'd you guess they were together?"

"Her laugh. The way you looked at the two of them."

"It wasn't always so obvious." Carmen opens the door to the gazebo. "And to answer your first question—who cheated first? I don't know. I think maybe it happened at the same time. One night. But there've been many nights since."

"And you and Katherine? How long were you together?"

"Oh, we were never together. Not like you're thinking. Katherine is never really with anyone."

Carmen walks inside the gazebo. When you follow her, a warm blast of air greets you. You pull off your Batman mask and rustle your hand through your hair. Potted trees and plants line most of the walls and the foliage fills many of the windows, making it seem as if you've just stepped inside a jungle greenhouse. In the center of the room two wicker sofas and a set of wicker chairs face a wicker coffee table. On one wall there's a small bar set up, and on the wall opposite the door there's a cabinet with a record player. Tiny lights twinkle against the glass outside. "This is nice."

"A private oasis." Carmen looks over at you. "I feel like I should be honest with you. Katherine and I have slept together off and on for the past three years. But when you ask how long we've been together—never."

"She likes the single married life?"

"She enjoys more than one lover." Carmen adds, "Conveniently, Katherine's husband is of a like mind. They have the perfect arrangement. I only wish my almost-ex would be so understanding. It would save so much paperwork."

"Do you think he'll notice that you slipped away?"

"He will. But he doesn't care. We haven't slept together in ages. All I agreed to do tonight was show up for appearance's sake." Carmen pulls the pins out of her bun, and her dark brown hair cascades down to her shoulders. She tucks a few stray strands behind her ear and then walks over to the gazebo door. She turns the lock and then leans against the doorframe, eyeing you. "Any more questions?"

You shake your head.

"Good. I'd rather talk about something else tonight." Carmen steps toward you. Her hands settle on your shoulders. "Or not talk at all."

Her lips are inches from yours as she unties your cape. The polyester ripples to the ground and her hands slip down your arms until she finds the gloves. She pulls them off one at a time.

"I would have liked to watch you play the piano. You have beautiful hands."

"Maybe I can play something for you later. After the crowd's gone."

Carmen touches the Batman insignia on your chest and then her finger slides down your front. She hooks your belt, tugging the clasp. "Can I convince you to take off more of this costume?"

"You're doing pretty well without my help."

Once she's pulled the belt off, she lets it dangle in the air for a moment. "I've watched you in class so many times..." The metal buckle clangs on the cement floor when she drops it. "And wondered if I could ever distract you. But I never thought to try."

"Why not?"

"You seemed focused on the workout," Carmen says.

"You're a good instructor. I'm always focused."

"I suppose I should be flattered." You feel a magnetic pull as she turns and walks away. She sets her glass down on one of the wicker end tables and then skims her hand over the sofa cushions as she glances back at you. "Music?"

"Sure."

An old record player is positioned against the back wall. Carmen thumbs through a pile of records until she decides on one. She slips the record out of its sleeve and carefully sets it on the turntable. The sound crackles, but then slow jazz fills the room.

"Katherine's taste," Carmen admits. She looks up from the record player. "It's rubbing off on me."

"Seems like Katherine can be influential."

"She is. In good ways and in bad." Carmen smiles and walks over to you. "Now, where were we?"

She lifts your hands up to her shoulders and then moves into your embrace. Her lips meet yours and the kiss deepens. You let your hands explore Carmen's body as she kisses you. The fabric of the orange dress is thin enough to easily find her curves underneath, and you feel a rush letting your hand travel down her back, over her hips and back to the round of her butt. Her tongue slips into your mouth and she moves against you, her breasts bumping against the padded Batman chest.

Without stopping the kisses, Carmen unties the chest plate and you slip it off. Under this, you're wearing a long-sleeve, tight-fitting black shirt. Her hands trail up and down your arms—nothing like the way she's touched you at the gym. Lips brush against your neck. The more she touches you, the closer you are to forgetting about the party in the mansion up the hill. And you long to feel her with no clothing between you.

"You know, I am going to have trouble keeping my hands to myself the next time you're in my class," Carmen says.

"Well, my positions do need a lot of corrections. You could put your hands all over me and you'd have a good excuse."

"Don't tempt me."

"Maybe I should set up a private class. One-on-one instruction."

"Katherine does keep a yoga mat out here." She looks over at the back corner of the room. A weight bench and a stationary bike are pushed against the wall, along with a rack of weights. "I'm sure she wouldn't mind if we borrowed it. But I'll need you naked for this class."

"Oh, really?" You laugh.

Carmen nods. Her expression is just as serious as it is during class. She slips her hands under your shirt. The next song begins and her hips sway to the music as she traces the curve of your bra. She follows the strap until she has it unhooked and then pulls off your shirt and bra in one move. With a smug look she draws a line down your belly. Her lips are soft and they brush against yours as if she's testing you. Not quite kissing you. The sensation leaves you tingling with want. You step forward, and the next kiss is deep. She moves into your arms. Through the thin gown, you can feel her nipples harden. She isn't wearing a bra. Carmen steps back from you and exhales.

"It's warm in here, isn't it?" She fans herself. "I think Katherine has those heaters turned up hoping she'd get someone to strip."

"I wouldn't mind taking off your dress."

"I don't think a student should be undressing their teacher," Carmen returns.

"And in what class does the teacher undress the students?"

"This class." Carmen clears her throat. "We'll start with a little work on your core. And I'll need you on your back for that."

"So, you want me naked and on my back. Was that spread eagle?"

"I haven't heard of that Pilates exercise," Carmen says. "But we could work on it."

She heads to the far side of the gazebo and pulls out a purple yoga mat. "Over here," she says, unrolling the mat on the tile. "And why are you still wearing those pants?"

You pull off the boots but hesitate with the pants. With the heat blasting you're more comfortable stripped down, but Carmen's still fully clothed.

"Don't worry, I've seen you naked before. The shower at the gym. You weren't modest then." Carmen winks. "Strip."

You don't mind Carmen ordering you to strip or the look in her eyes as her gaze travels over your body. Her desire has you eager to please. The pants come off as she watches, and she looks impatient when you tug off your underwear slowly. As you straighten up, her gaze appraises your body.

"Good," she says. "Now lie down."

You lean in to kiss her, but she turns and you only get her cheek.

She clears her throat. "On your back."

She's told you to lie down on your back before, of course, but you've never been naked. Reluctantly, you drop down to the mat. On your back, you keep your knees bent and fold your hands to partly cover your otherwise exposed middle. Carmen's gaze tracks to your hands.

"Nervous?"

You shake your head. But that isn't exactly the truth. You can see that she's scheming something. Naked, you're at a disadvantage. Still, you don't want to stand up and go for your clothes. Carmen plays a good game.

"You shouldn't be. You have nothing to worry about. I take very good care of my students." She walks around the mat, her heels clicking on the tile floor, and pulls out a wide foam roller from behind the weight bench. "I wish Katherine kept more equipment in here, but I think this is all we have to work with." She leans down and runs a cool fingertip over your knee. "It's a shame I can't have you naked in every class."

"You don't think you'd be distracted?"

"Not at all. I'm very good at focusing. And always staying professional." Carmen takes off her heels. You watch as she unzips the orange dress. The material slips off her body and you swallow hard, feeling the muscles in your groin clench.

"I don't think I'd be able to focus in class if my teacher was naked."

"You're going to have to try this time." Carmen kneels down next to you and pushes away your hand when you reach out to touch her. "I do the touching at the moment."

"That's not fair."

"Who said this was going to be fair?" Carmen moves to your feet, stretching each leg until you're flat on the mat. Then her hands travel from your ankles up to your thighs as she bends your knees. She leans over you and slips her hands under your butt, adjusting the position of your hips. Her lips brush below your belly button, barely kissing you. Her face is close enough to your groin that you can feel her breath. She straightens up but keeps one hand on you, just above the line of your short-trimmed hair. "I do love correcting your positions. Now tighten your abs and try a pelvic curl."

Raising your hips off the mat, you hold the pelvic curl for a second and then eye her full breasts. Carmen cocks her head when you drop the position and sit up. Patiently following her orders is simple in class, but here you can't make your body slow down and you're hungry for another kiss.

"That wasn't what I asked for," she chides.

"I know."

"I don't think you're focusing on your core." She tilts your chin up, shifting your gaze away from her breasts and then brushes her fingertip across your lips before pushing you back on the mat. She leans over you and kisses you hard.

When her lips pull away, you're out of breath and ready for more. "I don't think you're helping me focus."

Carmen straddles your hips, her naked thighs on either side of you. You reach up to caress her breasts, and she moves into your hand. "Try another pelvic curl." Her tongue slips over her lips. She can't hide how much she wants you. "Slow this time. I want to feel every muscle contract."

Seeing Carmen's desire makes you ready to follow her orders. You clench your belly into a tight washboard under her hands and then raise your groin up to meet hers one inch at a time. Her wetness mingles with yours as you hold the position until your muscles are shaking.

"Good," she says. "Now lower your hips slowly down to the mat. And repeat."

"How many times do I get to do that?"

"Until I tell you to stop," Carmen says. Her eyes narrow.

You try to focus on another slow pelvic curl, but Carmen distracts you with a kiss. Her lips linger on yours and then slowly she opens up, wanting your tongue. You push inside, feeling a surge between your legs as her hands move up and down the muscles of your belly. Too soon, she pulls away. She shifts back and crosses her arms.

"You're not focusing." She's still straddling you, but you can't feel her pussy against yours now.

"I'm trying," you argue.

She arches her eyebrows. You do another slow pelvic curl and then hold the position when your mound pushes against Carmen's butt cheeks. "Better?"

Carmen makes you wait for a long moment before she finally nods. "You've almost got it. Lead from your abs and tighten your core."

You drop your hips to the mat. "I think we should switch places so you can show me how I'm supposed to be doing this."

Carmen smiles. "You like to be on top?" She leans forward and pins your shoulders. "Too bad. I'm the teacher."

You try to shift free from her hold, but she has an advantage. Every time you move, her wet pussy slides on your belly, and you're soon too distracted to put up a fight. When you finally relax, she leans forward and kisses you. Then her hands are moving up and down your body. She breaks away from your lips to whisper, "I need to tell you something."

"Okay." Whatever she has to say, her tone suggests it won't be good news. But tempering the impulses in your body won't be easy.

"Katherine has cameras everywhere. There's probably one even here in the gazebo. Sometimes I make it a game trying to find where she's hidden the camera. Can you find it?"

You tense involuntarily when you see a tiny red light above the fan in the center of the room. You point it out and Carmen smiles.

"I figured." She sighs. "That's Katherine. Makes you think of secured assets in a new way. She watches everything."

"You think she's watching us now?"

Carmen shakes her head. "She's enjoying her party guests at the moment. But later tonight, I'm sure she'll scan the footage. Do you want to stop?"

"No. But maybe we should wave." You grin.

"We don't need to wave. She knows that I know about the cameras. But before anything happens, I wanted you to know."

"Before anything happens? I think your news is a little late." You smile and touch Carmen's exposed nipple. "Good thing I'm not modest. I'm lying naked on her yoga mat while one of her lovers has her way with me. Think she'll mind?"

"Not at all. And I have so much more in store for you," Carmen promises. She leans down and kisses a line from your shoulder down your collarbone. Then she moves lower and sucks your nipple into her mouth. Her tongue strokes until you've forgotten about the cameras and are completely focused on Carmen's rasping tongue.

Carmen lets your nipple slip out of her mouth and reaches for your hand.

She kisses each fingertip in turn and then slips the middle finger into her mouth. The muscles in your groin spasm to attention as she sucks your finger back and forth between her lips. When she lets your finger slide out, you feel your clit quiver. Carmen leans back, tracing the creases of your hand, her soft touch playing on the inside of your palm. She takes your hand and guides it toward her body. Already wet, your fingers dip inside. She arches back, moaning. You find her swollen clit and start to stroke. Carmen grips your wrist, controlling you still. She presses your fingers deeper into her and then comes in a sudden hard spasm. Her wetness spreads over your hand, dripping down her thighs and onto your belly. She holds you against her for a long moment and then suddenly pushes your hand away. When she looks up, her eyes are dark.

"Now it's your turn," she says. She moves between your legs, and you feel the pulsing start at your clit. Her hands slip under your butt cheeks and she tilts your pelvis up to her waiting mouth.

Carmen's tongue dodges side to side over your clit until you feel a tremor threaten. You try to slow your response and shift your hips back from Carmen's face, but she doesn't let up. Instead of a break, you feel her fingers. First one of her fingers and then another thrusts inside you.

You push up with another pelvic curl and Carmen adds a third finger. She pumps her hand hard into you, finding your g-spot and riding it with her knuckles. She thrusts deeper, her thumb stroking over your clit haphazardly. Then she sucks your clit between her lips. Her fingers still driving inside. Steady and unrelenting. You steal a quick glance down at Carmen. Her face is buried between your legs, and her hair is now a dark, tangled mess. You close your eyes as the climax hits, the wave spreading from your groin up to your clenched jaw. You squeeze your legs together as Carmen's fingers slide out.

Carmen comes up to kiss your lips, and then she stretches out across your body. You enjoy the weight of her. Firm muscles, heavy breasts, all of it pinning you on the mat.

"You've got that pelvic curl down now," Carmen says.

Carmen moves off your body and stretches out alongside you. After a while she begins to rub your shoulders and neck. Her touch is soft and lazy and the massage stops a few moments after it began. "I can't remember the last time I had sex with someone I hardly know. Usually sex these days is so polite. So expected. Sometimes I think I should schedule it on the calendar and say thank you afterwards. But you…were unexpected. And exactly what I needed."

"Are you going back to the party?"

"Maybe. Or maybe I'll spend the night right here."

"Do you think Katherine will like the show?" You point to the red light above the fan.

Carmen glances up. "She'll be upset that she missed the private party."

"We could invite her for more later."

"No. I'm not sharing you with Katherine. You're my secret student for the night." Carmen wraps her arms around you. "And I don't think I'll be letting you go back to the party."

"What's the next lesson?"

"Positions for multiple orgasms," Carmen says. Her tone is serious. She points to the thick foam roll lying by the weight bench. "And after that, we still need to work with the roller."

"When I'm sore later, I'm telling everyone it was my Pilates teacher's fault."

"You better." Carmen leans close and kisses you. "I can't wait to show you what we're going to work on next."

This is the end of your night's adventure.
Turn to Chapter Fourteen (page 229) to see what happens the morning after,
Or read on to Chapter Three to find out what would have happened if you'd chosen to play the piano.

CHAPTER THREE

Agree to play the piano

There's no use arguing. Your fate was sealed the moment Katherine asked. And maybe Carmen's offer will still stand after you've played—as long as you don't make a fool of yourself. "Two songs. That's all."

Katherine's smug look makes it clear she likes getting her way. She leans close to Carmen and whispers something. You glance at the crowd of people and your stomach sinks as you realize what you've gotten yourself into. Before you can come up with an excuse for the sudden affliction that's left your fingers numb, Katherine turns and makes her way over to the grand piano.

You wonder what Katherine whispered to Carmen, but you don't have time to wonder long. Katherine is talking to the pianist now. Ingrid glances over as Katherine points you out in the crowd. Apparently she didn't think to simply say that Batman would be taking over. You sigh. The pianist is nearing the end of Beethoven's long *Moonlight Sonata*. "Piano Sonata No. 14."

"I love secret talents. I can't wait to hear you play." Carmen touches your arm. "Good luck."

Carmen turns and heads back to the group she'd abandoned earlier. You stare at the silky draped orange gown exposing a good section of her back for a long moment and down the rest of your champagne. A waiter passes and you hand him your empty glass, then take a deep breath and make your way over to the piano.

Probably most people who play the piano as often as you do have a whole repertoire of songs memorized. Unfortunately, you don't. Without sheet music, you are reduced to Frank Sinatra's greatest hits. Frank Sinatra has always been your mother's favorite. Thanks to her insisting you play a dozen of his songs every Christmas, you have at least something to get you through tonight.

Ingrid gives you a sniff and a once-over as you approach the bench. She holds the last note and then abruptly stands. "I'm told that you're my replacement." Ingrid chuckles. "Good luck, my dear. I do hope you know what you are doing."

"I'm pretty sure I'm about to make a fool of myself."

Ingrid nods. "I've done worse in ten minutes."

As soon as Ingrid steps away from the piano, you clench your shaking hands. You sit down on the bench and then tug off your Batman gloves. Your palms are sweaty and you can count your elevated pulse by the whooshing sound in your ears. You take two deep breaths and imagine a Christmas tree next to the piano and your mother worrying about how long a turkey takes to cook. "New York, New York" is the logical choice. You could play that song with your eyes closed. Or, you hope, while wearing a hooded mask.

You stretch your fingers and then ball them into fists a few times before you strike the first note. For the first half of the song, you don't look past the piano. Maybe no one is staring at you. Then that thought, that question, makes you look up. A blurry sea of faces focuses into one person. Alison Greer. Her gaze is locked on you, and then suddenly she's walking up to the piano. She starts to sing and your breath catches in your throat. You try to swallow, nearly missing the next note, and focus on the keys again. Alison's voice might not be Sinatra's, but her notes are clear and the tone is warm as honey.

When you finish the song, you realize you haven't thought of what to play next. The crowd is clapping. A warm buzz fills your chest as she looks over her shoulder and smiles.

"I do take requests," you say. "But only Frank Sinatra covers."

"How about 'The Way You Look Tonight'?" Alison asks.

"Perfect."

You play the familiar notes, and Alison's voice burns a path right through you. She leans against the piano, her profile catching the light from the chandelier. Alison could have imperfections, but you haven't found one yet. Which is why you shouldn't think about what it would feel like to kiss her lips under any circumstances. Unfortunately, that thought is running circles through your mind. You look away from Alison's face and imagine a Christmas tree strung with popcorn and cranberries standing on top of the piano.

The applause breaks your concentration.

"Thank you," Alison says, meeting your gaze. "That was fun. I haven't sung Sinatra in ages."

Alison turns back to the crowd and does a half-bow, then starts to walk away from the piano. Someone shouts "Encore!" And then the word is a chorus. Alison glances over her shoulder at you.

One more song is tempting fate, yet you begin to play. "Fly Me to the Moon."

Alison comes over to the piano bench and sits down next to you. She watches your hands for a long moment, and then finally comes in at the last chorus. The feel of her body sitting so close—nearly touching yours—isn't what has your pulse racing so much as the sound of her voice.

When you finish the song, you turn to Alison. "If we had a little practice…"

"I couldn't remember the words to that one," she apologizes. "You had me distracted."

"I had you distracted?" You grin.

"Yes. How often do you see Batman playing the piano?" She tilts her head and adds, "And playing well."

"That's why I like to show up at parties dressed like this. Throws everyone off. It's my competitive advantage."

Alison laughs. "Okay, Batman, now that you've admitted you had an advantage, I want a second chance. Play that song again. I want to redeem myself."

"The same song?"

"Yes. I'll do better this time. It took me a minute, but I think I remember most of the words now."

If you couldn't say no to Katherine, there's absolutely no way you'll say no to Alison. Besides, Ingrid is nowhere to be seen. "Okay. But I get to have a drink with you after."

You don't give Alison a chance to argue. This time, she doesn't wait for the last chorus. Transfixed by her voice, the notes spill off your fingers, and you only realize you've reached the last stanza when Alison sets her hand on your leg.

"I've never had someone barter to get a drink with me," she says. "Nice work."

The applauding crowd saves you from having to answer. There's no way you could manage talking. Alison gets up from the piano bench and smiles at the audience. She turns to clap in your direction.

You return the gesture, clapping for Alison, and then stand and find your gloves. Your hands have stopped shaking and your adrenaline rush makes you feel as if you're floating. Ingrid settles into place on the bench and murmurs a thank-you. You pull on your gloves and float across the ballroom, fielding shoulder pats and grinning at the smiling faces that had you terrified ten minutes ago.

Alison meets you at the bar. "What are we having?"

"How about a martini with a twist of lemon?" the bartender suggests. She's already pouring gin into two martini glasses. Dressed in a tux with her blond hair pulled back in a low ponytail, she looks vaguely familiar, but she could be any soft butch that you've bumped into at a bar. She winks at Alison. A few strands have slipped loose from the ponytail. "They say Sinatra liked Jack Daniels best, but I think a martini fits the mood tonight. You've got an amazing voice," she says, blushing when Alison meets her gaze. "And you're not so bad on the piano," she adds to you. "Maybe you two will do another set?"

"I'm done for the night." Luck got you through one set, but you wouldn't count on that lasting through even one more song. And you've already made an impression on Alison. Why push it?

"Too bad." But the bartender is looking at Alison when she answers, not you.

Alison takes one of the drinks and hands the other to you. "Thank you," she murmurs, smiling at the bartender. Alison turns away from the bar and then leans close to you and says, "So, tell me. What was Katherine's bribe to convince you to play tonight? You didn't look too excited to play when you first sat down."

"You noticed?" The bartender has moved on to the next customer, but you can tell her attention is still trained on Alison. "Katherine did promise a reward. She wasn't specific on what that might be."

"Don't let her forget about the promise." Alison points toward the sofas by the fire and heads in that direction. "Having something you can hold over Katherine Flaggerty is gold."

"I'll keep that in mind."

There aren't any empty seats by the fire, but as Alison approaches, two men at the closest sofa stand and offer their spot. They flash toothy grins at Alison when she thanks them and then nearly fall over each other as they back away, their eyes still glued to Alison.

As soon as the two men are out of earshot, you ask, "Does it get annoying?"

Alison cocks her head. "What do you mean?"

"Men, women, falling over themselves to impress you all the time."

Alison shakes her head. "That is completely not what happens. Maybe tonight…and maybe at a party after a show. But most of the time, no one is trying to impress me."

"Maybe you don't notice it all the time, but I bet it happens more than you think."

"I noticed you trying to impress me."

"Katherine put me up to playing the piano," you argue. "And if I was going to try to impress you, that wouldn't have been my first, or second, plan."

"I wasn't talking about tonight. Last New Year's. Remember asking if I needed a coat?" Alison sips her martini and then pinches her lips together. "The bartender made this a little strong."

Of course you remember the New Year's party. Although you'd heard about Alison Greer before that night, you'd never met her. The party was on a yacht, and as soon as the rain started, everyone rushed into the enclosed area under the deck. In the crowd of people, you bumped into Alison. She was dripping wet and shivering. You offered her your coat, and she slipped it on. An hour later, someone handed the coat back to you, but Alison was gone. That was it. You decide to change the subject rather that bring up that night. "The bartender was trying to impress you. Did you see the way she poured the gin and then sliced the lemon, making sure you were watching the whole time?"

Alison laughs. "Okay, I'll give you that one. And she was cute. I should have asked her for a number."

"You could walk back over there now. You'd make her night."

Alison sighs. "I've never been brave enough to ask any girl for a phone number."

"Never? Maybe tonight you need to cross that off your list." You glance back at the bartender's station. "I could pass her a note."

Alison crosses her legs and leans back against the sofa cushions. She looks over at you and smiles. "With you in that costume...I feel like I've signed up for a relationship therapy session with a superhero."

"I have asked a lot of women for phone numbers. That is one talent I've mastered. But I wouldn't listen to any of my relationship advice beyond the first date."

"First date, huh?" Alison nods. "Okay, I don't have a notebook to write this down"—she smiles—"but if I asked for a phone number, and then actually called to ask her out, where should I take her?"

"We're talking about the bartender, right?"

Alison shrugs.

"Well, it's important to think about who they are, what they would like, when you plan a first date." You eye the bartender again. "Don't take her to a club, or a bar, obviously. And nights are probably out, but she wouldn't say yes to anything too early in the morning either because you know she probably works late." You deliberate. "Picnic lunch at the Japanese Tea Gardens. And if all goes well, you can walk a few blocks from the park to that little cinema over on Eighteenth Street and catch a four o'clock matinee."

Alison stares at you for a long moment. Finally, she glances back at the bartender. "But there are other questions I never know the answers to. Do I pick her up? Or do we drive separately? If all goes well, do you kiss on that first date? And am I the one who sets up the second date? Or is it her turn, since I asked her out? And should I ask if she's a vegetarian or is lunch a surprise?"

"Surprise her, but no meat, just to be safe. Buy a sourdough baguette and some cheese. Maybe a pear or strawberries, this time of year."

"And do I bring wine? Red or white?"

"Red. But only if you bring chocolate."

"Chocolate. Perfect. Thanks for the advice." Alison smiles. "By the way, what's your phone number and what are you doing this Tuesday?"

"Very funny."

"Don't leave me hanging," Alison says. "This is my first time asking for a number."

"This Tuesday?" You stall. It's hard to believe she's serious, but the look in her eyes confirms it. You grin. "Well, I'm pretty sure I'm playing hooky from work to go on a date. But I thought you were going to ask the bartender."

"She's intimidating. I feel more comfortable with you. And I like the way your jacket smelled."

"New Year's?"

Alison nods. "I never said thank you. I was freezing that night. I know, it was December, and we were out on a boat in the bay. Don't ask me why I thought it was a good idea to wear a sleeveless dress and leave my jacket in the car."

"You looked gorgeous that night. And ridiculously cold."

"Well, you look ridiculous tonight." Alison laughs. "So we're even."

The butterflies in your stomach are buzzing again. You glance at your glass, knowing you should eat something before you finish the drink, especially with Alison sitting so close.

Alison reaches across the sofa to touch your gloved hand. "I loved watching you play tonight. Especially in that costume."

You pull at the edge of your padded chest. Next to the fire, you're ready to strip all of it off. "I bet Batman is constantly sweating."

"I could use some air. Want to go outside for a minute?" Alison points to the French doors leading out to the lit-up patio.

Before you can agree, Katherine appears. At her side is a woman several inches taller than Katherine. Her features are all sharp angles but sexy in an unusual way and too interesting to ignore. Her jet-black hair contrasts her pale complexion. In a striking silver suit with a black blouse, she looks like she's about to strut down a runway. Considering that she's apparently Katherine's friend, you wonder if she is in fact a model. Her hands are on her hips as if she's ready to pose for the camera. You half-expect her chin to jut out and a lip pout to follow. Perfect for the front-page spread. She eyes Alison and then tilts her head to consider you. Or, more likely, your ridiculous costume.

"You're difficult to find," Katherine says to Alison. "One of the bartenders told me I'd probably find you with Batman, and turns out she was right. Alison, this is Amélie, the friend of mine from Paris that I mentioned. You'll be in neighboring rooms tonight, and I wanted you two to meet in case you bump into each other in the bathroom."

Alison and Amélie shake hands.

"And Amélie, you noticed Batman earlier at the piano, I'm sure," Katherine says.

Amélie nods. Her eyes catch you off guard. Deep blue and piercing. She seems to be sizing you up. The fact that Katherine doesn't use your name makes you wonder if she's forgotten it.

Amélie continues to hold your gaze until Katherine lapses into a conversation with Amélie and Alison in French. Suddenly, you feel out of place. Several minutes later, you stand up, ready to make your exit.

Alison catches your hand before you can leave. She continues speaking to Amélie, still in French, but doesn't let go of your hand. Katherine eyes Alison's hand latched on yours. Her lips pinch together in a thin line.

The French conversation continues. You manage to catch only the names of French cities, and then Katherine hands a slip of paper to Alison. Amélie and Katherine are turning to leave.

As soon as they've gone, Alison lets go of your hand. "Did you think I was going to let you walk away without getting your phone number tonight? We didn't set up a time to meet at the Japanese Tea Gardens." Alison folds the slip of paper that Katherine gave her and then passes it to you. "Would you hold this for me? Batman has to have some kind of secret pocket in that outfit, right?"

"No pockets. But there's a pouch for a cell phone on the utility belt."

"Utility belt?" Alison grins. "You come fully prepared." She waits for you to drop the note into the pouch and then continues. "Katherine's paranoid. She keeps the door to the private rooms of the house locked, and she changes the code whenever she has events like this."

"Are you serious about a date?"

"Why wouldn't I be?" Alison says something in French and then in English adds, "I still want some air. Walk with me."

Alison lets go of your hand as soon as you open the door for her. When you close the door, the soft sounds of a light breeze rustling through a willow and trickling water in the fountain at the center of the patio are a welcome change to the noise of the ballroom. Alison sits down on a stone bench next to the fountain. She shivers when the wind picks up.

"It's cooler out here than I expected."

You untie your cape and slip it over her shoulders, careful not to touch her bare skin despite your body's longing to do just that.

"If I asked, would you play another song for me?"

"Only if I had sheet music."

"I doubt Katherine has anything here." Alison sighs. "She's letting me spend the week here because my apartment building is being rewired. Some electrical issue."

"You got lucky on roommates for the week."

"Amélie or Katherine?"

"Or both?" You smile. "Nothing wrong with a threesome."

"Once I get over the first hurdle of getting a phone number, I'll consider branching out to threesomes."

"You've never had a threesome?"

"Don't look at me like that," Alison says.

"Like what?"

"Like I'm naive. I'm not." She shakes her head. "But go ahead and call me old-fashioned. I prefer one lover at a time."

"Okay. One at a time." You sit down on the bench. "So which one are you sleeping with tonight?"

"No one." Alison turns and pushes you off the bench. "I have to go on a date with someone before anything happens. And then maybe a second or third date. Old-fashioned."

The patio door opens and two women step out. You recognize the women in the leather jacket and red pants. DJ Dee. She mixes on Ladies Night at Rumors, the one gay club in town. The woman with her looks familiar, too. They walk toward the koi pond lit up with an orange light. Then DJ Dee turns and glances in your direction. Alison reaches for your hand.

"Kiss me," she whispers.

"What?"

Before you can argue, Alison stands abruptly and reaches for you. Her lips are close enough to kiss, but you hesitate. Only moments ago, she pledged to play hard to get, but now one hand presses on your chest as the other wraps behind your neck. Somehow, she's keeping you at arm's length while pulling you toward her.

Your lips meet hers. The outside sounds funnel away; the only thing you can hear is your heartbeat, and the only sensation is Alison's lips perfectly matching yours. You're light-headed and seeing stars. Alison doesn't stop at one kiss, and she keeps her hand on you to hold you in place. Another kiss and you're opening up to her, wanting the moment to never end. When she finally pulls away, she glances first over your shoulder at the women by the koi pond. Your heart sinks. She's left you breathless, and you were only a decoy.

You stand between Alison and the women by the pond, unable to move and unwilling to look Alison in the eye after her stunt. A door opens and closes. Only then does Alison take a step back. Her hand slips off your chest.

"God, I can't believe Becca has the nerve to show up here."

"Becca?" Then you recall the posters from the club. Becca Dee. Otherwise known as DJ Dee. You rub your lips, wishing you could forget the kiss. But that kiss, even if Alison was only acting, was unforgettable. "Is she an ex-girlfriend?"

Alison doesn't seem to hear the question. Or she's ignoring you. She's staring at the two women. They've already gone back inside the ballroom, but they're standing near one of the windows and you can easily see their profiles as they lean close to kiss. Alison turns away as their lips lock. Finally, she says, "Katherine must have invited her tonight."

"You're old-fashioned…and I'm gullible," you murmur quietly.

Alison looks over at you. "What'd you say?"

"Nothing." Clearly your kiss meant nothing to Alison—nothing more than a performance for a woman she's still hung up on. DJ Dee, or Becca, the ex. There's no way you can outcompete a DJ with a sexy bad-girl reputation.

"I'm sorry about asking you to kiss me. That was—"

"You don't need to explain," you interrupt. "I'm going back inside." You turn and walk toward the door, not caring if Alison follows or not.

"Wait," Alison says.

You keep walking. The door opens before you can reach for the handle. A crowd of five or six file past you, the men reaching for lighters and the women finding cigarettes before they've even crossed the threshold. You slip inside the ballroom. Ingrid is still playing. Mozart. "Rondo Alla Turca." The song's bouncy half-notes make you want to clap your hands over your ears. Chopin's funeral march would be more fitting with your mood.

Now is the perfect time to make your escape. No one would notice you slipping to the front door, and Janine can think what she might of your disappearing with Alison Greer. You cross the ballroom, and just as you near the hallway leading to the foyer, you spot Carmen. She's chatting with another woman, but you'll have to walk right past her to leave. You clench your fists, wishing tonight were a long-forgotten bad dream.

Before you can find a different way to the front door, Carmen looks up. She smiles when she sees you. When she hugs the woman next to her and then starts toward you, you realize you've missed your chance to leave unnoticed.

"The famous Batman pianist. Are your ears buzzing? We were just talking about you. Frank Sinatra gets me every time." Her voice could charm anyone. She smiles and then narrows her gaze. "What's wrong? You look like you're about to go kick someone's butt. Evil Joker on the loose?"

"No...Something came up. I need to leave early."

"I don't buy it. Who pissed you off?" Without waiting for your answer, she continues, "Let me guess. Alison Greer?"

You sigh and drop your shoulders.

"Don't worry. I'm not a mind reader. I saw you two go outside."

"Yeah. I was just played."

"You're not the first." Carmen touches your chin, tilting it up. The caress is as gentle as it is arresting. She stares straight into your eyes. "Alison Greer has half the women in this town begging for her attention, but then she crushes anyone who gets close. Congratulate yourself on figuring out her act in under an hour. Most people are stuck on her for months." She sweeps her hand out toward the crowd at the banquet tables. "But why leave now? So Alison played you. Go find someone new who won't play games. You had half the crowd eating out of your hand when you were sitting at that piano earlier. You won't have any trouble finding a replacement for Alison."

"I don't know what I was thinking."

"You weren't thinking. It happens to all of us." Carmen stops a waiter with a tray of appetizers. "Egg roll? You should try one. They're delicious. I've had two already."

You don't want to eat but you take one anyway, knowing at least part of your response to Alison was the fault of the martini on an empty stomach. And the champagne. You crunch on the egg roll. The crispy coating and sweet ginger flavor makes you want to lick your fingertips, but you're wearing gloves. Dinner is being served to the guests who have found their way over to the banquet tables, and the crowd in the main room has thinned out. The egg roll hits your stomach and you realize how hungry you are.

"Take my advice—unsolicited, of course—and find someone else to think about. As soon as possible. Don't let Alison Greer under your skin."

A man waves to Carmen and she smiles in return, then turns back to you. "That's my husband's associate. Unfortunately, I need to go be sociable with him." She touches your arm. "Don't leave because of Alison."

Carmen disappears into the crowd. Considering her advice, you glance around the ballroom. The thought of finding someone for a fling suddenly seems like too much effort. Janine is chatting with a group of friends from work. Forcing your gaze beyond her, you see Katherine. She's chatting with a couple by the fire. Amélie, the French model, is still hanging by Katherine's side. They stand close enough to be nearly touching, and you can't help but wonder if the French woman is another one of Katherine's famed girlfriends. Not for the first time tonight, you realize that you don't belong in this ballroom. You pull out your cell phone and send a text to your best friend, Maxine. Maybe she's up for company. After what happened with Alison, you're in the mood for watching a movie and making popcorn with Max. No surprises.

Maxine quickly responds. *Of course you can come over. But Roger's here.*

Roger is Maxine's boyfriend. Before you can slip the phone in your pocket, a hand grabs your arm. Alison. She holds out your black cape. It's five seconds too late when you realize that you're staring at Alison's ample cleavage instead of looking up at her eyes. You take the cape and swallow hard. Despite everything, Alison is still gorgeous.

"I heard Batman's cape is bulletproof."

"Not this one."

Alison looks in Carmen's direction. "For the record, Carmen hates me. I overheard her say my name." Alison's jaw clenches. "I'm guessing she told you I was scum of the earth. And I may have totally screwed up with you outside just now, but I'm not a horrible person."

"The move you pulled out there…"

"You didn't even give me a chance to explain. I was trying and then you took off. Maybe I had a good reason for what I did. Did you consider that?" Before you can gather your thoughts to respond, she waves dismissively. "Fine, I get it. I'm sure you've heard enough from Carmen to never want to speak to me again. Can I just have that piece of paper with Katherine's security code? Since I can't go home tonight, I'm going to bed."

Alison is still impossibly sexy. Your body is ready to forgive her even if your mind isn't. You fumble with the snap on the pouch and then pull out the folded note and read the numbers without thinking. 5-4-3-2-1. Before you can say a word, Alison snatches the note from your hands. She spins on her heel and is gone.

"Cream puff?" a server asks, holding out a silver tray with a dozen perfectly puffed golden pastries.

Do you:
A) Follow Alison (read on)
B) Wise up and take a cream puff (go to Chapter Five, page 68)

Follow Alison

There's no way to be sly about following Alison. She's cut straight across the ballroom and is already passing a throng of people near the entrance. If you take the long way and cut behind the bartender's table, she'll be long gone. You stride past Ingrid at the piano, pausing to compliment her on the piece she's just started. You've always liked Vivaldi's *Four Seasons* no matter how overplayed it is. Without waiting another second to question your sanity, you head straight for the foyer. The hallway is empty and Jim, the coat check man at the door, recognizes you instantly.

"How's it going out there, Batman?" Jim asks.

Alison is standing at the opposite end of the hallway by the doorway leading to the private section of the house. She looks up and meets your gaze at the same moment that Jim announces your presence.

"I've had worse nights," you say.

Alison taps a small computer screen mounted near the closed door at the end of the hall and then punches the numbers on the keypad.

"Wait, Alison," you say, crossing the foyer. "Give me two seconds."

Alison holds the door and counts out loud, "One, two." Then she lets go of the door and disappears to the other side.

"Not that I'm trying to compromise the security detail, but after the door closes, you've got about five seconds before it locks," Jim says. "I've always been a Batman fan," he adds.

You have to run, but you manage to catch the door before the bolt latches. You hear Jim cheering. Maybe you are crazy for chasing after Alison. Carmen's warning repeats in your head. But Alison Greer got under your skin the moment she sat down on the piano bench next to you. And even before that. New Year's. It was the way she looked straight into your eyes when she took your coat.

The hallway is dark on the other side and you take a moment to adjust. You hear a click as the door locks behind you.

"Nice move, Batman. You're quick," Alison says. She hits the hall light switch. "What are you going to do now?" She folds her arms.

Blinking in the bright light, you try to catch your breath while Alison stares at you. You hadn't thought out your next move, and Alison has a way of making you forget your words.

"What did Carmen say about me?" Alison asks.

"Carmen doesn't like you."

"Tell me something I don't know."

"Unfortunately, I like you," you admit. "And if we don't even get a first date, I didn't want to leave things the way we did."

"You hardly know me," she argues. "Maybe you should listen to Carmen."

"You're right. I don't know you. But why should I trust what she says about you?"

"Maybe you shouldn't trust anyone." Alison pivots and heads down the hall. She passes a living room and then stops at the second closed door. Before she opens the door, she looks back at you. "Good night."

"Maybe I was crazy for thinking that something was going on between us earlier. But I thought there was something," you say. "Anyway, I wanted you to tell me that I was wrong. I didn't want Carmen to be the one to tell me. Because otherwise, the next time I go to the Japanese Tea Gardens I'm going to be thinking about you. And wishing I was there with you."

"How often do you go the Japanese Tea Gardens?"

"So far?" You shrug. "Not once."

"You should take someone. That date sounded perfect." She leans against the doorway watching you. "You weren't crazy," she says finally. "I could have spent the rest of the night with you on that piano bench. Too bad you don't have more songs memorized. We could be out there still."

"What was the kiss about? I mean, I know you used me. I get that part. But why?"

"When Becca showed up with Courtney..." Alison shakes her head. "Do you really want to talk about what happened outside? Or can I just say that you're right. I used you."

"Maybe I deserve to know why."

"You do. But it's a long story. And I really don't want to talk about it now." Alison rubs her eyes. "Look, I'm sorry. And I'm sorry you took off before I could explain. And I'm sorry Carmen got to you before I could."

"What's going on between you and Carmen?"

"I think you should ask her that question." She takes a deep breath and exhales slowly. "Carmen has a grudge against me. It's possible I may have unknowingly had a long relationship with her girlfriend. And then that woman told Carmen. But, in case Carmen forgot to mention it, she happens to be the married one in this whole equation. I didn't do anything wrong. And I broke things off with the other woman as soon as I found out about Carmen. If Carmen had asked me directly, I would have told her my side of the story. There's always two sides." Alison pauses. "Anyway, you should go back to the party and find someone to go with you on that date. I'm going to bed."

"You're really going to bed?"

She nods.

"What time am I picking you up on Tuesday?"

A smile edges her lips. "I thought I was supposed to pick you up." She pushes the door all the way open. "Come here."

You cross the hallway, stopping a foot from Alison.

She reaches for your hand. "I'm sorry."

"Me, too. Think we could start over?"

Alison steps forward and kisses you. Her lips press against yours. She pulls away before you've had enough of her to satisfy your body's craving, but she's set you on fire again.

"You're a good kisser," Alison says. "I was only going for one little smack outside, but you drew me in and I couldn't stop."

"That's your excuse? Almost sounds like you're blaming me."

Alison smiles. She looks over her shoulder into the bedroom behind her. "Do you want to come in? We can talk."

"Setting ground rules?"

"I'm only saying that I'm not inviting you in to have sex with you. In case you're wondering."

"We hardly know each other. Of course I don't want to have sex with you tonight. Who do you think I am?"

Alison laughs. "You need acting lessons." She steps back from the doorway. "Come in anyway."

A desk lamp gives the room a pale yellow glow. Aside from the four-poster bed with a thick mattress and a downy comforter, the room has minimal furnishings. One dresser, one desk and one chair—clearly a guest room. Alison kicks off her heels and goes over to the writing desk. She fills a glass with water from a metal pitcher, takes a sip, and then offers the glass to you.

Alison opens a closet and takes out a nightgown and a white robe. "Do you want something to change into?"

You nod.

Alison pulls out a T-shirt and a pair of yoga pants. She hands you the clothes and then glances at the adjoining bathroom. "I'm going to shower. You can wait for me here or you can join me."

"Wait, what'd you just say?"

"I think you heard me."

"But are you serious?"

She doesn't answer, fishing through a dresser drawer for a toiletries bag. She pulls out a bottle of shampoo.

"What happened to the old-fashioned part?"

"Just because I don't want to have sex with you yet doesn't mean I'm a prude." Alison turns and walks to the bathroom.

"No," you murmur. "But it might mean that you're an incredibly good tease."

"I heard that." Alison leaves the door ajar, and you can see her reflection in the mirror as she begins to unzip her dress. She looks up and meets your gaze. The dress slips off her body, but she turns and disappears behind the shower curtain before you get a good look.

"Oh man." You glance at the door and then back at the bathroom mirror. All you can see now is a shower curtain. The shower turns on, and you hear Alison begin to sing "Fly Me to the Moon." Maybe Carmen is right. Maybe Alison is only playing a game with you. But you strip out of your costume anyway. Second-guessing Alison's motives doesn't make you less inclined to seeing her naked.

"Let me guess: No touching?"

Alison doesn't answer as you step into the steaming shower. It's a double-wide shower stall, all in marble with ornate gold water spouts. A bench lines the back wall and there are two showerheads. Plenty of room to keep your hands to yourself.

Alison turns into the spray of water and you get a good look at her backside—smooth light brown skin and perfect round butt cheeks. You'd love to run a hand over the curves. She looks over her shoulder and catches you staring.

You hold up your hands. "I'm not touching. But I can't take a shower with you and not look."

"Relax. You're not breaking any rules." Alison takes a step toward you and caresses your neck. "Yet."

Alison's touch leaves you anything but relaxed. She reaches past you and turns on the second showerhead. The water takes a chilly moment to warm, and as you turn into the spray, you feel Alison's hands on your back. She massages your shoulders with a bar of soap and steps right up against you. Her breasts brush your back as she massages your arms. You swallow hard.

"I think I need the rules written out."

"No sex. Everything else is up for discussion."

"Everything?" You turn around and meet her lips.

Alison's body presses against the full length of yours. "Mmmm. I like you even better naked."

"Than as Batman? Thank you, I think."

Alison smiles. "I want to go to the Japanese Tea Gardens with you. And then I want to go see a movie. What's your phone number?"

You kiss Alison's lips. The kiss deepens and you wrap your arms around her body, opening up as her tongue brushes against yours. You reach for Alison's soap and caress the angle of her hip with the bar, leaving a swath of suds on her skin. She glances down at your hand.

"Are you going to stop me?" Waiting for her answer, you trace down the length of her thigh with the soap.

"Not yet."

Her eyes lock on yours as you bend down, making a soapy path all the way to her toes and then back up her other leg. You stop when you reach her hip again and she hands over a washcloth and turns around, presenting her backside. You lather the soap into the washcloth and then rub her shoulders, lower back, butt cheeks, and finally her thighs.

"You missed the calves," she says.

You squat down to finish the job, but she turns around and you're suddenly nose-level with her knees. "You're making this hard."

You lean forward and kiss one knee, then as you straighten up, you make your way toward her middle with kisses, narrowly avoiding the one place you'd love to touch. As you pass over her groin, she draws in a quick breath. Her breasts, full and round, push forward as you kiss her belly.

"You're making it hard for me to follow my own rules," Alison says, her fingernails massaging your scalp.

"You could break those rules."

The washcloth slips over her breasts. With Alison watching, you lean forward to find her nipple with your lips. Her back arches, pushing her other breast into your hand as your mouth works the first nipple. You shift to the other nipple, feeling her need grow as the rock-hard tip responds to your tongue. When you straighten up to find her lips, she reaches between your legs. Waiting for her hand to dip inside, you can hardly concentrate on kissing, but she only teases, tracing your edges.

"I'm not the person that has sex with someone I hardly know," she says temptingly.

"If I stop, you have to, too." You glance at Alison's hand. She still hasn't pressed inside, but her touch is dangerously close. She caresses up and down your inner thighs while your swollen clit begs for attention. "And if you go much further, there's no way we can say that we didn't have sex."

Alison pulls her hand away. She turns into the shower spray and closes her eyes. You see her chest heaving and know that she wants exactly what your clit wants.

You brush your hand over her butt cheeks and up her back. She moans in response. "I won't tell if you don't," you offer. "If anyone asks, I'll say that Alison Greer is old-fashioned. No sex before the first date."

"A real prude." Alison steps out of the stream of water and pushes you back against the marble wall. Her kiss is hard and full of desire. Her hand pushes your legs apart and two fingers press inside. Every nerve fires and Alison groans with satisfaction as she feels your response. She covers your mouth with hers. You can hardly breathe as her fingers circle, edging you closer and closer. Her breasts fill your hands and as you pinch her nipples, the rush of an orgasm spreads through your body.

Alison holds you against the wall, kissing you as her hand still works between your legs. Weak-kneed, you worry that if she lets go of her hold on you, you won't be able to stand. She's trying to get you off a second time, and her fingers have you dangerously close. One lick from her tongue and you'd come. Again. Breathless, you push her hand off your clit.

"That wasn't fair," you say.

"Who said life was fair?" Alison replies. Her look is smug. She turns off her showerhead and steps out of the stall before you can move.

A tremor races through you, and you reach down to squeeze your clit. Alison left the shower curtain half-open, and you watch her rub a thick green towel over her skin and then wrap another green towel around her body. You long to pull her towel off. In two steps you could have her back in the bedroom and spread out on the bed. Bracing your hands against the back wall, you step into the stream of water. Your clit is still pulsing, asking for Alison's touch.

Unfortunately, seeing Alison naked wasn't enough. In fact, it only made you want her more. And she knows it.

This is the end of your night's adventure.
Turn to Chapter Fourteen (page 229) to see what happens the morning after,
Or go to Chapter Five (page 68) to see what would happen if you picked a cream puff instead of Alison.

CHAPTER FOUR

Go find Katherine to ask for a change of clothes

Two hallways lead out of the marble foyer. An opulent glass chandelier hangs at the center and plush burgundy settees, each with a pillow featuring embroidery reminiscent of Georgia O'Keefe, form a sitting area under the light. According to Jim the doorman, one hall leads to the crowded ballroom, the dining area, and beyond this, the fully staffed kitchen. The other leads to the private areas of the house. Bedrooms, library, office, gym (because apparently Katherine needs to work out at home as well as at the club), and two living rooms.

You stop at the entrance to the ballroom and scan the crowd. The room is buzzing with the sound of competing voices. There are at least fifty people clumped in groups around the room and another half-dozen waitstaff zipping about with trays of wine or appetizers. You spot Alison, predictably in the center of the largest group, and then you notice Janine. She's off to the side talking to a woman you recognize from the gym. She bench-presses a hundred pounds to warm up and you've affectionately dubbed her "Muscles." Muscles is now standing a little too close to Janine. And Janine is laughing. You sigh and glance away. If you could find Katherine you'd have a chance out there. As it is Janine has already won tonight's contest. You are officially jealous.

"Who are you looking for?" Katherine, suddenly standing next to you, gives you a sly smile.

"I was looking for you," you admit. "But so much for my Batman senses. I didn't hear you come up behind me."

"I was channeling Cat Woman," Katherine says. "When I saw Janine making friends without you I thought you'd left. I'm happy to be mistaken."

"Making friends. That's one way to describe it. She's trying to make me jealous."

"Why?"

"It's a contest. We're both trying to make each other jealous tonight. And if it doesn't work..."

Before you can go on, an older woman with ash-blond hair swoops through the entrance to the ballroom. She comes straight for Katherine and clasps her hands. Her sequined burgundy gown catches the light.

"Katherine, there you are! Lovely party as always. It's been ages since we've gotten together, hasn't it? I was just telling Dean that we've got to find a time to get you out on the yacht. You and..." The woman hesitates, gaze narrowing in on you. Her brow furrows.

"Batman." You raise your hand. "And thank you for the offer, but I don't do yachts."

Katherine pushes your hand down and quickly interjects, "I'd love to get out on the water, Linda. Let's set something up. Maybe next month?"

"Perfect. I'll tell Dean."

As soon as Linda turns back to the ballroom, Katherine asks, "Why don't you do yachts?"

"Have you ever seen Batman on a boat?"

"I've never seen Batman at one of my dinner parties either. Clearly I have a lot to learn. Any other secrets I should know about you?"

"At the moment, I'm wishing Batman's outfit breathed a little better."

"Sweating under all those muscles?"

"It's not the muscles." You tug at your outer briefs until the molded plastic jock cup shifts. "Who knew Batman wore a jock strap?"

"The things you learn." Katherine smiles. "So is that why you were looking for me?"

You nod. "I was hoping you'd have something else I could wear. I'd take pretty much anything over this."

"Anything?" She tilts her head to the side, considering. "I can think of a few things that might work for you."

Her hand touches your utility belt. You hold your breath as her finger traces the belt buckle. She moves up your padded chest to your shoulders.

"I was trying to remember where I knew you from. And then it came to me. The gym. I've seen you in the Pilates class." Katherine's hand trails down your arm, feeling your muscles and bringing a warm buzz to your chest. "And in the locker room a few times, too. You look good in a towel."

"So do you."

Katherine's coy smile suits her. A waiter crosses the hallway with a tray of champagne and Katherine beckons him over. She takes two glasses and then hands one to you. Her eyes hold you captive as she takes a slow sip. You try to sip the champagne just as slowly.

"Is this the first time you've packed at a formal dinner?"

"I'm not packing tonight," you admit.

"That's too bad." Katherine clears her throat. "We should change that."

Katherine looks over the edge of her glass at your briefs. The suggestion in her gaze makes you weak at the knees. You feel a flush travel up your neck to your cheeks and are temporarily thankful for the mask. She reaches down to touch you, one finger pressing against the jock cup.

You swallow hard as a throb starts between your legs. Before you can enjoy her touch, she pulls her hand back and takes another sip of her champagne. She glances out at the crowded ballroom as if nothing happened. "This crowd is boring, don't you think? Sometimes I wish I didn't have to invite half of the people on the guest list."

Your pulse is still racing, but Katherine seems calm, cool. You try to watch the crowd, wondering if you read too much into Katherine's attention. There's a chance that she was only teasing. Tempting but not promising.

"I don't know about boring. But I wish someone else was in costume. I feel overdressed."

"You should have read the invitation a little more carefully. It clearly stated this was formal dress."

"It's a long story."

Katherine taps your padded chest. "That outfit has potential. Next time, I'm having a costume party. You've convinced me." Katherine's tone is all business despite her lingering hand on your chest. "But I think we can find something else for you to wear tonight. Follow me."

Before you can argue, Katherine's arm is slipped through yours and you're heading back through the foyer. As you pass the front door, Jim the security guard holds up his thumb. Fortunately, Katherine doesn't seem to notice. She leads you down the second hallway to the private rooms of the mansion and pauses by a keypad screen near the door to tap her nails against the keys. The lock clicks and Katherine opens the door. Once inside you hear a series of clicks and realize the door has locked behind you.

A new hallway leads to a green living room complete with dark green carpet, wood-paneled walls, and dark green sofas. Katherine continues through this living room to yet another hallway. You pass a series of closed doors, and Katherine finally stops at the fourth closed door. She opens this door, and beckons you to follow.

A four-poster king-size bed complete with a canopy in red velvet and dangling gold ropes claims center stage. Brown, burgundy, and golden threads course across the bed duvet and overstuffed gold pillows line the headboard. In front of the bed is a wide wooden chest and an ornate Chinese rug.

Katherine walks over to the chest and spins numbers on a lock until the latch pops open. She reaches inside and pulls out a black leather harness and a dark red dildo. "Would this fit?"

Do you:
A) Reach for the harness (read on)
B) Tell Katherine you were thinking of something a little more formal (go to Chapter Six, page 83)

Reach for the harness

The butterflies in your stomach give way to a pulsing sensation between your legs. You eye a short whip and handcuffs in the chest. "What about those?"

"I like the way you think." She smiles. "We could talk about that."

You pick out the velvet-covered handcuffs. "I used to have a pair like this."

"Fond memories?"

You nod, testing the short strap between the cuffs. Despite the soft exterior, once the cuffs are in place, they are as effective as their metal counterparts. You reach for the harness.

Katherine pulls back her hand. "Not so fast. I didn't give you the ground rules yet."

"You should be asking what my rules are."

Katherine's cobalt eyes are fixed on yours. She opens her mouth as if to argue but only stares at you for a moment longer. No stranger to power plays, you hold her gaze. Establishing roles is only step one. You have to be prepared to follow through, and there's no doubt in your mind that you're up for the challenge. Finally, she lowers her hand. You reach for the harness and dildo and this time she only looks up at you, lips parted.

"You are an unexpected surprise," Katherine says. "Usually, the guest list is full of company execs and finance managers who are a complete bore."

"What about Alison Greer? How does she fit in?"

"I noticed that you couldn't keep your eyes off her earlier. I know how you feel." Katherine smiles. "Alison and a few others are on the invite list to balance out the bankers. I always have two different lists when I have a party. The ones I have to invite and the ones I want. And you—"

"I didn't make it on the guest list," you interrupt. "I'm here because of Janine."

"Janine doesn't keep very good track of her date. But she does have good taste. What would she say if she knew you were in my bedroom?"

"We have an agreement."

"Good. I like to have those things settled up front. I want to know if I'm going to have enemies later." Katherine brushes her fingertip over your lips. "In the future, you will be on the guest list." When she touches your chest, you push her hand away. She sighs. "Do I beg?"

"Not yet."

"I think I should ask about the rules of this little game."

Handcuffs, whips, and clamps used to be some of the favored tools of one of your exes, and you guess by the nervous energy in Katherine's eyes that you have more experience with these toys. "I tell you what to do. And you do it."

"And I'm supposed to pick a safe word?" She laughs.

"You can if you want to."

Katherine cocks her head at the serious tone of your voice. She steps forward and plants a kiss on your lips. She tastes like champagne. Good champagne. You slip your hand behind her neck and pull her into another kiss just as she starts to pull away.

"You're my present for being good all week." Katherine runs her tongue along the edge of her lips.

You touch Katherine's gold necklace and then draw a line down to the start of her cleavage. Your fingertip traces the fabric over her breasts. "Who says you've been good? I saw you with the Pilates instructor in the locker room on Monday. You two were standing awfully close. Just friends?"

"You saw that?"

"Turn around," you say. The huskiness has already settled in your voice. Simply thinking about strapping on the harness and the dildo has you dripping wet. You want her naked and then you want inside. The sooner the better.

She slowly turns and you are greeted with her naked back. "That Pilates instructor is waiting for me out in the ballroom. Carmen. But I was planning on sleeping with Amélie tonight. And then maybe Alison if she's in the mood. Of course I'd like to see the two of them together."

"I like your appetite." You start with kisses on her neck and shoulders as your fingers search for a way to get the dress off. Moving down her back, you find the zipper hidden at the side of the gown and tug on the clasp. The material falls to her feet and Katherine turns to face you. She's wearing a cream-colored lace thong and a strapless bra that slips off easily. When you brush a cool fingertip over her nipple, she shivers at the touch but masks her nerves with a smile.

"The bartender was tempting. Did you see her? Slim, short blond hair...She asked if I was going to be alone later. After the party." Katherine's words are as forced as her smile. She squares her shoulders and stares back at you. "What?"

"You're trying to keep up that player attitude—as if you could turn around right now and walk out of this room, as if you could do anything you want without my permission." Katherine's jaw clenches and she shakes her head, but you continue, "Maybe you didn't understand what you signed up for. You happen to be mine tonight. Those other women will have to find someone else to keep them occupied."

"Oh, I'll have time for one of them later," she returns.

"Not tonight." You reach for the handcuffs and then cover her wrist in kisses as you latch first one cuff and then the other. She tenses up with the touch and you turn her face toward you, wanting her lips. The fire in her kiss only fuels your desire. "Lay down."

Katherine looks up at you as if she's ready to argue, but she slowly steps out of her heels. She pushes the bedcovers aside and sinks down on the bed. "I'm usually the one giving orders. I'm not sure if I like being told what to do."

"I think you'll change your mind. Lay all the way down." You wait for her to stretch across the bed and then reach for her handcuffs. The gold ropes dangling from the bed canopy are at the perfect height. Looping the rope around the short strap between her cuffs, you tether Katherine exactly where you want her. You cinch the knot on the gold rope and eye Katherine. Your mouth is watering already.

Katherine tugs on the handcuffs, but the ropes hold her in place. She complains about the chafing but you ignore her. She'll soon be thinking of other things. Her hands are above her head and her body is exposed, waiting for you. Her nipples are hard pink buds and her chest quivers when you reach for the whip. You snap it once and then trace the leather tip up from her toes to her panties and back down again.

The only sound in the room is her breathing. Her chest rises and falls quicker now that you have her attention. You touch the tip of the whip against her thigh and then snap it once more. She cries out and strains against the cuffs. Then her lips curl up in a smile.

"You've done this before," she says.

"More than once." You go over to the bedside table and pick up a black silk eye mask. "Yours?"

"I have trouble sleeping."

"You won't after this." You slip the mask over her head and cover her eyes.

"What are you doing?" she asks.

The nervous breathiness in her voice makes you realize that she doesn't know what to expect. "This is your first time being tied up." You wait for her to argue, but she doesn't respond. "First time being submissive, first time playing this game? It's not just that you aren't used to being told what to do, is it? You have all the toys…but you couldn't find a willing partner."

"My husband thinks I'm crazy for wanting something like this."

"What about your girlfriends?"

She tries to pull her hands down, probably to take off the mask, but the cuffs hold her in place. She exhales, long and slow.

"It takes a minute to relax." You run the leather strap along her calf. "But you will. You'll soon realize that you don't need to be the one in control…Everyone has a first time." When she doesn't strain against the rope, you lean down to kiss her neck.

"I've thought about paying someone," she says. "But it seemed ridiculous...To want something and not be able to ask a lover for it."

"You have to know the right people." Your hands trail along the inside of her thighs, skipping over her center.

"Maybe I'll start a list," Katherine says.

"Maybe you'll only need my phone number."

You brush your lips over her cheek. She takes a sharp breath inward as you nibble at her neck and she strains against her tether. Her chest trembles as she takes a breath.

"Don't worry," you whisper into her ear. "I'm going to take my time. And I won't hurt you unless you want that."

She shudders and then licks her lips. "I want it...but..."

"Only a little?" You chuckle. "We'll go slow. I've got all night."

You eye the harness and the dildo lying inches from Katherine's body. But you want to take Katherine as yourself, not as Batman. You slip off your mask and run your hand through your hair. You search the room with your eyes until you spot a closet and then another door that isn't the one you came through. Without a word to Katherine, you pick up the harness and dildo and then try the door.

The bathroom is just as ornate as the bedroom. After you turn on the shower, you light one of the candles on the counter. Katherine calls you from the bedroom. The image of her stretched out on the bed fills your thoughts as you eye the harness. Instead of answering her, you step into the shower.

After a rinse, you dry off with one of Katherine's plush towels and then try on the harness. The leather straps rub comfortably against your thighs. Thick and with a promising weight, the dildo takes some force to fit into the harness ring. The pulse in your groin returns as you stroke the shaft, shifting the dildo into position.

Katherine pulls against her tethers when she hears you in the room. The light from the candle casts a weak glow to the bedroom. She left the chest at the foot of the bed unlocked and you rifle through the toys until you find a bottle of lube. She sighs when you settle onto the bed beside her.

"Were you worried that I wasn't coming back for you?"
"Maybe."
"I wouldn't leave you like this. Tied up. Completely naked. Not for long, anyway." You feather her nipple with your finger, softly enticing the tip until you're ready to pinch. You squeeze hard, not letting up as she complains, straining against the cuffs and threatening to pinch you back. But you follow the pinch with soft licks and then a bite when her pelvis arches up off the bed.

"Too bad you don't have nipple clamps. These nipples are so tempting. So responsive. One little pinch and I have your attention." You trace the curves of her breasts. "You'd like the way a clamp feels. Just enough pain. Maybe I'll buy you a couple. For next time…"

You play with the other nipple until Katherine is moaning and trying to shift her pelvis toward your hands. But you won't touch her there yet.

You take off her blindfold and she blinks in the weak light. You lean down to kiss her and she parts her lips, opening up to you. Your kiss deepens as you search her with your tongue. She is ready to give anything to you, wordlessly begging you to top her in every way. You pull the blindfold back over her eyes.

You slather lube over the tip and shaft of the dildo and then push Katherine's panties to the side to slip your lubed fingers inside her. She wasn't expecting it, and she arches up and moans at the sudden touch. Every one of her finely sculpted muscles is taut. She shudders as you pull the panties off and move between her legs.

"I want you inside. I can't wait," she begs. She twists on the bed, fighting the cuffs.

You kiss her belly and make your way up to her neck. When she complains again, you reach for the whip and tap it lightly against her thigh. "Roll over."

"When do we get to the part where you fuck me?"

"When I decide that I want to fuck you." With the tip of the whip, you draw a line from her hip along the side of her belly to her ribs and then up to her armpit. She writhes on the bed as you rake the whip down the underside of her arm. "Roll over," you say again. "That isn't a request."

With her hands in cuffs and her wrists crossed, it takes a moment for her to shift onto her belly. When she does, you kiss her cheek. "I do love your backside." You run a fingertip down the line of her spine and then between her butt cheeks. She shifts and tries to roll over. "Stay right there."

You tap the whip against her butt. A moment later a murmured moan slips out of her lips. You snap the whip again, light against the back of her thigh, and get a whine in response.

"Oh God. I want you to fuck me," she says, looking over her shoulder at you. "Do I have to say please? Because I will."

"Will you tell your husband about tonight?"

She doesn't answer.

"Get on your knees."

She does, and you push her legs apart, then settle in behind her. The gold cord is pulled taut, holding her cuffed wrists on the pillows. She pushes up onto her forearms and tugs against the cord. Testing the cuffs again, she eyes you. Still defiant.

"Do you want me to untie you?"

She nods.

"But then this little game of ours would end..."

Katherine looks back at her hands.

"And when you're tied up like this I can fuck you any way I want to. Or not fuck you at all."

She licks her lips and her head drops to the pillow. You push her hips up and move between her legs. Her wet clit is staring at you. Pink and round and swollen. Parting her wet lips, you finger her for a moment.

"But you want me to keep going, don't you?" You pull your hand out from between her legs. "Because the truth is, you like being tied up. You've been waiting for this. Fantasizing about it. And you need someone who knows how to fuck you until it hurts. And then fuck you a little more." You stroke the inside of her thighs. "Tonight, I get to do whatever I want with you. Until my appetite is satisfied."

Katherine murmurs "Please" and tries to shift back onto your finger. She's slick and wanting. But you wait until she asks again. When she does, you slide inside with two fingers. She groans and begs for you to touch her clit, but you pull your fingers out of her and wipe the slick juice across her back. The smell of her musk is intoxicating. You grab a hold of her hips and she looks back at you, opening her mouth as she feels you shift forward. With a thrust, the tip of the dildo finds its way roughly inside her opening. Katherine closes her eyes and moans as you push the head of the dildo past her rim. Your shaft glides inside in one smooth push. You sink deep until the base of the dildo presses against your clit and Katherine cries out, clutching her pillow. You let her hear your pleasure with your own low moan.

"God, you feel good. You're clenching on me. You're gonna feel every thrust." You rock against her hips until you are dripping with cum. You lean forward over her, her back pressed tight to your chest and her butt pushed against your hips, and pump the dildo, riding her hard.

When you hear her breathing change and know her climax is close, you straighten and slide nearly all the way out. Katherine's gaze darts up to yours. She's worried that you're about to pull out, and her muscles are tense. Ready to come. You're still inside her with the tip, and you rock side to side against her rim, knowing she'll feel it on her g-spot. "You like this big cock, don't you?"

Katherine nods.

You pull all the way out suddenly. Katherine gasps as the head bucks out of her. She drops against the mattress, but you slip your hand under her belly and pull her back up again.

"I'm not done with you," you say. She pulls herself forward. Her eyes are wild. Angry. Before she can say anything, you grab her thighs and pull her back against you. The tip of the dildo bumps against her opening. "You still want it rough? Because this is gonna hurt. And you can tell me to stop any time. But I haven't heard you say the word." You wait, but Katherine only opens and closes her mouth. You lean close and kiss the back of her neck. "I'm gonna make it hurt. But only a little," you whisper. "And I know you want it." You thrust forward, forcing the cock into her. As she takes it, she groans low, clutching the sheets. "You like it?"

A weak nod.

"Good. That's how I like to fuck." You thrust your hips against her, riding the dildo in deep. Every time you pull back she sticks her pussy up, begging you to drive deep inside her again. You work her until her arms are shaking and her breath comes in quick gasps. "Tell me you want more."

"Oh God," she says. "I want more."

You push again. She's moving up and down now, bucking her butt up to take the shaft all the way inside and pushing back with enough force to make you brace your toes against the footboard at the end of the bed. She'll be sore later. Every step she takes tomorrow will remind her of what you've done to her tonight. And how much she wanted it. You feel your climax hit suddenly. The tremor races up your chest and you can't breathe. You hold on tight to Katherine, riding her still but numb to everything except the surge. You manage to reach around her hip to press your finger hard against her clit.

"Oh, ohh," she moans. She comes in a spasm that rushes through both of your bodies. She yells loudly enough that you wonder if a security guard will be tapping at the door. And then she's squeezing her legs together, trying to hold you inside. You stay, giving her a long moment to enjoy being filled, being fucked completely, but you're weak from your own orgasm and you pull out before she starts to relax. She groans when the tip comes all the way out.

"I want you back inside," she whines. She tries to break the cord between the handcuffs and then groans when it holds tight. "Why'd you pull out? Just put something inside. Anything. Put a finger in me."

You shake your head. You're too breathless to answer, and your clit is pulsing. Katherine collapses face down on the bed. You roll onto your back and reach down to finger your clit. An aftershock races through your body.

When the wave has passed, you lay quiet for a minute, listening to Katherine's breathing. Finally, you shift onto your elbow and reach up to unclasp the handcuffs. She rubs at her wrists and rolls onto her back. Her breathing is still ragged, and you watch her breasts, perfectly shaped mounds with nipples you'd love to nip, rise and fall rhythmically.

Several minutes pass before she glances over at you. "I'm not telling him, in case you really wanted to know. We've been separated for years now." She sighs. "I never see him. He's been living in England for the past four years. And he's got a lover there. Or two, or three. I don't even know. And I don't care." She pushes up on her pillow. "We have an agreement. And I've always found ways to entertain myself."

"Think your guests are entertaining themselves?" You touch her cheek and she looks over at you. You wonder if this is only a one-time thing with her. You could imagine having her three times a day every day for the rest of your life.

"Don't worry. This isn't the first time I've disappeared from my own party before dinner was served." She eyes the bedside clock. "And I could still make an appearance for dessert. If I got out of bed now…"

"Your guests may have to wait for their dessert. I'm not done with you yet." You move on top of her body and shift between her legs as you do. Her skin is sweaty against yours. You reach down to position the dildo, maneuvering the tip between her legs.

"Again? Are you kidding?" She laughs and shakes her head.

"I want you to remember tonight when you wake up tomorrow."

"Trust me, I will. I won't be able to walk without thinking of you."

"Good." You push the tip inside.

"Oh, God…" She moans and raises up from the pillows. Her hand presses at your chest. "I don't think I can take you inside me again. Not yet."

You pull back and finger her clit. "I think you can."

Her smile is tense. She's worried you're going to hurt her. And wanting the pain. "I don't know…"

You watch her a moment. "Tell me to stop and I will." You wait for her to answer, but she lays perfectly still under you. You lean forward to kiss her lips, and the dildo inches inside her.

"Fuck me," she murmurs.

You rock your hips against hers and the dildo sinks all the way in. She gasps and you start to pull back, but she shakes her head.

"Don't pull out." She reaches for your harness. Her fingers curl around the leather, pulling you back toward her. "Maybe you've convinced me."

"I like the way you say maybe."

"Maybe," she says again. She smiles. "I like the way you handle me."

"Tonight, I own you. I can do whatever I want with you." You sit back and stroke the shaft of the dildo, lathered with her cum, the tip still inside her.

"I liked to be owned." Her fingers still grip the harness. She watches your hand on the dildo. "Will you promise not to pull out this time?"

"No." You push her back against the pillows and then slip all the way inside again, watching her face as you do. Her lips part as she moans. Her fingers clutch the sheets. You pump the dildo, building speed as her cries intensify and her nails rake your arms.

"Fuck, I'm going to come again," she complains. She shifts her hips up, pushing against yours. "What are you doing to me?"

"Giving you what you need."

She licks her lips and squeezes her legs tight around your body as you slide in and out of her. "I need you to touch me," she begs. "Please."

You lick your finger and reach down to touch her, circling her engorged clit and then stroking until she's squeezing your hand and panting. You ride in and out of her, feeling another climax. As soon as you're close, you pinch Katherine's clit. She grabs your shoulders, pulling you tight against her as she moans. A minute passes before you feel her relax. She drops back on the pillows, her body limp under yours. Spent. Slowly, you sink down on top of her, your chest pressed against hers and the dildo buried deep inside. Your bodies are tied together.

After a long moment she moves under you, trying to push you off. You kiss her breasts, her neck, and then move up to her lips until finally she gives in and starts kissing you back. You shift your weight so you aren't pinning her, and she looks up at you.

"Screw the phone number," she says. "I want your address. I'm showing up unannounced whenever I want you."

"Whenever you want? You think that's how this is going to go?" You start to sit up, and the dildo slides nearly all the way out.

Katherine tries pulling you back into her. "You said you wouldn't pull out."

"No, I didn't. And maybe you forgot, but you aren't in charge."

She murmurs an apology. Contrite. When you don't lay back down, she says, "Let me try that again." She sighs. "Can I have your number, please?"

"Better."

You shift your weight on Katherine, rocking the dildo side to side inside her. Katherine purrs and pulls you tight against her body. Your clit is buzzing, ready to come again if you work the dildo in just the right place. You rock side to side again and then sink in. She takes it deep and then shoves her mound upward. The base of the dildo presses against your groin exactly where you want it.

"Keep that up and you'll have me again," Katherine murmurs.

Her eyes are closed and her lips are parted. She's beautiful. And she's all yours.

This is the end of your night's adventure. The party's over by the time you finish with Katherine, but you didn't miss anything important.
Go to Chapter Fourteen (page 229) for the morning after.

CHAPTER FIVE

Settle for a cream puff

"Cream puff?" the server asks, repeating the question.

"Yeah, sure. Thank you." You hesitate in picking out a puff, your hand hovering over the serving tray as you watch Alison slip out of the ballroom. She hurries through the foyer and then passes Jim the doorman. The hallway bends and she's gone from sight. Every fiber in your body longs to follow her, but your brain keeps your feet weighted in place. Her kiss on the patio makes your lips tingle still but you've lost any chance with her.

"They're all the same," the server adds.

"I know," you answer, watching the foyer and silently willing Alison to reappear.

"So, would you like one?"

You glance at the server. "A cream puff?"

She laughs. "Yes. What else?"

"I'd like a date." You see Janine talking with a woman you don't recognize. They are only talking. For the moment. "She doesn't need to be beautiful. Or smart. Just good company. And I wouldn't mind a good kisser."

"What if she was delicious?"

"Delicious?"

The cream-puff server directs a shy smile at you. This particular server, you notice, is very easy to look at. She has one dimple and light brown hair in a pixie cut. Freckles dot her cheeks. She wears a knee-length black skirt and a white tuxedo shirt with a black bow tie. A red serving towel hangs in the crook of her elbow and she holds the tray in one hand as if she's had a lot of practice despite the fact that she looks fresh out of college. Or maybe still in college. A coed between semesters.

"Try one. These make up for being single." The server leans in to add, "Don't tell my boss, but I've already had three. And compared to my ex-girlfriend, these things are way more satisfying."

"At least there's a good reason why she's an ex."

"Many good reasons."

Finally, you choose one of the puffs. The toasted shell is exactly the right texture, light and crisp, and the bottom half is dipped in a rich chocolate. As you bite into the pastry, the sweetened cream fills your mouth. "Oh, those are good," you admit. The bittersweet chocolate compliments the cream and the flavor lingers on your tongue after you've swallowed. You wipe crumbs off your lips. "Perfect, in fact. Who was the genius who decided to add chocolate to a cream puff?"

"Better than most dates, right? Go ahead and take another. I won't tell," she offers. "Besides, they're small."

You reach for a second. "Okay, I agree with you. They're good. But they aren't better than a good date."

"Better than any of the dates I've been on lately," she admits.

"Clearly you need to bring chocolate on your next date."

"Maybe." She sighs. "Sometimes even chocolate won't save a bad kiss."

"Sounds like you're going out with the wrong women."

"Is that an offer?"

You shake your head. "I'm too old for you."

"So, why are you in a costume?"

Tired of giving the same excuse, you say, "This isn't a costume."

She laughs. "No wonder you don't have a date."

"Who's your manager?" you ask, wagging a finger at her.

"This gig is a part-time thing. I don't care if they fire me." She continues, "I used to play the piano. In high school. Do you know anything besides Sinatra?"

"Not really."

"I'm not a jazz fan," she admits. "Especially the old stuff."

"Sinatra's not just a jazz singer. And he's...timeless," you argue. "How old are you?"

"Twenty-one."

"Too young."

She grins, and the dimple is back. "I'm not too young. You're too old."

You point to a couple standing off to the side of the bartender's station. "I think they need cream puffs over there."

She hands you a napkin. "Anyway, I liked the songs you played. Even if it was only Sinatra. You've got a little powdered sugar, right here." She touches your cheek. "I'm Mckenzie, by the way."

"Mckenzie with the cream puffs. Got it." You wipe your cheek and point again to the couple. "You're too young to appreciate Sinatra, and I'm too old to be dressed up in a costume."

"But you look good in it."

You meet her gaze, and she blushes.

"Don't worry. I was joking about finding your manager. You don't need to try and win me over."

"I mean it. You look good. How old are you, anyway? You can't be over thirty."

"Come back and find me when *you* turn thirty. Then we can flirt. Until then, you need to find someone your age."

"Who said I was flirting with you?" Mckenzie huffs.

You shrug, and she turns away. Her hips swish as she walks off, and you can't help noticing how nicely she fills out her skirt. "Twenty-one," you remind yourself. Mckenzie stops in front of the couple you'd pointed out. They each take a cream puff, and before she moves on she glances over her shoulder to wink at you.

You wave her on. Mckenzie with the cream puffs would be a nice distraction. If she were five, ten, or maybe twenty years older.

It doesn't take you long to spot Janine. Somehow you weren't thinking of her for the past half hour, but a hollow feeling hits your chest now. She's sitting at one of the banquet tables with two of her coworkers—unfortunately the sexy-single and possibly not straight Sarah is in the chair closest to hers, along with a few other couple you don't recognize. Likely rich clients. Or prospective rich clients.

"Hey, Batman."

You smile as Jim the doorman walks up. He holds his ear and then speaks into a microphone on the collar of his jacket. After a moment, he looks over at you and smiles. "How's your night going?"

"Good. Have you tried the cream puffs?"

"I'm off sugar." He holds his ear again and then speaks into his tiny microphone: "I'm heading that way. Give me a minute and I'll give an all clear after I've checked out the back." He strides past you to check one of the back doors leading out to the patio, then doubles back. As he nears your spot, he slows down. "Have you seen Mrs. Flaggerty?"

"Not recently. Why?"

Jim clears his throat before saying, "An alarm was triggered. We're doing a security sweep and we can't get to the other side of the house…Never mind. Just come find me if you see Mrs. Flaggerty."

As Jim walks away, you wonder why Katherine Flaggerty would need to hire a security crew for a dinner party. Having a key code for her private rooms seems strange, but maybe, you guess, when you're as rich as Katherine, you have enemies.

You hear loud voices coming from the foyer and decide to check it out. Jim is animatedly talking to a tall black woman in the marble hallway. The woman is at least two inches taller than Jim and disarming in a tuxedo that fits her slender frame perfectly. Jim sees you coming and lowers his voice. The woman turns to look at you.

"She's fine," you hear Jim say. "She's on Mrs. Flaggerty's list."

The woman's cell phone rings and she answers it, quickly turning away from your gaze.

Mrs. Flaggerty. You've never heard anyone call Katherine Missus anything. And you wonder what list Jim could be referencing. Guest list? But then everyone at the party would be on it. And your name wasn't specifically on the invitation list anyway. You were only invited because of Janine. Or so you thought. But the invitations were sent months ago and you never saw them anyway. If you had, you would have realized it was formal dress, not fancy dress. And now you are scratching your head wondering how Katherine would have had you on any list at all.

"Someone try to break-in?"

"We had an alarm go off by the garage," Jim says. "It's over on the far side of the house. We didn't find anything amiss, but we have to check everything."

"Your boss looks like she can handle anything."

Jim nods. "Tasha Wilcox. Ex-marine. Don't get on her bad side."

"Wouldn't think of it."

Tasha Wilcox eyes Jim. She speaks into her cell phone, "Yes, one of the house alarms was triggered so we are doing a security sweep...But I don't have access to half of the house and I am trying to locate Mrs. Flaggerty now."

You glance at Jim. "The house alarm was triggered? Why would anyone try to break in when the place is full of people?"

"We're trying to figure that out. My guess is a kid threw a rock at one of the windows. A neighbor told one of the valets that kids were setting off fireworks. Could have been that...But the back door of the garage was triggered. Probably only kids causing trouble."

"Doesn't sound dangerous."

"You're right," Tasha Wilcox says, suddenly turning back in your direction. She pockets her cell phone. "There's a report of a couple broken car windows and one stolen car. We probably don't need to call Batman in on this one." Her serious expression wavers and then slowly she breaks into a smile. "But if anything changes…Actually, maybe you could help with one thing. Katherine's hired us to be in the background, and I know she isn't going to want a scene. She won't like it if Jim or I walk in and interrupt the party. Can you find Katherine and tell her that I need to talk to her out here?"

Someone knocks on the door and Jim says something into the microphone on his coat. A moment later you see both Jim and Tasha tilt their heads, listening to their ear buds. You wait in the hallway long enough to hear Tasha handing out orders to whoever she's talking to over the radio. You'd love an excuse to spend more time watching Tasha, but a sharp look from her sends you off to find Katherine.

Katherine isn't in the ballroom. You crisscross from one end of the room to the other and ask a half a dozen people but only get shrugs and sideways looks in response. As a last-ditch effort you decide to ask the bartender.

"Any chance you've seen Katherine Flaggerty? She's the host."

The woman with the short blond hair nods. "If you're looking for Katherine, you might want a drink first."

"Did you see where she went?"

The bartender points to a back hall. "She was headed that way earlier. But who knows if she's still back there."

"Okay, thanks." You start toward the back hall, but the bartender steps out from behind the table and signals you over.

"She wasn't alone. And the woman she was with…they looked like they wanted privacy when they walked off."

You glance at the hallway and then back at the bartender. "The security guard asked me to find Katherine."

"Suit yourself," the bartender says. "But I've heard that she can be difficult. She might decide to shoot the messenger."

"I'll take my chances."

The bartender's warning seems to echo everyone's opinion of Katherine: *Don't cross her.* She clearly has a reputation, but in this case, you have nothing to lose. You head down the back hallway, passing an open doorway to a large noisy kitchen with a handful of servers and a cook shouting orders. Mckenzie suddenly steps out of the doorway. She's carrying a full tray of cream puffs.

"Coming to help in the kitchen?"

"Cream puff girl." You smile. Unfortunately, Mckenzie would be perfect. If she weren't still in college. "Did you happen to see the host? Katherine Flaggerty?"

"Cream puff girl?" Mckenzie narrows her gaze. She holds up her middle finger and tries to move past you.

"So you didn't see her?"

"Oh, I saw her. She took the last cream puff off my tray. I had to go get a refill."

"Where was she?"

Mckenzie shrugs. "Sorry. I'm just the cream puff girl."

Playing hard to get is always a turn-on, and Mckenzie is laying it on thick. You try to ignore the chemicals in your brain asking you to reconsider a twenty-one-year-old. "I'm sorry. I know your name—Mckenzie. You're right about what you said earlier. It's not that you're too young. I'm too old. But I still think you're cute. No hard feelings?"

Another server steps out of the kitchen with a tray of shrimp. He eyes Mckenzie, but before he can say anything, Mckenzie turns back to you and says, "You wanted a cream puff?"

"Yes, thank you."

You both wait for the other server to move on, then Mckenzie glances over her shoulder at the kitchen. She points down the hallway behind her. "There's an office at the end of the hall. She went in there. But she wasn't alone. There was another woman with her. Tall."

"Did she look like a model?"

"That's the one."

"Thanks, Mckenzie." You start down the hallway, but before you pass Mckenzie, she steps forward and kisses your cheek. Her hand catches yours.

"I'm off at ten, by the way."

"And you're twenty-one." You skirt around Mckenzie's tray. Admittedly, Mckenzie's peck made you catch your breath.

But she caught you off guard, and you argue that was the only reason. "Twenty-one," you repeat.

The hallway ends at a closed door. You raise your hand to knock and then stop yourself when you hear the sounds coming from the other side. You can't make out the words, but the general intent of the voices is clear. Whoever is inside isn't likely to be fully dressed. Or wanting an interruption.

Do you:
A) Tempt fate and knock on the door (read on)
B) Go back to the foyer and face the security crew without completing your mission (go to Chapter Eight, page 131)

Tempt fate and knock

Your fist raps against the door. You wait ten seconds, and when there's no answer, you try again.

"This better be good," Katherine says, opening the door only wide enough to see your face. She tilts her head. "Oh. I wasn't expecting you. The secretive pianist. Coming to discuss your reward for entertaining the guests?"

You shake your head.

"What happened with you and Alison?"

"She went to bed early."

"You pissed her off?" Katherine asks.

"The feeling was mutual."

Katherine chuckles. "Sounds like Alison. She's mad at me tonight as well. I invited Amélie to come for a visit. I thought the two of them would hit it off. Turns out Alison doesn't like sharing."

"Sharing?"

"Sharing me." Katherine opens the door a few more inches, and you relax when you realize that she's fully dressed. Apparently you were mistaken about the sounds you'd heard.

Behind Katherine you can see a big desk with an old-fashioned oil lamp casting the room in a dim yellow glow.

One wall is covered in books and another is all windows with a French door out to the back patio. You suddenly spot Amélie. She's naked. Stretched out on a long black leather sofa, one of her hands rests on the arm of the sofa while the other lazily fingers her nipples. Her legs are parted. She meets your gaze but doesn't move to close her legs. Then she says something to Katherine in French, still watching you. Katherine answers her and then turns to you.

"What was it you needed?" Katherine asks.

You clear your throat. "Tasha Wilcox wanted to speak with you. Tasha—the security guard." You manage to keep your eyes focused on Katherine though you long to see if Amélie is still prying her nipples.

"I know Tasha is my security guard." Katherine smiles. Of course she can tell that you're distracted by Amélie. And it seems that she's enjoying watching you begin to sweat. "Why did she need to talk to me?"

"Apparently there were some kids breaking into cars. And one stolen car."

"One of my cars?" Katherine asks.

"No. But an alarm was triggered on the house. Over by the garage. The guards called the cops."

"Apparently Miss Wilcox misunderstood her job requirements. I hired her to take care of security tonight," Katherine says. "And I chose her specifically because she said she could take care of everything…so I could focus my attention on other things." She motions to Amélie.

"Clearly."

"Then you understand that I can't be interrupted at the moment?"

"Of course. I'll let her know."

Behind Katherine, you hear Amélie speak up again. Katherine glances over her shoulder and then a smile edges her lips. "Amélie says that you shouldn't leave."

"What about the security guards?"

"What about them?" Katherine pushes the door all the way open and turns back into the room. "Tasha can figure this one out without us. But if she has any trouble she can't handle, she knows about the security cameras." Katherine flicks her wrist upward and signals the fan on the ceiling. "Only my bedroom doesn't have cameras. So why don't you come in and relax? Tasha can track me down if she really needs to."

"Cameras?" Amélie asks, her French accent testing the word.

Katherine nods. She walks over to the sofa and leans over to kiss Amélie on the cheek, then whispers something into her ear. As she straightens up, Katherine moves Amélie's hand off her breast and places it between her bare legs.

The only French phrase you can think of, "*Voulez-vous coucher avec moi ce soir*," slips off your lips. Loosely translated, it means *Would you like to sleep with me tonight?* Thank you, "Lady Marmalade."

Amélie glances at you and murmurs something in response. French. You wish you had more than song lyrics to pull from.

"Close the door," Katherine says. She goes over to the desk and picks up her cell phone. You watch her type something on the screen and guess that she's sending a text. Maybe to the security crew. If not, Tasha Wilcox is going to have a good view if she decides to check the security cameras to track Katherine down. The fan is directly above the leather couch. Amélie's eyes are closed and her head is back against the arm of the sofa. She tilts her hips up and fingers her lips.

You swallow. *Ménage à trois* comes to mind. Appropriate that you can only think of French phrases having to do with sex... From down the hall you hear footsteps and spot the cream puff girl—Mckenzie—coming toward you. She stops five feet away, a question on her lips. You shake your head and point to the ballroom, mouthing the words "Go back." Her tray is still full of plump crisp pastries.

"What are you doing?" she whispers, starting toward you anyway.

You meet Mckenzie halfway, snatch up three puffs, and then quickly spin her about, hoping you've moved fast enough to keep her from peering into the office. "Go back to the ballroom. We'll talk later."

Before she has time to argue you step into the office and pull the door closed behind you. Amélie cocks her head and then says something to Katherine. You set the puffs on a glass end table and then pull off your gloves.

"Take off your mask next," Katherine says. She drops her cell phone on the desk and then leans back in her chair. "And you might want to lock that door. In a few minutes, you and Amélie might not want any unexpected visitors."

Katherine's tone makes your heart skip a beat. It's too late to wonder what you've gotten yourself into. You pull off the hooded mask and then run your hands through your hair. Without questioning Katherine, you go to lock the door. The key turns in the door handle.

"You can give that to me," Katherine says. She's standing by the sofa now and stretches out her hand. You pass her the key and watch as she slips it into the bodice of her dress. "The belt next."

Katherine murmurs something in French as you pull off the yellow utility belt, and Amélie smiles. For once you wish you'd taken French instead of Spanish in high school.

"Keep going." Katherine motions to your padded chest.

You take each piece of the costume off until you're wearing only the long-sleeved black shirt and the Lycra pants. Katherine walks over and slips her hand under your shirt. She smiles when you tense up.

"Nervous?"

You shake your head, lying.

"Good." Her hand settles on your breast and her eyes lock on yours. A fingertip circles your nipple. "I've watched you in Pilates…and thought about what I'd like to do to you. But I never thought the opportunity would come up. Tonight is a pleasant surprise."

You move into her hand, enjoying how she's made both of your nipples hard and already wondering what her lips will do. She steps forward and kisses your neck, then continues feathering the tip of your nipple with a lazy touch. As soon as you start to relax, she pinches down. You gasp and she smiles with satisfaction. Her hand slips out from under your shirt as she steps away.

"Amélie can help you finish undressing," Katherine says. The look on her face is undeniably smug.

Katherine turns to Amélie and says something in French. Amélie's eyebrows arch. You feel your breath catch when Amélie stands and walks toward you. Katherine's cell phone buzzes.

"You can take everything off. It's warm in here." Katherine heads back to her desk. But of course she's fully dressed. Clearly this is her power play.

Amélie helps you out of your shirt and bra. She murmurs something that sounds like tits as her hands cup your breasts. Then she sucks your nipple into her mouth and you feel a nerve race straight from your breast to your groin. Amélie kneels in front of you. Her face is right at your waist as she inches your pants, with the underwear, off your hips. Her breath is hot against your thighs. She pulls your pants down to your ankles and waits for you to step out of the clothes. Katherine comes behind Amélie, pausing long enough to say something, again in French, to the kneeling woman. Amélie glances first at Katherine and then at you. She runs one fingertip from the inside of your ankle up to your thigh and then stops. Your heart is pounding.

"Too bad you don't speak French. You might enjoy hearing what I just told Amélie to do to you," Katherine says. "Part your legs."

Your groin is already pulsing. As soon as you move your legs apart, Amélie wraps her arms around your thighs. She pulls you toward her mouth and her tongue pushes in. You gasp and grip Amélie's shoulders, somehow keeping your balance as her tongue sends your clit into a spasm.

Katherine circles behind you. She leans close to whisper in your ear, "She is very good, isn't she? I noticed that you were eyeing her earlier, and I thought this might be perfect...But then you slipped off with Alison." Katherine touches your lower back, sending a shiver up your spine. "I told you that I'd find a way to repay you for the piano performance. The guests did enjoy that. Maybe you can play something just for Amélie and me later? I'd enjoy seeing you naked on my piano bench."

Amélie's tongue changes from circling to stroking and your swollen clit is nearing the edge. You glance down at her face between your legs. The jet-black hair is all that you can focus on.

"Tell me." Katherine settles in on the leather sofa with a tumbler of what you guess is whiskey. "Do you like toys?"

Katherine's watching you, waiting for an answer, but you can hardly breathe, let alone form a sentence. You manage a nod. Toys are good, you think, but tongue is better. You feel your climax coming. Amélie sucks your clit between her lips and her chin juts up, pushing into you. You come hard, a sudden rush travels from your groin up to your jaw. You clench your teeth and ride out the cascade of firing nerves.

When you open your eyes, Katherine is staring at you. She smiles and says something to Amélie. Amélie wipes her lips and looks up at you.

She stands up and grazes her fingertip over your lips. Then she kisses your cheek. Katherine holds out her glass, and Amélie goes over to the sofa. You watch her take a long sip. Your legs are shaky and your clit pulses. Amélie's tongue was experienced, and you're already wondering what more could be in store.

"The toy chest is over there." Katherine motions to a large wooden box on the bottom shelf of the wall of books. "Pick out one that you think Amélie might like."

Katherine reaches for a cream puff. She bites it and places half on Amélie's waiting tongue. Amélie sits down on the sofa, her legs on top of Katherine's. You watch the two women. They finish their cream puff and then Katherine pulls Amélie toward her, covering her mouth with a deep kiss. You linger, watching their lips open, imagining the feel of their kiss. Finally willing your body to move and your eyes to look away, you go to the bookcase.

Katherine's toy chest is painted black and lacquered to a brilliant sheen. Intricately carved and layered with bits of abalone shell and onyx, the lid depicts a scene of two plump women, their bodies entwined as they bathe in a pool of shimmering water.

You unclasp the lock and open the box. Lined in dark red velvet, the inside of the box is nearly as beautiful. You brush your hand over the velvet, enjoying the sensation, and then sort through the treasures inside. You choose a small flexible pink vibrator and a firm blue dildo. Tiny bottles of flavored lube tempt you. Vanilla bean, mocha, raspberry... You pick all three.

You walk over to the sofa and set your treasures on the end table. Katherine pushes Amélie back against the sofa. Amélie murmurs an argument, but Katherine ignores her as she surveys your prizes.

"No harness? Hmm. Maybe later..." Katherine reaches for the pink vibrator and then motions for you to take the dildo.

You squirt raspberry lube on the tip of the dildo and smear it down the shaft. You taste the tip—tart raspberries. Amélie is watching you. She lays back, her head against Katherine's chest, and then stretches across the sofa. Holding your gaze, she parts her legs and rocks her hips up. Lubed and perfectly shaped, the bulged tip pushes inside and the slender shaft follows. You hold the flat base, stroking in and out a few times, and then pause and dip your head to taste her. Amélie pushes back against Katherine, moaning her enjoyment.

"Not so fast," Katherine says, moving your head away from Amélie. "She comes too quick if you let her."

Amélie complains, trying to pull your head back between her legs.

"What?" Katherine asks. She listens to Amélie's response and then shakes her head. She adds something in French that makes Amélie's lips purse and then slips the vibrator on Amélie's clit. A low hum starts when Katherine presses the bright pink button. "She wants your tongue. I told her to convince you to spend the night with us. Then she can have you between her legs when she wakes up tomorrow morning."

"Ah," Amélie moans. She grinds down on the dildo. Katherine holds the vibrator as Amélie rocks up and down.

You thrust the dildo faster, watching Katherine. Amélie is stunning. A perfect French model. But you find your body lusting after Katherine even more. Her eyes are locked on yours and you wonder if she will let you work the dildo in her next.

You shift forward and kiss Amélie's lips. Katherine's lips are so close to yours. You look up at her and she cocks her head as her lips part. You close your eyes, dizzy with lust, and find her mouth. Her tongue pushes forward.

Amélie moans, her cries gaining volume. You pull away from Katherine's lips and pump the dildo faster and deeper inside, knowing that Amélie is close. Katherine pulls off the vibrator and her fingers taunt Amélie's swollen clit. Then she sets the vibrator back in place and Amélie pushes against it. She climaxes hard, yelling as she does, and sits up to grip your hand, the dildo buried deep inside her. She kisses your lips and says something to you in French. When she falls back against Katherine, a tremor races through her body. She is still for a moment after, then pushes the vibrator away and squeezes her legs together around the dildo.

You hazard a glance at the fan above the sofa. You'd forgotten about the camera. Now the blinking red light reminds you that all of this has been recorded. When you look back at Katherine, she smiles, maybe guessing at your thoughts. Amélie is relaxed. She stretches her lean body lazily and turns her lips to Katherine. Their kiss is fierce and it's a long moment before they part. Finally, Katherine reaches down and pulls the dildo out of Amélie. She hands the wet dildo to you.

"In case you were thinking of leaving…don't. We're keeping you all night," Katherine says. "I have plans for both of you… Besides, I have the key. Now go find the harness. And a bigger dildo. We have to taste all the other flavors you've picked."

This isn't the end of your night's adventure. But this is the end of the story.
If you want a morning after, turn to Chapter Fourteen, page 229. Otherwise, good night.

CHAPTER SIX

Tell Katherine you were thinking of...

"I was thinking of something a little less binding. Something more formal, maybe." You reach out to touch Katherine's harness and run your hand up and down the leather straps. "I can't believe I'm saying no, but..."

"You don't want to say no."

"You're right." You look up at Katherine and feel a tug. Janine gave you permission. And yet she also has permission. "My heart is telling me to go back to the party. If I don't, I think I might lose Janine. But every other fiber in my body is telling me to take that harness."

"I make a habit of never letting my heart become involved where sex is concerned. It's such a common mistake." Katherine drops the harness and the dildo into the chest. She brushes her thumb over your cheek and then crosses her arms. "Are you in love with Janine?"

"Maybe. I felt sick when I thought we were breaking up. But I don't know if that means I'm in love with her, or if I just don't want to let her go." Katherine's touch has you second-guessing your priorities. And her eyes won't let go of yours. Her dress would be easy to slip off her slim shoulders. You take a deep breath and try to focus. "I want her. But I don't know if I love her."

Katherine smiles. "That might sum up every relationship I've had to date."

You laugh, feeling the tension ease. "Janine wants to play this game tonight. We're supposed to pretend that we aren't together, flirt with other people, dance with other people…She thinks a little jealousy is a good thing." You sigh. "And then we meet up tomorrow to talk about whether we are going to break up or not. But what if she's the one? What if I screw it up by not saying something tonight? What if someone else sweeps her off her feet?"

"What if? Would you be sad? Angry? Do you want to fight for her? There's other fish, you know." Katherine steps closer to you, inches away from your lips. "If Janine's really the one you want, why do you keep looking at me like you want to take off my clothes?"

Suddenly the room is too quiet. Katherine doesn't make the first move. She waits for you, maybe knowing that you can't resist. When you lean in, warm lips open to yours. She presses against you, parting enough to offer exactly what you want without making you ask. Another kiss, deeper, and Katherine's hand settles on your chest. You rest your hands on her hips. Thoughts of undressing her, of where she will let you touch her, make you dizzy with want as she keeps you occupied with her lips. Too much time passes before your resolve kicks in and you force your body to pull away.

When you open your eyes, she's staring at you. "You're very good at that."

"I know I am," she says.

Katherine holds your gaze. There's no use weighing your options—sleeping with Katherine versus winning back Janine. The two can't be balanced. And the longer you hesitate, the more likely you'll lose everything. But you slip into figuring a risk–benefit analysis. "Any chance you'd consider a rain check?"

"If you don't win Janine back tonight?" Katherine laughs. "No." She closes the lid on the wooden chest and the toys disappear. "But I'm willing to help you get her back. And then maybe we can talk. I won't turn down a threesome."

Katherine crosses the room and opens a door. She flips a light switch and motions for you to follow her inside. Her walk-in closet is the size of your bedroom. Suits line one side of the closet, but the rest of the space is filled with rows of dresses. Shoes fill racks along the bottom. In the middle of the closet is a long padded leather bench. The back wall has a floor-to-ceiling mirror.

Katherine stops in front of a small rack of men's suits. She pulls out a black suit and holds it up, eyeing it for a moment and then glancing back at you. Katherine tosses the suit on the padded bench along with a pressed white shirt still hanging in a garment bag from the cleaners. She goes to the opposite side of the closet and pulls out two dresses, one dark blue and one black.

"Strip."

Despite the fact that you can't shake the feel of her kisses on your lips, or maybe because of that, you begin pulling off the Batman costume as Katherine settles in on the bench.

"My advice is play Janine's game. Walk out there and let her see you. Then find someone else to kiss. With her watching."

"That's not exactly fair to whoever I kiss tonight."

"Pick someone who isn't really available," Katherine says. "I have a list of exes with issues I could give you."

"You do have a reputation."

"Well deserved, I suppose." Katherine glances at your half-naked reflection in the mirror. You see her smile in the mirror. Of course she's enjoying herself. "The question is, do you only want to make Janine jealous or do you want to really enjoy yourself tonight?" She watches until you're down to a bra and, fortunately, your sexiest pair of underwear, and then she hands you the dark blue dress.

Do you:
A) Try the dress (read on)
B) Tell Katherine you prefer a suit (go to Chapter Seven, page 112)

Try the dress

You eye the tags on the dress. "You haven't even worn this?" "It didn't fit." Katherine motions to her ample breasts. "Too tight around the chest. I never got around to taking it back. I bought it in Rome."

You slip the dress on over your head and Katherine comes up behind you to help with the zipper. Once the zipper is fastened, her hands linger on your hips. You turn to face her and she steps back and looks you up and down, then nods.

"What do you think?" She points to the mirror.

You glance at the mirror. Batman is gone. The blue dress clings to your body, making you feel exposed and invincible at the same time. You run your hands over the silky fabric hugging your hips. "I love it."

"It looks like it was made for you."

You turn back toward Katherine, and her lips meet yours. Again. The kiss is over too soon; this time, she pulls away first. You find yourself wanting another. But Katherine is already searching through her rack of shoes. She pulls out a pair of blue pumps.

"These might be a little big, but try them on."

You reach for the shoes. "I think I made a mistake. I don't think I should have turned you down earlier."

"You're following your heart, remember? And maybe it will turn out better for you than it usually does for me." Katherine continues, "Try those on."

The shoes are at least a half-size too big, but with a pair of nylons stuffed in the toes you can manage. And they're perfect with the dress.

Katherine stares at you as you try a test walk around the bench. "No dancing. I don't want to be responsible for a twisted ankle."

"Deal. I'd rather do other things anyway." You glance at Katherine. Your lips are still buzzing from her kiss. "I've never had a threesome. Do you take turns?"

"You've never had a threesome?" She whistles softly. "What a loss." She runs her hand along the neckline of your dress. When a phone rings, Katherine glances back at the bedroom. "Someone has finally noticed that I'm missing out there. Anyway, we need to get you to the ballroom."

Katherine's hand slips down the side seam of your dress. Then she steps forward and meets your lips. She cups your chin before she pulls away and you regret the moment she lets go. She turns and heads back to the bedroom.

You stand still, watching your reflection in the mirror, and then touch your lips. Maybe that last kiss was meant for good luck, but Katherine's lips have managed to make you doubt your goals. Maybe your heart has no business getting involved where sex is concerned.

After a stop in the bathroom to splash water on your face and let Katherine test a puff of perfume on your skin, you make your way to the ballroom. Katherine's hands lingered on your skin in the bathroom and again in the bedroom, but by the time you pass into the foyer she keeps her distance. Your body is convinced you're making a mistake turning down her offer. But the bright lights in the foyer and the classical music snap you back to reality. Katherine only wants a one-night stand. With Janine you could have a relationship that would mean something the morning after.

Before you cross the threshold to the ballroom, you spot Janine. You take a deep breath. She's sitting at one of the banquet tables with the woman from the gym. Muscles. As you watch, Muscles leans close and whispers something in Janine's ear. And then they kiss. It's only a peck, but your heart sinks.

Katherine glances at you and clicks her tongue. "Looks like you've got your work cut out for you tonight if you're still set on that one. But if I were you, I'd go say hello to her." She points to the bartender's station. "Blond hair. Ponytail. Looks like a soccer player. She's easy on the eyes and not a bad kisser."

"You kiss and tell?"

Katherine ignores your question. "She's not the only one I can recommend. There's Carmen." She points to a woman in an orange dress. "Our Pilates teacher, of course."

"She looks amazing. I hardly recognize her."

Katherine nods. "And she's very good with her tongue. Carmen's in the middle of a divorce from her husband and is up for anything. Plus, she's mentioned that she thinks you're hot. I guarantee she won't turn you down."

"Carmen mentioned me? I saw you together in the locker room after the Pilates class the other day and wondered if there was something going on between you two." Seeing Katherine lean to whisper something into Carmen's ear had sent a flush through you that had nothing to do with the workout. "But I thought she was straight."

"Most women are straight until they start kissing other women." Katherine's confident look makes you realize she's probably led more than one *straight* woman astray. "There's also Alison Greer. I know you two are acquainted." She points out Alison, who is predictably in the middle of a crowd of women. "She mentioned you earlier as well. You've been the talk of the town."

Alison Greer is an unexpected curve ball. You stall for a moment. "I think she's hot, but who doesn't? She wouldn't go for me."

"You're wrong." Katherine meets your gaze. "But my point is, Janine looks like she's having a good time on her own. Maybe you should do the same."

And then Katherine is gone. You watch her slip into a crowd in front of the fondue fountain. She dips a strawberry into a river of chocolate and then bites it in half. A man comes up behind her and says something to make her laugh. Katherine's last kiss is still fresh on your lips, but you have a feeling you won't be getting another from her. You glance back at Janine. Muscles has her arm around Janine's chair.

Two bartenders are working: the woman Katherine pointed out and an older man with a buzz cut. The line at their counter moves quickly. Before you have a chance to think of something witty to say as an introduction, the woman with the short blond ponytail is wiping the counter in front of you. She's about your age and definitely easy on the eyes—exactly as Katherine promised. But there's something familiar about her, and you have a nagging feeling that you know her.

"What can I get for you?" She sets a napkin down on the counter.

"I wasn't really coming for a drink," you admit. The longer you stare at her sparkling dark blue eyes, the more convinced you are that you know her. "Katherine told me I should meet you. But I feel like we've already met. I just can't remember where. Or when."

The bartender squints for a moment and then smiles. "Jeez, it's been a long time. UCD, Dorm Three. We were on the same floor freshman year, remember?" She extends her hand. "Lara."

"Lara. Of course! It's great to see you again." You clasp her hand, noting her strong grip and the unsteadying smile she has fixed on you. Lara was your favorite player on the rugby team. And not because of how she played.

"It's been a long time," she repeats. "I remember you used to play that old piano down in the rec room for hours. I loved hearing you play. You know, you were the reason I passed physics."

"After you'd missed every class and came to me for the notes."

"Because of you, I scraped by with a C." Lara grins. She glances at the bartender next to her. "You okay with me taking a minute over here?" He holds up his index finger. Lara turns back to you and continues, "Do you work with Katherine or are you friends?"

"Not exactly either," you admit. "But she loaned me a dress."

"It's a good pick. You look gorgeous." Lara flashes her perfect smile and then reaches for a glass. She picks up a sprig of mint. "Can I make you a drink? Back when I used to do this gig full time, mojitos were a special of mine."

Lara crushes the mint with a wedge of lime and is liberal with the rum. You have no intention of turning her down but make a mental note to go slow. You've still got a buzz going from the tall glass of champagne on an empty stomach.

"So, what happened to you?" Lara asks. "How'd you end up here?"

"I could ask you the same. Last I heard, you dropped out of college sophomore year. Everyone on the rugby team was mad at you. You were their star player."

"I miss rugby. But not the bruises." She laughs. "I made a few mistakes back then. One of which was thinking that I didn't need a degree. I dropped out and got a job. But I went back to college eventually. Now I'm in grad school." She shakes the ingredients of the mojito in a tall metal shaker and then pours the contents into your glass, sprinkling a few mint leaves on top. "Tell me what you think."

You take a sip. The lime juice makes your cheeks purse and the rum is strong, but the sweet mint aftertaste is perfect. "This is good." You take another sip. "Perfect, in fact. What are you a grad student in?"

"Law."

"A lawyer, huh? I wouldn't have guessed."

"You say that like it's a compliment." Lara grins. "Don't worry, I get it. But I'm not going to be that kind of lawyer."

"Which kind?"

"You know, the ones who chase after ambulances or get wet when couples argue about divorce." Lara adds, "Those guys are out there. But that's not me. Anyway, at the moment, I make mojitos and read legal briefs."

You hold up your drink. "I'm sure your friends enjoy studying with you. Mojitos always help."

"Exactly." Lara glances down at your hand, maybe looking for a ring. "I haven't seen anyone from UCD since I left. And I can't believe you're the one I run into now." She shakes her head. "Remember that girl who used to snort Mountain Dew?"

"Her girlfriend thought it was sexy." Lara laughs with you and her eyes sparkle. "Those two were crazy."

"So what happened to your girlfriend?"

"We broke up junior year. I didn't keep in touch."

"Her loss," Lara says. "Any chance you're single now?"

"If I was, would you give me your number?"

"If you were single, I'd ask you out tonight." Lara cocks her head. "So are you?"

The confidence that made Lara fearless in college and sexy as hell hasn't changed. And you can't stop smiling at her. She's got you hooked again. But your heart interrupts your thoughts. "It's complicated. My girlfriend and I agreed to take some time off. One week. And when that week ends, we decide if we are going to break up or not."

"When's the week over?"

"Tomorrow."

"Then technically you're single for one more night."

You nod.

"Is your girlfriend here tonight?"

You turn to point out Janine. She's still sitting with Muscles, but the banquet table has filled with six other dinner guests. "She's the one in the red dress." Servers are bringing out plates of salad. You look away and sip the mojito.

Lara leans on the counter, studying the table you pointed to. "And how do you feel about the idea of her going home with that dyke who's about to kiss her now?"

"I don't want to see." You close your eyes.

"I'm joking. No one's kissing. They're eating salad." Lara laughs. "Your girlfriend's hot. Maybe you should go over and join their conversation."

"I'd rather talk to you," you admit. Lara's charisma hasn't faded one bit. Nor has her confidence. Her gaze is fixed on you, and you can't bring yourself to look away.

"Good. Want to go out with me tonight?"

"At midnight?"

A customer comes up to the counter. You recognize the woman but can't recall her name. She immediately says your name, smiling as if you're close friends, and you manage to compliment her rhinestone-studded heels before turning back to Lara.

"I should let you get back to work."

"Wait," Lara says. "You didn't answer my question." She turns to the customer at the counter. "What can I get for you?"

"Scotch. On the rocks."

Lara scoops two ice cubes into a glass and then reaches for a bottle of scotch. She holds it up and the woman nods. Lara chats with the customer, and your gaze wanders back to Janine. Katherine has walked over to Janine's table.

When the woman with the scotch leaves, Lara turns to you. "Do I have a date tonight?"

"I don't think so."

"Well, your girlfriend's hot. I guess I don't blame you. But I had to try." She reaches for something under the counter and then takes your napkin. She writes her number on the napkin. "In case you change your mind or you just want to catch up... I'd love to hang out sometime."

You take the napkin and fold it in half. "Thanks for the drink. It was really nice seeing you."

"Maybe we'll see each other again."

As you turn to leave, you nearly collide with Janine. You manage to catch her arm, steadying her. She draws a quick breath in and adjusts her dress as she straightens.

"That was close. Thank you for catching me." She clasps your hand. "I was on my way to get a drink, but maybe that champagne was enough. I can't believe I'm already tipsy."

"I think it was my fault," you admit. "These heels don't really fit...Are you okay?"

"I'm fine. Really." Janine smiles. "I see Katherine set you up nicely."

You glance first at Lara and then, feeling a sudden blush, realize Janine meant your dress. "Yeah, you should see her closet. She has everything. And more."

"I've seen it. Katherine's taste is stunning and she's got the pocketbook to back it up," Janine says. "But I think I would waste more time than ever wondering what to wear."

"You're probably right." You wonder why Janine would have been in Katherine's closet. Before you can think of a good reason to ask, Janine is pointing to your drink.

"Since when do you drink cocktails?"

"The bartender convinced me to try this."

"That bartender could get me to drink just about anything she put in front of me. What is it?"

"A mojito. Want a sip?"

Janine takes a sip, and her face pinches. "Whoa, that's strong. Watch out, you'll be going home with anyone who asks by the time you finish that drink."

"I'll try to use discretion."

"Looking as good as you do in that dress, you're going to have more than one offer. I can tell Katherine has her eye on you. And that bartender's staring at you now, too. How does it feel to be available to so many eager takers?"

"I'm not sure how I feel. I guess it's nice. But I keep thinking about you."

"Good. I keep thinking about you, too." Janine glances back at the banquet table, and her gaze finds Muscles. "But I think I'm going home with Mac. Are you okay with that?"

Muscles. You force a smile. "Do I have a choice?"

"Find someone to kiss. You have plenty of women interested." Janine touches your arm. "We'll talk tomorrow."

Janine doesn't give you a chance to argue your case. She walks right past you to order a glass of red wine. From Lara. You stare at Janine's back, the spaghetti straps of the red dress and then the slit up the side of her thigh. Unfortunately, she's going home with Muscles.

Lara chats as she pours. Comparing Lara and Janine is apples and oranges. You've never kissed Lara, never slept with her, never had a long conversation in bed with her. A comparison wouldn't be fair. Yet you find yourself comparing the two women anyway. They're both attractive. Fit. Outgoing. Engaging. Although you'd love to know Lara better and her unknowns are enticing, you still find Janine interesting after five months of dating, still have questions about her, still wonder what she thinks about when the lights go dark. All of that might be worth more than the excitement of a newcomer.

Lara has Janine laughing now. You take a sip of the mojito and look away from the bar. Your gaze settles on a small crowd gathered by the fire. And then you see Katherine. She's leaning on the arm of a love seat and ostensibly engaged in a conversation with two men who, from fifty feet away, seem to be one-upping each other for Katherine's ear.

Then you spot your Pilates teacher. Carmen. She walks up to Katherine and distracts her from the men's conversation. Anyone would be distracted looking at Carmen. Her orange dress is stunning on her perfect body. You force your gaze away from Katherine and Carmen and down the rest of the mojito.

You set your empty glass on a tray and head over to the fondue table. The choice of apple slices, strawberries, or pineapple chunks is a breath of fresh air. Easy. Strawberry. Maybe you shouldn't sleep with anyone tonight, you think, skewering an extraplump strawberry. Maybe you are meant to leave the party alone.

You can't help wondering what Max is doing tonight. Maxine, your best friend, would have a field day teasing you about tonight if only she knew. If only. The dull ache in your chest comes on suddenly. Max. You've avoided her for the past two months, but you haven't admitted why. And she's still your best friend. You reach for your phone to text her, but it occurs to you that you've left your cell phone and keys in Katherine's closet. Probably for the best, you realize. Texting Maxine with the full strength of champagne and a mojito coursing through your brain along with loneliness clouding your thoughts might spell disaster.

"So what'd the strawberry do?"

You glance up and see Alison staring at the mess of strawberry in your hand. You've managed to not only transect the fruit with the bamboo skewer, but also to eviscerate the thing.

"I guess it was too ripe." Reaching for a napkin, you swipe the mess off your hand, wishing anyone except Alison could have caught you indisposed with the strawberry slime.

"Or maybe you don't know your own strength."

"I'd blame alcohol before that. Clearly a mojito after a glass of champagne is too much for me."

"They're making those mojitos strong," Alison agrees. "You look good in blue. But why the sudden costume change? I kind of miss having Batman at the party."

"Turns out this wasn't a costume party." Alison's compliment has you fighting back a blush. You try to seem nonchalant as you toss your napkin and miss the trash can. Alison notices and grins. You walk over to the trash can and toss it again, chuckling as you miss a second time. Now Alison is laughing too. At you. You sigh and finally manage to get the strawberry-covered napkin in the trash.

"How strong was that mojito?"

"Too strong." You walk back over to her, wondering why she's stopped to talk to you at all and not in the middle of a crowd of fans. "Turns out I've made a series of bad decisions today. Only one of which was skipping lunch."

Alison reaches past you for a skewer and a strawberry. With one move she has the fruit skewered and dipped in chocolate. She hands you the skewer and waits for you to take a bite. "I find that I make better decisions after I've eaten something. Particularly chocolate."

"To better decisions, then." After you finish the strawberry, you stab an apple slice and dunk this in chocolate too. Your stomach growls, and you eye the banquet tables. The servers are making the rounds collecting salad plates and dishing out cuts of steak and creamed potatoes. You rarely eat steak, but the aroma is suddenly enticing.

"That steak smells delicious," Alison says.

"I was just thinking the same thing."

"But I can't bring myself to sit down over there," she admits.

"Why not?"

"Aside from the fact that my doctor has warned me that my cholesterol is too high for red meat, there's certain people here tonight that I'd like to avoid." Alison sighs. "Three different women, in fact. If I sit down alone, I'm one hundred percent certain that one, or all three, will sit down at my table."

"All three?" You smile. "Exes?"

"I've got bad luck with women." She shakes her head. "I could tell you more, but it would take all night."

"Are you the heartbreaker?"

"Not exactly. I'm the reality check. For some reason, everyone I date wants to live in a fantasy world where you don't have to deal with any problems." She eyes a passing waiter with a tray of heaped dinner plates.

"We could sit together at a table that's nearly full. Then there wouldn't be any room for exes." You stop as soon as you realize that you've just asked Alison to eat with you. Alison Greer. Somehow, for the last several minutes, you've forgotten to be tongue-tied around her.

"It's risky..."

"But maybe worth it." Blaming the mojito, you continue, "Or we hide out here, stick to a fruit and chocolate diet and enjoy the smell of the steak without the cholesterol."

"I bet this fondue has cholesterol, too. We might as well be eating steak."

You wave a skewer. "Don't ruin this chocolate fondue for me." You try a pineapple chunk.

Alison skewers a pineapple as well and dunks it in the chocolate. She takes a big bite and ends up with a drip of chocolate on her chin and a smear on the side of her cheek. "We can pretend this is cholesterol-free fondue. Oh, God, there's Becca. I'm going to hope she keeps walking."

"One of your three exes?"

Alison nods. You eye the woman Alison is watching. She's got a crew cut and flashy dangling earrings. Latina butch but fashion-forward, you think, assigning a label to someone who probably hates labels. She's notably handsome in a stylish leather jacket and a pair of red jeans that show off her butt, but it's her swagger that seems to have everyone looking her direction. She cuts through the ballroom as if she's on a catwalk. And then you recognize her. "Isn't she the DJ from Rumors?" Rumors is the gay club downtown.

Alison nods. "DJ Dee. Otherwise known as Becca Dee."

Becca glances over at the fondue table, and you remember the chocolate on Alison's face. You grab Alison's arm and spin her toward you so that she has her back to Becca. "Pretend like

I'm the most interesting person here. Whatever you do, don't look back at her. You've got chocolate all over your face." You touch Alison's chin and then her cheek.

"Oh God. Thank you." She laughs as she tries to swipe off the chocolate. When she only manages to smear it, you take the napkin and help.

"I figure the last thing I'd want my ex to see is my face covered in fondue." You dab the two spots until the chocolate is gone. "There. Now you're perfect again."

Alison's eyes crease as she smiles at you. Then she shakes her head. "Thank you. I'm far from perfect."

"Not far," you argue. Feeling a sudden undeniable urge to kiss her, you step back. You quickly point to a passing waiter with dinner plates laden with steak. "Too bad we only get to look."

"I've never wanted steak as much as I do right now," Alison admits.

A server passes the fondue table. He's carrying a tray of dirty salad plates en route to the kitchen. "I've got an idea. Follow me."

The server with the dirty plates cuts behind the piano, passes through the middle of the ballroom, and then just as he's past the bartender's counter he turns and disappears down a hallway. You follow his path, slowing as you cross through the line at the bar. Lara is pouring wine. She looks up long enough to meet your eyes. You wave, and her lips turn up in a smile.

Alison notices the exchange and says, "You made friends with the bartender? I don't blame you. She's cute."

"We knew each other in college." But the truth is you made friends with the bartender because she was cute. The fact that she happens to be an old friend is a good excuse. "Almost there," you say to Alison, turning down the narrow hall.

"Where are we going?" Alison wonders.

You spot the server halfway down the hall just as he pushes through a door into a noisy kitchen. Before you reach the door it swings open and a young woman with a tray of cream puffs emerges.

"We need a favor."

"Um, okay." She glances from you to Alison.

She's young and impressionable. And from the short haircut and the way she's looking at you, she might even be queer. Perfect. "We're avoiding the banquet tables. Any chance you can steal us two dinner plates. Steak?"

The server nods. "No problem. Here, hold this."

You take the tray of cream puffs, and the server slips back to the kitchen. Alison reaches over and picks out a puff. She takes a bite, and her eyes close.

"Oh. Dear lord." She pops the rest of the puff into her mouth, and you watch as she moans her enjoyment. She licks her fingers. "You've got to try one of these. Maybe we should skip dinner and run off with this tray."

Just then the cream puff server pushes out of the kitchen with two dinner plates complete with slabs of steak, creamed potatoes, and sautéed green beans.

"I stole a puff," Alison admits immediately.

"Orgasmic?" The server grins and her dimples show. "I didn't make them. But I've eaten three. So far." She hands Alison the dinner plates and two sets of utensils rolled in cloth napkins. Then she turns and takes the tray of cream puffs from you. "If you want more later, just ask for me. Mckenzie."

As soon as the server heads back to the ballroom, Alison says, "This was a good idea."

"We still need to find a place to sit down. Without exes."

"I know where we can go." Alison hands you one of the plates and then continues down the hallway. At the end of the hall is a closed door. Alison knocks once and pushes open the door. Inside, an oil lamp dimly lights a small office. Books fill one wall, and windows line the other. Aside from a large desk, a leather sofa, and a coffee table there's little room for anything else.

Alison sits down on the sofa and sets her plate on the coffee table. "Perfect table, right?"

"No exes in sight."

She sighs. "Thank God."

"So, how'd you know about this room?"

Alison shrugs. After you sit down, she says, "You know how I said that there were three people I was avoiding tonight? One of them is Katherine Flaggerty."

"But you still show up at her party?"

"Long story." Alison picks up her fork and knife and starts to cut the steak.

You settle back on the couch. "We've got all night."

Alison takes a bite of steak and chews. She dabs her lips with a napkin and then looks over at you. "Katherine and I get along great as long as we aren't sleeping together. In fact, I'm spending next week here while my apartment is renovated, so I couldn't exactly turn down this invitation, but then when I realized two of my other exes were also here tonight...I almost went back to my torn-up apartment." She sighs. "What do you think of Katherine?"

"What do you mean?"

"Do you think she's attractive? She likes you. She's mentioned you more than once. You're the hot dyke from the gym—her words. And then when you came in the Batman costume tonight...I think she had plans to get you in her bed."

"I noticed. She let me borrow this dress, but I think she would have preferred me wearing a sex toy."

Alison laughs. "That's Katherine. Don't tell her I told you, but I have to admit, she's fun to have sex with. As far as a girlfriend goes, however, she's terrible."

"Sometimes all you need is good sex." You reach for your napkin and unroll your knife and fork.

"And then other times you want commitment. Katherine doesn't do commitment. She lives in a fantasy world where she doesn't need to commit." Alison pokes at her potatoes. "Unfortunately, she's the only one I've ever really fallen for. And all she wants is sex. No relationship."

"That's not a bad reality."

Alison waves her fork at you. "Don't get me started." She sighs. "Katherine doesn't take her car to the shop when a check engine light comes on. She goes to the dealer and buys a new one. She doesn't commit to anything."

"And you still love her."

"Yes. And I hate saying no to her. But she won't really say yes to me. Not completely. Pathetic, right? Sometimes I wonder what's wrong with me. Women are a pain in the ass, you know that?"

"But this steak is delicious." You chew on your bite.

"So are the potatoes," Alison agrees. "Although, not as good as the cream puffs. And that server was a cutie."

"Cute. But a little too young. And too eager."

Alison grins. "Tell me about the bartender."

"What about her?"

"Are you two really old college friends? Or is there more to the story?"

"That's it. At least at the moment."

"For the moment?" Alison laughs. "You're blushing."

"She's..." You hesitate. "Maybe something will happen. I don't know. She gave me her number. But I think she was just being nice. Flirting's your job when you're a bartender."

"Uh-uh. She wasn't doing her job when she stopped and stared at you back there. She almost spilled the wine she was pouring." Alison pokes your arm. "She's into you."

"Maybe. But I've got a girlfriend. So I'd only be looking for a one-night stand." You shake your head. "Plus she's in law school."

"And you don't like lawyers? For one night, I think you can handle it." Alison pauses. "Wait a minute, aren't you a lawyer?"

You grin. "How'd you know that?"

"Katherine mentioned it. Like I said, she has a thing for you." Alison continues, "You don't want to get involved with another lawyer, even for a one-night stand? Two lawyers, one bed...you'd probably argue over who was calling the shots all night. And then fight over the pillows."

"No. I'd let her top me."

Alison laughs. "You're blushing again. Clearly you are into her. What's the issue?"

"The truth is, I think she's looking for more than a one-night stand," you admit. "I don't want to lead her on. I'm only single for one night."

"Are you sure you don't want to sleep with Katherine? You two might be perfect together."

"You're going to set me up with the woman you love?"

Alison shrugs. "She's going to sleep with someone besides me tonight. Might as well be you." She scoops up a bite of green beans. "At least I like you. Most of her other lovers drive me crazy."

The door to the study opens and Katherine is standing in the doorway. She glances from you to Alison. "Look who's hiding out here. As soon as I saw you two together in the foyer, I wondered…"

"Don't even start, Katherine," Alison says.

"Don't *start*? Then why don't you explain so I won't have to *start*?"

Alison drops her fork on her plate and wipes her mouth. She levels her gaze at Katherine. "Look, I know this might sound crazy to you, but two people can be alone together without it leading to anything. For your information, all we're doing is talking." Alison's tone cuts through the room. "And eating dinner."

Katherine's smile is tight-lipped. "Apparently, you missed all of the banquet tables in the ballroom and thought this was the best place to eat?"

"Yes, I'm hiding out," Alison counters. "But there's nothing going on. If you must know, I'm avoiding my ex-girlfriends. All of them."

Katherine mutters something under her breath. Her jaw muscles are working and her fists are clenched. Clearly Alison has touched a sensitive spot. And maybe Katherine isn't as unflappable as her reputation.

Katherine looks at you. "Would you mind giving us a moment alone?"

"Don't leave," Alison says. She turns back to Katherine. "I said no to you tonight. And now you're going to make a scene about it?"

"The only one making a scene is you," Katherine says. A phone on the desk rings and Katherine crosses the room to pick up the handset. She hangs up the line without answering and then sinks down in the large leather chair behind the desk.

You set your fork carefully down on the plate so it doesn't clatter. "I think I'm full." You stand up.

"You don't have to go," Alison says. "Everyone always does what she says, but you don't have to."

You meet Alison's eyes. "I think I should. Maybe you two can talk."

As you head for the door, Katherine motions to your dress. "That's perfect on you. Keep it."

"Thank you." You glance from Katherine to Alison and then step out of the office and close the door. The words are muted but you can hear Alison first and then Katherine's raised voice. You let go of the door handle when the voices go silent. Maybe they're kissing now. Or else they're both too angry to speak.

"Hey."

You look up and see Lara standing in the hall. She's just stepped out of the kitchen and has a bucket of ice.

"Everything okay?"

You nod and then add, "Not really. Is it midnight yet?"

"Not even close. Why?"

You think of your breakfast date with Janine and take a deep breath. You can second-guess your hormones tomorrow. Tonight, you only want to act on them. "How do you feel about random hook-ups?"

"Are you propositioning me?" Lara laughs.

"Maybe. But I don't want to wait until midnight."

Lara cocks her head. "Well, damn. I wasn't expecting that."

She steps forward and meets your lips. You close your eyes. Her lips tempt and push at exactly the right moment. Her hand slips behind your neck and guides you into a deeper kiss that makes you tingle all the way down to your toes. When you finally part, her eyes are locked on yours. She knows she's a good kisser. With her confidence, you fully expect her to be good at other things as well.

"So is that a yes?"

"Let me drop off this ice and tell Joe that I need a break. It's slowed down out there anyway. Don't go anywhere." Lara turns and heads back to the bar. When she reaches the end of the hallway, she glances over her shoulder and smiles.

The door behind you bursts open and Alison storms out. She's crying. Katherine follows her. You step to the side of the hallway, out of their path. Katherine catches up to Alison before they reach the ballroom.

"You didn't let me answer," Katherine says.

"You didn't need to," Alison argues.

Alison tries to pull her arm free from Katherine's grasp. The two women stare at each other and then Katherine steps forward and covers Alison's mouth with a deep kiss. Alison pulls away and turns the tables, pushing Katherine against the wall. She holds her at arm's reach. "Damn it. Why are you so difficult?"

Katherine tries to pull Alison into an embrace, but Alison pushes away. She wipes her eyes and cusses. "I hate that I still love you," Alison says. Then she turns and slips out of Katherine's grasp.

Katherine slumps against the wall. Her gaze follows Alison until she's passed the end of the hallway and is lost in the crowded ballroom.

"I don't think she's just saying the words," you say. "I think she really does love you."

Katherine presses her hand to her temple. She seems to be holding back tears. She slaps her hand against the wall and then straightens up. "Damn it." When she looks back at you a second time, her eyes are clear and there's no sign of any residual emotion on her face. She's steeled it all away.

The kitchen door pops open and the cream puff server appears. She looks over at you and then at Katherine. "Cream puff?"

Katherine doesn't answer, but the look she gives the server has the girl shrinking back in the doorway. Katherine storms down the hallway. You hope that she'll find Alison and that her temper will push her to finally admit her emotions. Or at least they'll have good sex.

Lara appears in the hallway. You feel a flush when she strides up to you.

"Dinner break starts now. Want to keep me company?"

"I'd love to."

"Good." She takes your hand in hers. Her skin is warm. Fingers chafed and sure of their grip pull you toward her. You love the rough edges of her as much as the desire in her eyes. "I'm not planning on eating dinner. You have me too distracted to eat. I keep thinking of college. Things we did back then. And the things we didn't do...I can't believe we bumped into each other again now."

"I hope you're thinking of doing more than reminiscing about college tonight."

Lara smiles. "You don't want to reminisce?" Her lips brush against yours.

The quick kiss is enough to give your body a kick start. You're already wet at the thought of her hands on you. "How long's your break?"

"I've got to be back at the bar when the dancing starts." She scans the hallway. The server has slipped away with her tray of cream puffs, but the kitchen door threatens to open at any moment. "Any ideas of where we could go to be alone? Some dark corner, maybe?"

"I've got something better."

You keep hold of Lara's hand and lead her back to the office. Lara waits for you as you try the door. Katherine didn't lock it. You walk in, eyeing the room with a new perspective. The sofa could work.

"I like this," Lara says, letting go of your hand. She starts loosening her tie. "Maybe we should lock the door."

You turn the key to lock the door and feel your heart skip. Janine gave you permission, you remind yourself. She practically insisted. But Lara isn't exactly a stranger. There's history. At least on your end. She's someone you've fantasized about more than once. Especially when she was in her rugby uniform.

All nerved up, you hesitate before moving closer to her. You could blame the past and all the insecurities of college or maybe it's the undone tie hanging around her neck. She's gorgeous, and you can't wait for her to touch you. But she's waiting for you to make a move. Finally, you reach for the ends of her tie. She lets you tug on it, keeping her eyes on you as she starts unbuttoning her shirt. She tosses her shirt and her bra down on the coffee table. With her chest bare the ends of the tie hang between her breasts. You reach out to touch her nipple, but she brushes your hand away. It's too late: with one light caress the soft tip hardens to a tight bud. Her broad shoulders always made you a little weak and her arms are just as strong as you remember. Cut muscle. Rugby arms. You wonder how she keeps in shape now. You wouldn't mind watching her lift. Or maybe she still throws a football. Reaching for her belt, your fingers slip around the leather.

"Any chance you're packing?" The thought is too delicious not to ask aloud.

"Not tonight. But I can make up for that." She moves into your lips, kissing you hard as her hands hike the length of your dress up to your hips. Your muscles quiver with her touch and suddenly you're a novice in an expert's hand. If she keeps up with her lips, the kissing alone will make you come.

When she pulls away you gasp involuntarily. Hungry for more, you try to move into her again but she holds you at arm's length, surveying your body. Her blue eyes darken. She turns you around and her hands move up and down your back. She kisses your neck and then your shoulders.

"Do you know how much I wanted a chance with you back in college?" She kisses the back of your neck again. "But you had a girlfriend then…And I guess you still have a girlfriend. You sure your girlfriend's okay with this?" Lara finds the zipper at the back of your dress and starts to tug.

You murmur "yes." You can think about commitment tomorrow. Tonight you aren't anyone's girlfriend. The material gapes at your chest and Lara runs her hand along the edge of your bra. Then she pushes the dress all the way off and turns you to face her. You're exposed down to your bra and the silk underwear. Lara surveys your body. Her tongue slips over her lips. You start to touch her chest, but she pushes your hand down.

"I like being in charge."

"Oh, really?" You laugh softly. She grabs your wrist when you try to touch her again. She holds on, kissing the underside of your arm.

"Yes. Really."

When she pushes you back against the desk and moves against you, a moan catches you off guard. Your body wants to obey. She could ask you to do anything tonight and you'd consider it. Her finger swipes over the thin cloth covering you, and her lips part. Your knees nearly buckle as her mouth works down your neck to the edge of your bra. She unhooks your bra and slips it off your shoulders. Then she takes a nipple into her mouth. She sucks until your breast is tingling. Her leg slides between yours, sensing exactly what you need, and she lets you grind against her thigh for a moment. She pushes her leg hard into you and you feel a surge of heat that makes sweat bead up on your back. Before you can sink down on her thigh again, she moves away. You moan plaintively and she chuckles.

"I love how much you want this." She steps back and rubs her groin. "And you've got me so wet..." Lara reaches out and brushes the tip of your hard nipple. "I've always liked women who know what they want and ask for it. It's very sexy." Her finger moves to your lips. You slip your tongue down to her palm and then she pushes inside your mouth, watching as you suck. She pulls her finger out. "But what if I want more than one night with you? What if I'm greedy and ask for your number?"

"Maybe you should stop thinking about what-ifs and fuck me."

Lara's lips turn up at the corners. "You don't know how much I want to do just that." She presses you hard against the desk, then pushes your underwear to the side as her fingers plunge inside you. She thrusts in and out, her eyes closed as she enjoys your wetness. She finds your lips and covers your mouth with a hard kiss. She only lets you come up for air when she steps back suddenly. Her fingers slide out and she wipes the wetness across your nipples.

"You're dripping," Lara says. Her finger runs along the edge of your underwear and then tugs on the band. She lets go and the elastic snaps against your skin. "I like your underwear. Would you mind if I tore it a little?"

"I don't have another pair to wear home."

"What a shame." She slyly works her fingers under the band again and then with a jerk, rips the seam. The underwear drops off your hips and Lara smirks. "Sorry."

"You're not sorry."

"You're right."

But you aren't upset. The raw desire you feel in her touch is enough to excuse her. She plays with the edge of the torn cloth and then bends down to inch the underwear over your thighs and past your knees until it falls at your ankles. Slowly, she straightens up, running her hands along the inside of your legs as she does.

"I'll make it up to you," she promises.

One kiss follows another. She lifts you up onto the desk. The polished wood is cold under your butt, but before you can complain Lara pushes your knees apart and moves between your legs. The metal of her belt buckle scrapes your thighs as she covers your mouth with hers. Her tongue pushes in on yours. She wants to overpower you, and you have no desire to fight back. She can take you any way she wants.

You feel her finger circling your clit. First one and then two fingers slide inside. She groans with satisfaction. "You're so wet."

"It's your fault."

"I know it is." Lara shifts back, leaving a gap of six inches or so between your bodies. "You want to watch?" she asks. "Your clit can't wait to be fucked. Look at how swollen it is." She flicks her index finger over your clit. "You want this bad." Lara's free hand pushes your knees further apart, and your clit throbs in response. She's right: you want this fuck so much you can't think of anything other than what her hands will do to you next.

When Lara thrusts inside you again, you push papers off the desk, grasping for a hold until you're balanced with your butt on the edge. You lean back and rock your hips up to Lara. Her eyes close and her lips part as she murmurs something about fucking you. Over and over. All night.

The hand that isn't inside you has your chest pinned against the desk. The muscles of her arm are taut. Her strength is perfect; she can hold you in place even if you resist. But you want to give her everything she wants.

She strums your clit until you're creaming on her. Then she pushes a third finger inside and steps forward, jamming her thighs against yours and closing off the view you had of her hand.

"You like what I'm doing, don't you?" Her voice is husky.

"I like it," you murmur. She's good and she knows it. There's nothing sexier. She strokes faster, deeper, and you moan at the pain she's causing. But you're close to an orgasm and you overlook the way her hand smarts with every thrust.

"I like your moans," she says. "But don't come yet. I want to fuck you more." Grinding down on her hand, you feel her thumb slip down your perineum to press on your anus. She circles around the hole. "And I want this, too."

Her thumb inches in and you gasp. Gripping her shoulders, you pull her chest against yours and moan into her arm. When she goes deeper, your anus clenches in response. You nip at her flexed bicep and try to buck back, but she holds you in place.

"If I had my cock with me, I'd put that inside you, too. But we'll save that for later. I'll take you home and fuck you all night. Give you everything you want." She leans into you, her arm pumping faster as your muscles clench. "I've got you," she breathes in a low voice. "I know you want come. I can feel your pussy on my fingers. You're tight. But I think you want a little more, don't you?" She drives in harder and you feel the wetness increase between your legs. "I want to hear you ask for it."

"I want it," you manage.

You moan as Lara pushes in the rest of her fingers. She grips you tight. Yes, you want her hands doing exactly what she's doing. Filling you. Yes, you want her pushing you farther. Taking you all the way. She's thrusting faster now and you want her more than ever—exactly like this—taking you completely. Rubbed raw and numb from her hard thrusts, you ache for more.

She touches your face, cupping your chin and guiding your lips into another kiss. "You want to come?"

You nod, not trusting your voice.

"Because I could keep doing this to you all night. Not letting you come until I was done with you…"

You nod again. She can keep doing this. But you are going to come. There's no way to stop the climax that's pushing at your seams. She dips her head and her face disappears between your legs. All you can see is the short blond hair. All you can feel is the swipe of her tongue and the pressure inside. She strokes faster. The pressure and the pain has you worked into a haze of lust.

Lara's hand moves faster, not giving your nerves time to think about what she's doing to you. Her tongue has you pushed as far as you can go. Everything hurts, but you don't want her to stop. You want more. And somehow she's giving you more. She sucks your clit between her lips and then tilts her head back and drives her fingers in again. When she sinks down hard on your swollen clit, the climax radiates from your groin to your fingertip and down to your toes. You can't breathe. You clench your teeth and squeeze your eyes closed.

Lara pushes you all the way back on the desk. You stretch out across the cold, hard surface and let your knees gape open. Her hand is still inside you. She's standing, gazing down at your naked body spread just for her. Her eyes are still hungry for you. Impossibly hungry. This time, when she starts thrusting again, she's got her fist positioned against the zipper of her pants. Every thrust rubs against her own crotch.

You moan and close your eyes. Lara wants to come, too. You're spent, but she's going to use you now to get off. You'll give her every bit of satisfaction. She's working harder now, shoving into you, her eyes half-closed and mouth open. You try to grip the edge of the desk and accidentally push a stapler off, along with more papers and a canister of pens. Lara's metal belt buckle cuts into the back of your thigh. From the low groans you know she's getting close.

You weren't expecting it, but another climax is building between your legs. She's got you on the edge. Again. Finally she thrusts hard and drops her weight into you, moaning low as she comes. A wave races through your trembling body. Your fingernails dig into the polished desk; you hope you make marks in the wood, deep gouges that Katherine will wonder at but never know. The second orgasm is short and you feel the stinging pain more than anything else. And yet you wouldn't change a thing. Lara's got you good. Exactly as she promised. Her weight between your legs is satisfyingly heavy.

She wraps one hand behind your neck as the other hand repositions between your legs. She shifts her hand and you squeeze your knees against her shoulders. There's no pain now—only satisfaction. When you shudder, she pulls you tight against her chest.

"I've got you," she murmurs.

And she does. You want to savor all of it: the hard desk; the edge of her metal buckle still gouging into the inside of your thigh; the spent look in her glazed eyes; her strength pinning you in place. Still breathless and quivering, you hope that Lara doesn't move a muscle. Not yet.

"I was a little rough. Sorry. I got distracted there for a moment." Her satisfied and slightly guilty look confirms that she got herself off in the process of fucking you.

"I could tell." You smile and touch her cheek. "You had your way with me. I feel…used. In a good way."

With another distracting kiss, she eases her hand out and then slides you off the desk and into her arms. She's still wearing her pants—and shoes. The belt's still fastened. But you're naked and weak. She guides you over to the sofa and you curl up on your side.

Her fingers trace your spine lightly in a slow, tender massage. Then she sits down next to you. Her hand drapes over your hips. She knows that she owns you. But it's only temporary.

"I missed out in college not sleeping with you." She smiles. "But you're more beautiful now than ever. More angles, more secret places that others have touched…and I love that you'll let me do whatever I want with you." She runs her hand down your thigh. "I wonder what would have happened if we'd hooked up way back then. I probably wouldn't have dropped out."

Lara pushed too far, and you loved every second, but now you can hardly move. You're going to pay for her attention tomorrow. When she glances at her watch, you want to whine. How can she leave you like this? "You have to get back to work, don't you?"

She nods.

"Quit."

"Turns out I need the money."

"Law school's not that important." You hate that she's reduced you to begging, but you don't stop the request from slipping out: "Please stay?"

"I wish...I'm off at midnight and I'll take you home then. Wait here for me. Take a nap, so you're ready for more later."

"Only if I get to strip you first. I can't believe you're still wearing your damn shoes."

She grins. "Once you strip me, what will you do?"

This woman is practically a stranger and can nearly kiss you to an orgasm. If you spent a month with her, it wouldn't be enough. You'd make love every day and not be satisfied. You'd always want more of her. When you think of Janine, your throat tightens as you realize what you need to say. Tonight has to be enough. "I can't go home with you."

"Why not?" Lara's smile slips off her face.

"If I go home with you, we'll both want more. One night won't be enough. And I have a girlfriend."

"Will you call me?"

"Tomorrow, I belong to someone else."

"What if I want you more than she does?" Lara sighs. "I could help you forget about her."

Do you pick Lara? If so, she's yours for the night and your adventure ends here.
If you turn Lara down, go to Chapter Fourteen, page 229.

CHAPTER SEVEN

Tell Katherine you prefer a suit

"That's not exactly my style. But I'd love to see you in that dress. The fabric's gorgeous."

Katherine shakes her head. "Sadly, this little gem doesn't fit me."

You walk over to the bench and pick up the suit. The pants look a bit long, but the waist is your size.

"Some women can be convinced to go both ways. Top or bottom...pants or dresses." She eyes you as you slip on the pants. "You'd be surprised how much fun you could have in a little piece like this."

You zip the pants and then reach for the shirt. "Next time we can have a fashion show. I'll let you dress me up in anything you want."

"Careful what you promise." Katherine touches your cheek and turns your face to hers. "You've got nice angles. I'll hire a photographer for our show. And invite a few other women. Not too many, of course. We'll keep it small." She walks over to a cabinet and opens a door to reveal a line of hanging ties. She glances back at you and then picks out a tie. She opens a small drawer and finds a pair of cuff links. "Janine is invited, too. But only if she'll let me undress you."

"I'm sure she wouldn't mind." You slip the shirt on and start with the buttons, thinking of Janine's response to Katherine eyeing you earlier. Making Janine jealous could be fun. And the payoff might be double.

Katherine comes over to help you with a pair of onyx cuff links. You wait for her to slip the cuff links through the holes, unable to slow the stirrings in your chest. She finishes with the cuff links and then loops a black tie around your neck. As she starts to cross the ends of the tie, she meets your gaze. With one tug she has your face inches from hers.

"You have to stop looking at me like that," Katherine says.

"Do I?"

She nods. "Or I won't be held accountable." Her lips press into yours. She has firm lips full of desire, but she pulls back before you're ready to let her go. "You're going to have to tie your own damn tie. Or we won't get out of this dressing room."

"I made a mistake turning you down." You want more. Not only more of her lips but more of everything about her.

Katherine nods and finds your lips again. One long kiss and she's opening up, inviting your tongue in. Your hands run up and down her curves until you slip over the zipper on her dress. It would be easy to undress her. As soon as you tug the clasp she pulls back and shakes her head.

"I think you're forgetting about your heart. Remember Janine? We have to get you out to the ballroom." Her hand slips down your chest. "But I hate to let you go." She sighs and turns to reach for the suit jacket. The jacket dangles from her hands like bait. "Maybe I can help make Janine jealous. Do you know how to dance?"

"I can lead."

"Ask me to dance later."

You reach for the jacket but Katherine keeps hold of her end. After a moment, she lets go. "You can find your way out?"

You nod.

"Good. Finish getting dressed and come show off. I want to see you out there."

As you pass through the foyer, Jim gives you a nod.

"Nice suit," he says. "What'd you give the lady of the house to get that hook up?"

"I bet you'd love to know."

He laughs. "I'll miss Batman."

You pass through the foyer and enter the ballroom. The pianist is playing Beethoven. A chocolate fondue fountain is set up across from the piano, and you spot Katherine there. She's skewering an apple slice and talking to a tall woman in a silver suit. The woman looks like a model and you watch the pair for a moment until you realize that you aren't the only one in their audience. On the other side of the table Alison Greer is watching Katherine as well. Or maybe she's watching the model. A dance with Katherine seems as far-fetched as another conversation with Alison.

"There you are," Janine says, linking her arm through yours. "I was looking all over for Batman. Someone told me that they'd seen you slip away with Katherine. And I started to wonder... Now I see why. I like the suit."

Your shoulders relax at the sound of Janine's voice. At the feel of her body near yours. You meet her gaze. Green eyes draw you in.

Those eyes were the first thing you noticed about Janine when you bumped into her on the sidewalk outside of her house. She was carrying groceries in from her car and you were texting on your cell phone. And then as you both bent down to pick up the spilt groceries, Janine suddenly stopped and looked right at you. She said your name and then recounted the dinner party you'd both gone to a month earlier and an introduction you'd forgotten. Everything clicked into place after that. She cooked you dinner that night and you stayed late for a glass of wine. She joked that she was pleased with her clever move to catch you—the accident of bumping into you. But the truth was, you wanted to be caught. And you didn't want her to let you go home that night. Or the next night.

The cascading neckline of her red dress distracts your thoughts. "I should have told you earlier—you look gorgeous tonight. That dress makes me think thoughts I probably shouldn't have...considering we aren't together tonight."

"Dirty thoughts?" Janine laughs. "Do tell."

"Well, first off, I can't help wondering if you're wearing underwear." When Janine only smiles in response, you continue, "And if you won't tell me, then what's the chance that I get to find out for myself? Just thinking of someone else sliding that dress up past your hips...It isn't fair to play this game of yours when you're wearing a dress like that."

"This game of ours," Janine corrects. "We both agreed to the rules. And I was beginning to wonder if you'd already won. You should know, disappearing with Katherine made me more than a little jealous."

"Were you hoping to be the one who slipped off with Katherine?"

"She snatched you up quick. Sometimes when she finds something she wants, she doesn't let go." Janine clears her throat. "I wasn't sure I'd see you again tonight."

"You didn't answer the question."

"You're right." Janine touches your tie. "I was on my way to get a drink. Thirsty?"

Two bartenders are working the line. When you and Janine step up to the counter, the bartender with the short blond hair glances quickly at you and then turns her attention to Janine. The bartender looks familiar, but you can't think of where you've met her before. Maybe a club.

Janine is her usual friendly self and the bartender is soaking up the attention. You take a deep breath and exhale slowly.

"Practicing those deep-breathing exercises?"

You turn to see your Pilates teacher, Carmen, smiling at you. She's wearing an orange dress that shows off her cleavage and hugs her ample hips. Perfect hourglass. You glance up quickly from her breasts, hoping she hasn't noticed. "Carmen, I almost didn't recognize you without your usual workout gear. That dress is stunning."

"Thank you. And you're looking dashing tonight. I like you in a suit."

"Better than a sweaty tank top and yoga pants?"

"Better?" Carmen laughs. "I don't know about that. I always enjoy seeing you dripping in hard-earned sweat."

Janine glances back at you and Carmen. She's still chatting with the bartender but you can tell she's listening in on your conversation as well and carefully appraising Carmen. Finally she takes her drink from the bartender and turns to slip her arm through yours. You're quick to introduce Carmen and Janine.

After a few minutes of small talk Carmen heads to the bar for the drink she was waiting in line for and Janine leads you toward the banquet tables.

"I want to talk about the rules of our game," Janine says. "I think I should have veto rights on who you pick tonight."

You reach the nearest banquet table and pull out a chair for Janine. "Worried I'll pick Carmen?"

"Yes." Janine sets her glass of wine on the table and looks over at you. "She was ready to eat peanut butter out of your hands."

You grin, trying not to laugh. "I think you mean she was putty in my hands."

Janine waves off the correction. She loves American expressions but often jumbles the meaning. You can't shake the image of Carmen eating peanut butter out of your hands and let a couple chuckles slip.

"Don't push me." Janine swats your arm. "You're the one who showed up in a Batman costume tonight." She touches your tie. "And now you look too good in that suit. If I let you loose, you'll have a roomful of women watering at the mouth."

The image of a crowd of drooling women comes to mind and you can't help but smile. "What's wrong with that?"

"I've decided that you have to tell me who you are going to sleep with."

"Okay. So is Carmen off the list?"

"Yes. And Katherine's off the list, too. She might have let you go once, but I know she's keeping tabs on you now."

You lean back in your chair. "Anyone else?"

"Alison. Apparently she thinks you're the eye candy for the evening."

"Alison Greer doesn't even know who I am."

"Maybe not yet, but she wants to know you. I overheard her say how much she liked a woman in a suit the moment you walked in wearing that. And she was staring at you. But don't let it go to your head."

A server walks past with a tray of egg rolls and Janine waves her past. Janine clears her throat. Her gaze drifts over the crowd. You want to distract her with a kiss. The change in her rules means that you've managed to make her jealous, but that doesn't feel like success when you know she is scoping for someone to sleep with even now.

You brush a loose strand of red hair behind her ear. "I like the streak. Red suits you." Janine smiles at the compliment but doesn't look over at you. Now you're convinced that she's upset. But this was her game, you argue silently. "So, what about you?"

"What do you mean?"

"Can I keep you on my list?"

Janine takes a sip of wine and then swirls the dark red liquid in the glass. She runs her finger down the narrow stem of the glass and then circles around the base, still avoiding your gaze.

"I want to pick you." When she doesn't respond, you continue. "You're the one I want to go home with tonight. The one I want to wake up with in the morning. We can have our coffee in bed and read the *New Yorker*."

Janine shakes her head. "I'm not on your list."

You fight the urge to argue. Once Janine has her mind made up, you know how hard it is to change. And there's your pride to consider. If her answer is no, you don't want to push it. You take a deep breath.

"How are you? I missed you this week. I kept wanting to call and ask how your day was." You force a smile when you want to yell instead. Her strong will might be an asset in her business dealings, but you wish she'd bend a little now. "I know we're not supposed to talk about anything serious tonight, but a week goes by slow without you."

"You could have called. We didn't have a rule about calling." Janine looks over at you. Her eyes glisten. "My week was terrible. In fact, I can't remember the last time I've felt worse."

Her words hit like a brick on your stomach. She doesn't have to say that she felt terrible because of you. Because of what you said. You can see it in her eyes. "Janine, I think we made a mistake. All week I kept regretting that conversation we had. And I know I brought it up, but I think I was wrong. I think we're supposed to be together. Let's call this thing off. Let's go home. I want to hold you. I want to—"

"No." Janine holds up her hand. "I'm not your date tonight." She pushes her chair back from the table. "After what you said that night, I was so angry I couldn't talk to you. Now...I don't know how I feel. Don't try and act like this game is all me. This started with you. You were the one who said you thought things were moving too fast. That maybe we should see other people. So, now here we are. You don't get me tonight."

You watch her jaw muscles working, clenching back more words. Clenching back tears. Your stomach's tightened up in a ball and you struggle to think of what to say. Maybe it's too late to say anything.

"How could you pull a stunt like that without any warning? I thought everything was good. One day we're talking about moving in together and then the next...You tell me that you want to slow down and maybe, maybe, date other people. Maybe? Screw you."

"But you agreed with me," you argue. "I thought—"

"Yeah, I agreed with you. Because I didn't want you to be the one deciding all of it. I wanted it to be mutual. That was me being tough and rising to the fucking occasion." Janine rattles of a long string of words in German. You recognize more than one cuss word. "I'm not on your list tonight." She reaches for her wine glass and stands up. "You know, I don't even care who you sleep with tonight. Don't tell me."

You don't watch her walk away. You lean back in your chair and stare at the empty seats around the table. "Fuck."

"Is this seat free?"

You look up and see a woman with blond curls dropping past her shoulders, tanned skin, and a tight black dress that outlines perfectly grab-able curves. Exactly the type of woman you don't need now.

"Um, no. It's taken."

She sets her cocktail down and then motions to the other empty seats around the table. "Let me guess, those are all taken, too?"

"Yes. All taken."

"Perfect. Then we can be alone."

There's no denying that she's beautiful, but at the moment, you aren't interested. Still, when she smiles at you, you find yourself smiling back. You chastise your unstoppable hormones and point to the next table nearest yours. "There's empty seats over there."

"But I want this seat." She sits down in Janine's seat. "I'm Courtney."

You grudgingly introduce yourself.

Courtney nods. "I already knew your name."

You glance at her again, trying to recognize her face. Maybe you've seen her before, but she'd be easy to confuse with any other pretty white girl in a room of femmes. "I'm sorry, have we met before?"

"No." She holds on to the tiny pink umbrella as she sips her cocktail. "Nice party, right? I feel like I'm in an episode of *Lifestyles of the Rich and Famous*. But I can't imagine living in a house like this. Too many bathrooms to clean." She scoots her chair a few inches closer to yours. "So how do you know Katherine?"

"We're in the same Pilates class." This is true, of course, but has very little to do with why you're at the party.

"I thought you were going to say that you worked for her. Half of the people here seem to work for Katherine. What do you do?"

"I play the piano."

Courtney tilts her head. "Really?"

You nod. You do play the piano, but it's only a hobby. And obviously that wasn't what she was asking. But you hate telling people that you are a lawyer. Questions follow, or else stories of how some lawyer screwed them over.

Courtney reaches across your lap and takes your hand. She stretches out your fingers. "You do have nice hands. I'd love to hear you play sometime. They say pianists make good lovers."

"Where'd you hear that?"

"Someone did a study. Can you imagine the research for that study?"

Her fingers moves up and down yours and you feel uncomfortably stimulated by her touch. She seems to know what she's doing and gives you a half smile when you shift in your seat. "How'd you know my name?"

She shrugs and releases your hand. "I asked around. Apparently you're a lawyer. And a good one at that." She winks and takes another sip of her drink.

You clench your jaw and lean back in your seat. Caught. "I do play the piano. Every night before I go to bed. It's how I unwind." You squeeze your hand into a fist and then relax your fingers. "I don't like to talk about my real job."

"I don't talk about my job either."

"What do you do?"

She reaches for the umbrella in her drink and sucks the pointed end between her lips, pulling off the cherry. "I'm a dancer."

Suddenly it hits you. You've pushed a twenty under the elastic band of her thong. And she kissed you. It was only a few weeks ago, but the night was a blur of too many martinis. Courtney was dancing on a pole at Rumors, the gay nightclub. You take a deep breath. "Oh, shit."

"Now you remember." Courtney smiles. "So, where's your girlfriend?"

Janine was the one who convinced you to tip Courtney. You'd been watching her, out of all the others on stage, and then Janine had pushed a twenty into your hand and dared you to slip it under Courtney's thong. But that wasn't the end of it. After the dance show ended, Courtney had changed into a pair of jeans and a loose tank top that showed off her bra underneath. And then she'd joined you and Janine on the dance floor.

"Janine's here. Somewhere..." You glance around, not really looking for Janine. Courtney's eyes are still on you. You meet her gaze and feel a flush come up your neck, remembering the kiss you shared on the dance floor as if her lips were still pressed against yours. Janine had pushed you to kiss Courtney. She wanted to watch.

"I've seen you in the club a handful of times." Courtney grins. "Does it make you uncomfortable that I wanted to come talk to you?"

"Does it make you uncomfortable that I touched your butt?"

"You weren't my first."

"But for some reason, you remembered me. You have a nice butt."

"I've heard that before." Courtney laughs. She polishes off the last bit of her cocktail. "So why are you sitting here alone? Antisocial?"

You nod. That's the easiest answer, and it isn't exactly a lie. When she sat down, you were feeling particularly antisocial. Although her attention is wearing down your resolve to be depressed.

"Let's go outside then," she suggests, standing. "I heard Katherine's garden is amazing. Fountains, ponds, even a gazebo...I want a break from this crowd."

"I'm enjoying this table. And if I get up, someone might take my chair."

Courtney reaches for your hand. "Come on, I need a chaperone. And I picked you. Any chance you have a cigarette?"

"I don't smoke."

"Me neither," Courtney says. She pulls on your hand. "Come on."

You sigh and finally stand. Maybe Courtney is exactly what you need tonight. She is quite good looking, you decide, now that you are eye level with her and her face is inches from yours. You catch the faint scent of her musky perfume and recall the feel of her shapely backside. If Janine is planning on breaking up, you might as well find a temporary distraction. Courtney could be more than suitable. Her full, glossed lips are definitely kissable. You can ignore your heart tonight.

"If we don't smoke, we need some other excuse to go outside."

"I don't think we need an excuse," you say. "Who's gonna ask?"

"Your girlfriend," she says.

"She doesn't care what I do." In fact, she'd probably hate the fact that you are going outside with Courtney. And thinking about kissing her. After what just happened, you should be sulking in a corner. But the only reason you're thinking of kissing Courtney at all is because of what happened. "What about you? Do you have a girlfriend keeping tabs on you tonight? Or a boyfriend?"

"My girlfriend's talking to her ex at the moment," Courtney says. "Anyway, we're in an open relationship."

"Then we don't need an excuse."

You follow Courtney through the ballroom without looking at the faces you pass. When you step outside, the quiet of the courtyard is a stark change from the noise inside. A breeze makes Courtney shiver and move close to you.

"This is nice," she says, taking your hand. She circles around a fountain in the center of the courtyard. The sparkling lights strung overhead illuminate her skin. When she glances back at you, you think of Janine again. You swallow hard, trying to push away any thought of what might happen tomorrow.

"I liked kissing you. And your girlfriend," Courtney admits. "But Becca wasn't happy about it."

"Becca?"

"My girlfriend. She's one of the DJs at Rumors. DJ Dee."

Everyone knows DJ Dee. Her signature leather pants, crew cut, and confident strut would make her stand out even without the tattoos of naked women that cover her arms. But she's also known for her temper. If a fight breaks out at Rumors, DJ Dee usually has something to do with it. "You said you were in an open relationship. Does it matter to her who you kiss?"

"She can kiss whoever she wants, apparently, but she thinks I need to ask permission. Whatever. I don't ask."

"So if she sees you with me, or if someone saw us leave together and tells her…"

"Don't worry. She's not crazy," Courtney says. "She wouldn't be happy about it, but I'm not happy with her at the moment. I doubt she's still only *talking* with her ex."

"You're using me, aren't you?" You smile. "Good."

"Good? You don't mind?"

"Not tonight."

You reach for Courtney's hand. The warmth of her touch fills you with a rush of desire. Guilty desire. You shouldn't want someone new so soon. And yet you do. She steps toward you and your pulse races. When she leans forward you find her lips and savor a perfect kiss. Then you remember that she gets tips for her kisses. Of course they're going to be good.

Courtney pulls away and looks back at the ballroom. Faces are blurred but figures move in front of the door. And then loud voices break the quiet. Two couples coming out for a smoke.

You glance at the path behind you. The cobblestones lead down a slope to a lit-up cascading waterfall and pool and, beyond this, an enclosed gazebo. The gazebo is half-covered in vines and Christmas lights are strung on the roof. "Want to go check out the gazebo?"

Courtney doesn't argue when you pull her hand. A winding brick path follows a narrow stream. You cross two footbridges before reaching a waterfall and the black-bottomed pool.

Courtney stops at the pool and dips her hand in the water. "Perfect." She gazes up at Katherine's mansion perched at the top of the slope. The glowing ballroom seems miles away. "This whole place is perfect."

"Do you want to go back to the party?"

"No." She stands up and walks over to you. "I want you to help me forget about the party."

The door to the gazebo is unlocked. You step inside and Courtney follows. The twinkling lights around the windows give the space a soft yellow glow. Flowering plants and ficus trees encircle the room. A patio furniture set is positioned in the middle with a view of the waterfall and pool.

"This is perfect, too," Courtney says. "Our own private cabana."

You walk over to a cabinet on the opposite wall and open one of the doors. Shelves are lined with glasses. A bottle of rum and a bottle of tequila are on the counter. "Want a drink?"

Courtney shakes her head. "That bartender made my last cocktail a little strong. She's a flirt."

You close the cabinet and lean against the counter. The glow from the ballroom reminds you again of your conversation with Janine. If you blew your chances with her last week, why did she act like she still wanted you in the foyer earlier?

Courtney walks over and touches your arm. "You okay?"

You nod. But you can't stop thinking of Janine.

"Why don't you let me give you a massage? That's my other job. Dancing doesn't pay all the bills."

You don't argue as she pulls you over to the sofa. You watch her fingers as she loosens your tie, the tension in your muscles already easing. When the tie is undone she starts working on your shirt buttons.

"Do you want to talk about it?" she asks.

"No." You lean into a kiss. Her lips help you forget Janine's words.

Courtney undoes the last of your shirt buttons and then pushes your shirt off. Her hands trail over your biceps and shoulders. You slip off your bra and she brushes her fingertips lightly down your chest.

"You have to lay down for me to do this right."

You kick off your shoes and she points at your pants. "You want me naked?"

"It works better that way." She slips off her dress and then motions to your pants. "Strip. If you take too long, I might change my mind."

You can't resist smiling, but you follow her orders. Stripped down, you stretch across the sofa on your belly. The sofa cushion is a rough canvas that smells sweet like cut grass. You close your eyes when you feel Courtney's hands on your shoulders. She straddles your thighs. Her legs and center are shaved clean and feel perfectly smooth as she inches up to your butt. The feel of her naked skin against yours is more arousing than relaxing, but you swallow and try to breathe as her hands begin to knead up and down your back.

The minutes pass and you feel your body unwind, lulled by her touch. She works on the knots in your neck and slowly moves to your head. Fingers comb through your hair and then her nails scrape along your scalp. You roll over, wanting to see her body on yours. Her nipples are each pierced with a silver bar and her full breasts hang distractingly close.

She covers your lips with hers. Her touch is full of desire but promises only one night. Tomorrow you'll be strangers. You reach for her breasts and she moans as you play with the silver bars. Her nipples harden with the slightest touch. You suck one tip into your mouth and she murmurs her pleasure. She rubs her wet pussy up and down your thighs.

"I can come if you keep that up," she says.

Courtney shifts her body so her groin is riding your thigh. You have to go up on your elbows to reach her lips. She presses one of her breasts into your mouth and starts to rub on you again. Enjoying the weight of her breasts, you knead her until she moans while your tongue works the metal piercing. She buries her fingers inside her folds and bucks faster. You suck hard on her nipple, knowing she's close. Her legs clench on your thigh and her chin juts up.

"Oh, oh," she moans.

She rubs her wetness up and down your thigh, groaning with pleasure. Watching her come, unabashedly using you to satisfy her need, is unexpectedly gratifying. It's impossible to call her a stranger now, but if you bump into her again the closeness of this moment will have to be a forgotten secret. As she exhales, she stretches her body over yours. Her arms wrap around you and she drops her head on your chest. She shudders and then clenches you tighter, holding onto you as if you're keeping her from a fall.

Her perfume fills your senses and you're acutely aware of her breasts pressed against your chest. The blond curls are tousled and her lipstick has left marks on your arms, and probably other places too. As her breathing slows, she looks up at you.

"That was nice," she says. "You want a turn?"

When you nod, she kisses your lips. Then you hear the unmistakable sound of a door opening. You pull away from Courtney's lips and feel your heart jump to your throat. Becca. DJ Dee. Leather pants and all. "We have company," you whisper.

Courtney looks over her shoulder and her face drops.

"Courtney?" Becca's voice booms. "What the hell are you doing?"

Behind Becca is Alison. She looks like she's trying to shrink out of the room, but Becca has her hand in a vise grip. In an awkwardly long moment, everyone in the room seems to take a collective breath as if trying to fit pieces of the puzzle into some pattern. Then Becca lets go of Alison and charges forward. A fraction of a second later, you realize she's charging toward you. She stops at the coffee table as if she's not sure what she intends to do next. Courtney shoots off you and reaches for her dress. You sit upright, pulling your knees to your chest as cuss words fly. Courtney scrambles around the far side of the sofa, pulling her dress over her head as she does.

"Don't even act like you weren't coming in here for the same reason!" Courtney shouts.

"To talk," Becca screams back. "Let me guess, that's all you two were doing down here? And then one thing led to the next and—"

"No. I knew exactly what I was doing." Courtney pulls her dress down over her breasts. Her bra is still hanging off the armrest of the love seat closest to Becca. You stare at the bra, unwilling to make a move for it but wishing it would magically disappear.

"Where are my damn shoes?" Courtney shouts.

You reach down and pick up Courtney's heels. She passes in front of the sofa and snags them out of your hands. Then she throws one at Becca's chest. Becca dodges to the side, narrowly missing the silver-tipped toe. She straightens up, cussing.

"Yeah, go ahead and yell," Courtney yells back. "I found something I wanted and I went for it. Just like you always do."

You gulp as Becca's eyes burn through you.

"This?" Becca wags her finger at you. "You could have this any day of the week. And better. Why do it here? To humiliate me?"

"I could ask you the same goddamned question." Courtney waves her finger at Alison.

Becca's jaw is working overtime as she grinds her teeth. "Don't bring her into this. We were coming here to talk."

"You're protecting her? I'm so done with your games," Courtney says. She heads for the door, and Becca grabs her arm. "I'm done," Courtney says, tugging her arm free. "Sleep with someone else tonight. You'll find a different woman tomorrow. Or two or three."

"Wait," Becca says. "I don't want other women. I want you."

"Don't tell me that now," Courtney says. "It's too late."

"It's not too late. But I should have told you it before now." Becca steps forward. Her face is inches from Courtney.

"Let me go," Courtney says. Becca doesn't budge. Courtney presses her eyes, holding back tears. "Becca, I can't do this anymore. I can't do an open relationship with you. You have to choose. If you really want me…"

Becca closes the gap between their lips. Her hand slips behind Courtney's neck as their kiss deepens. You glance over at Alison, acutely aware of the fact that you are completely naked. Alison watches Becca and Courtney for a moment, then meets your gaze. She looks as if she's about to burst out laughing. Possibly at you. Possibly at the entire situation. She points to the pants on the floor in the middle of the room. Maybe she's on your side by default. Regardless, you need someone on your side. You reach down and find your underwear, trying to slip them on without attracting Becca's attention. The pants are too close to Becca's feet.

Becca notices you pulling up your underwear. She starts toward you, but Courtney quickly intercepts, turning Becca's face back to hers. "I want to go home with you," Courtney says.

"What about this?" Becca asks, waving at you.

"What about it?" Courtney's chin juts up. Becca starts to argue, but Courtney interrupts. "I'm tired of playing games. I want you."

Becca pulls Courtney into another deep kiss. When they part, Becca leans down to pick up Courtney's heel. She hands off the shoe and then glares at you. "We aren't finished." Becca heads for the door with Courtney in tow.

"Sorry about tonight," Becca says to Alison. "We'll have to talk later."

"Hell no," Courtney says. "You're done *talking* to her."

When the door closes behind Courtney and Becca, you take a deep breath. "I guess I'm not getting my ass kicked tonight."

"You've got balls having sex with Becca's girlfriend," Alison says. "And the next time you see her, I'd run." She walks over to the end table and picks up your pants. "Missing something?"

You wait for her to throw them to you, but instead she walks around the end table and sits down on the sofa. She hands you the pants and looks down at your underwear. "Nice panties."

"Thanks." You step into the pant legs, avoiding Alison's eyes. Of all the people to see you naked, why did it have to be Alison? "Were you two really coming here to talk?"

"What do you think?"

"Maybe I should be apologizing to you. Not Becca." You pull up the zipper on your pants and then search the floor for your shirt. "Where'd my shirt go?"

"On the other side of the couch," Alison says, pointing over her shoulder. "You two were getting crazy down here."

"I didn't even get off," you admit.

"Becca's gonna beat you up and you didn't even get off?" Alison starts to laugh. She covers her mouth with her hand when you look over at her. Her eyes sparkle. Gorgeous as always.

You sigh. "Yeah. Thanks for that reminder." You find your bra tangled up with your shirt and then sink down on the sofa. Still shirtless, you glance over at Alison. "Should I join a boxing gym? Start training now?"

"Move to a new city. You don't have a chance."

You drop your head as Alison begins to laugh again.

"I made so many mistakes tonight."

"I still think you're cute," Alison says.

"Apparently that's what got me into this mess." But you can't ignore the compliment. You pull on your bra and then your shirt. Alison leans across the sofa to help with the buttons. It's too late to be embarrassed. The smell of Courtney's perfume lingers on your shirt, but the feel of her hands on your back is a distant memory. Now all you can think of is the fact that Alison is helping you get dressed. Not undressed. But she doesn't seem to be in any hurry to leave.

"So you and Becca?"

"Yeah. Exes." She shakes her head. "I've made a few bad decisions with her since we broke up. You saved me from another morning of regret."

"You're welcome."

Alison smiles. Then she leans over and kisses your cheek. "Thank you."

Before you can respond to her kiss, Alison bends down and picks up your tie, half sticking out from under the end table. She smooths the silk. "This is nice," she says. "It's not Batman but..."

"Katherine hooked me up."

"Katherine's good at that." Alison's tight-lipped smile makes you wonder what she isn't saying. She loops the tie around your neck. "Going back to the party?"

"Only long enough to find Katherine. I need to get my wallet and my keys. Then I'm going home." You make a knot and cinch the tie up to your collar. "How do I look?"

"Like you were just having sex with a pole dancer." Alison grins.

"Oh, God. What was I thinking?" You sink back against the sofa cushions. "And I've got to walk through that ballroom and find Katherine. If Becca's up there waiting..."

"She won't be," Alison says. "She was horny. I'm sure she and Courtney are already busy. Anyway, you can get to Katherine's room without going through the ballroom."

"How? Katherine's got a special key code for her bedroom."

Alison nods. "I've got the code."

"You and Katherine..." You glance over at Alison, wondering what exactly to ask. Are they together? Or only sleeping together? Alison's silence is enough of an answer.

You follow her gaze out the gazebo window, beyond the waterfall and the pool, to the faint glowing lights of the ballroom. Now the jealous look Katherine first gave you when she thought you'd come in with Alison makes sense, along with the possessive way Katherine linked her arm in Alison's in the foyer.

"She's my most recent ex," Alison says finally. "But she thinks we're still dating." She looks over at you and then smiles. "I still can't believe Becca caught you and Courtney down here...in the middle of it."

"After tonight, I'm swearing off women. For at least a month."

"That's too bad," Alison says. "I was just about to ask you out on a date."

"You're teasing me now? After everything tonight?"

"Oh, you can handle it." Alison laughs.

She reaches over and straightens the knot on your tie. When she looks up, you feel your breath catch in your throat. Her fingertip brushes over your lips. She pulls her hand away.

"You are trouble," she says. "You look innocent, but now I know..." Her eyes crease with smile lines. She takes a deep breath and looks up at Katherine's house. Finally she stands up. "Come on. Let's get out of here. Tomorrow we can both forget what happened."

"There are parts I don't want to forget," you admit.

"Oh, I'll remember certain parts, too," Alison says, pointedly looking at your chest.

You cover your face and she laughs again.

Turn to Chapter Fourteen, page 229.

CHAPTER EIGHT

Go back to the foyer

You've never been one to interrupt. Besides, the warning from the cute bartender has you thinking. Staying on Katherine's good side might be the best plan. You turn away from the closed door and the sound of lovemaking to head back to the foyer.

Tasha Wilcox is waiting for you. She looks up as you enter the foyer and holds a hand up to silence Jim. "Did you find her?"

"Yes. But I wasn't able to talk to her."

"Why not?" Tasha shakes her head. "Never mind. Where is she? I'll go talk to her myself."

"Wait." You stop the security guard before she crosses into the ballroom. "She's in her office. But she's not alone." In a lower voice, you add, "And from the sound of it, she isn't going to be happy if you interrupt her."

Tasha's brow scrunches up and then she paces the hall. "Well, how the hell am I supposed to do my job if she hasn't given me the damn code to get into half of the house?" She waves her hand at the locked door at the end of the hallway. "I can only do a security sweep from the outside."

"I know the code," you volunteer. "5-4-3-2-1. I think there was a pound sign at the end."

Tasha's scowl slips away. She goes over to the computer screen and taps it awake, then punches in the code. The door clicks and she reaches for the handle. "That was it. Katherine said only three people had the code tonight. And I already met the others. Why do you have the code?"

"It's a long story."

"How the hell does she expect me to run security if she lets everyone else have the damn code but doesn't give it to me?" She curses under her breath. Then, motioning to Jim, she heads down the dark hallway.

Jim catches the door, wedging his foot in the doorjamb. He keeps one eye on the foyer and one on Tasha and leans against the doorway.

"I thought you said the alarm was triggered by the garage," you say. "Isn't the garage on the other side of the house? By the ballroom?"

Jim nods. "We still have to check out the whole place."

The image of Tasha knocking on Alison's door springs to mind. Alison in a nightgown and Tasha in her uniform... Unfortunately for you, the image is too perfect. Alison might finally get her chance to ask a woman for a phone number. Any sensible hormone-driven lesbian would ask Tasha out if they had a chance.

Mckenzie suddenly appears in the foyer. She glances at Jim and then you. "I thought you left."

"Not yet." You notice Mckenzie has a purse hanging over her shoulder. "You're leaving early?"

"My boss had more servers scheduled than we actually needed tonight. Dinner's finished, and the rest is only cleanup." She hesitates in the doorway. "Anyway, see you around."

You feel a tug as Mckenzie walks out. All you'd have to do is follow her and your night's entertainment would be set. The door closes, and you sigh. "Oh well."

"That one, too?" Jim laughs. "How many women are you trying to pick up tonight?"

"Only one." You think of Janine. "But more than one wouldn't be a problem."

"I'm wearing a Batman costume to the next party I go to." He laughs again. "But I never get invited to parties like this."

Tasha Wilcox reappears in the doorway. Jim scoots out of her way, straightening up as she passes. He closes the door and waits for the latch to lock.

"All clear on the west end of the house," Tasha says, speaking into the microphone on her lapel. "I checked the rooms. Windows are closed and external doors are locked. Can we get a sound-off on locations?"

You watch as both Jim and Tasha tilt their heads, cupping a hand over their ear to hear the radio. Tasha and Jim both echo, "All clear." You wonder if that means Alison got a wake-up knock or if Tasha simple peeked in on her sleeping form. You know there's no way to go back and change what happened with Alison, but part of you longs to do exactly that. Or at least have another turn on the piano with her next to you...

"Alarms are all reset." Tasha turns to you. "Thank you for the help. I owe you."

"No problem." Not *we owe you*, but *I owe you*... You doubt her word choice was intentional, but you'd like to think it was. Too bad Tasha's attention seems to be focused on work. You listen as she rattles off instructions to Jim and then she's off for another sweep of the house without even a glance back in your direction.

As you head back to the ballroom, you notice the music has changed. The pianist has retired from her station and most of the banquet tables have been cleared to set up a dance floor. A DJ has set up in the back corner and the music is top forties remix. Danceable, but not anything you're going to miss if you leave early. You decide on another drink, but before you've reached the bartender's table, you spot Janine. She's headed straight toward you. She's holding a nearly empty wine glass, and judging by the flush in her cheeks, you guess that she's polished off more than a few drinks.

"Why are you alone? I've seen you with quite a few women tonight. I'm surprised one of them hasn't snatched you up yet."

"I thought you were getting along pretty well with a few women as well. Where's Sarah? She seemed particularly interested."

"She's gone to find a restroom," Janine says. "Are you staying for the dancing?"

"I don't think I can bust a move in this."

Janine grins. "But I'd love to see you try."

Before you can answer, Sarah walks up and links her arm through Janine's. She glances at you. "Ah, the masked piano player." Sarah's tight-lipped smile does nothing to improve her look. You're certain Janine could do better. "That was a nice little performance. And in full costume. Do you play often?"

"Depends on my mood. The piano helps me wind down after a long day at work." *But I play even better after mind-blowing sex. Janine can tell you all about it.* You stop yourself from saying the rest of your thoughts aloud. She's made you jealous. Mission accomplished. You wonder if Janine can guess.

"Maybe we'll hear you play some more later?" Sarah turns to Janine. "Still want to dance?"

"Uh…" Before Janine can finish, Sarah begins to sing along with the DJ's song choice.

Breaking from the song, Sarah says, "This is one of my favorites. Let's go dance."

You force a smile when Janine's eyes dart up to yours. "Don't let me stop you. Enjoy your evening."

The pair walk toward the dance floor with linked arms. Of course they'll go home together. And then somehow you'll have to face Janine tomorrow morning at the café. You sigh. Maybe Batman always ends up alone.

"Hey."

Mckenzie. The fact that the twenty-one-year-old is a welcome sight makes you wonder at your own possible character flaws.

"First off, I know what you're thinking," she says. "And for the record, no, I'm not desperate. And I'm not trying to chase after you."

"Then why are you back?"

"Don't look so smug. My car won't start." She holds up jumper cables. "Any chance I can get a jump?"

"How long have you been working on that pickup line?" You grin.

"Shut up." Mckenzie pushes your shoulder. Her dimple is back when she looks up at you. "So, is that a yes?"

You take the cables from her. "I'm over this party anyway."

Jim is still in the foyer working the door. He glances at Mckenzie and then at you. You can guess at his thoughts. Before you're out the doorway, he holds up his thumb. Fortunately Mckenzie doesn't look in his direction.

"Have a good evening," Jim says.

You wave over your shoulder. A cool breeze stirs, clearing your thoughts. You push away the thought of Janine and Sarah dancing together. They will be doing more than dancing by the time the night is over, but now at least you have an excuse to not hang around watching as their evening progresses. You glance over at Mckenzie. She's attractive as hell. Unfortunately, she's barely legal to buy a drink.

"Where are you parked?"

You point to the right.

"Good. Me too." She sighs. "Thanks for helping me out. I hope this won't take long."

"Don't worry. I was looking for an excuse to leave that party. I'd rather be jumping a car than pretending to have a good time. At least I'm hanging out with someone interesting."

"You don't have to lie. I'm sure you think I'm a waste of time. Twenty-one and all."

"Ouch." You reach your car and stop, searching the utility belt pocket for your keys. "I know this might sound crazy, but some of us don't think about sex all the time. I like talking to you."

Mckenzie smiles. "I like talking to you, too. And I think about sex all the time."

"Twenty-one."

"Shut up, Batman," Mckenzie says, laughing. She continues walking several steps past your car and stops when you hit the unlock button. The brake lights flash, and she glances at the car and then at you. "You drive this?"

You nod.

"Somehow I didn't picture you in a sports car. Especially one this nice." She steps off the curb and then circles around the car. "This is a Porsche, right? Why the hell do you drive a Porsche? It's such a statement."

"A statement? How about this: I like nice cars." You open the passenger door. "You can say no if you don't want to be seen in a statement, but I'm offering a ride to your car just to be nice. Not because I'm thinking of having sex with you or because I am trying to impress you. I'm only trying to be nice."

Mckenzie walks over to the door and then hesitates. "I don't know. If it was a Batmobile, I'd consider it."

"Get in the damn car before I change my mind."

Mckenzie steps forward and kisses your cheek. "Thanks for helping me out." She climbs into the passenger seat. "I drive a Honda Accord. 1997. You'll recognize it because the fender is blue and the rest of the car is red."

"Got it."

You close her door and walk over to the driver's side, rubbing your cheek. Somehow you've got to convince her to stop sneaking kisses. Your body is beginning to take note of her lips.

"Well, it isn't the battery," you say, wiping grease off your hands. Three tries later Mckenzie's old Honda hasn't given one hiccup. You unhook the cables and close the hood on her car. "Maybe the alternator?"

Mckenzie looks at you through the windshield. "I'm broke. Don't tell me it's the alternator. That sounds expensive."

You've already taken off the hooded mask, cape and, gloves. But you're still sweating. You pull off the fake arm muscles, the utility belt, and the padded chest, then toss everything into the backseat of your car. You walk over to Mckenzie's car and lean against the door.

Mckenzie is slumped against the steering wheel. She looks up and bangs her fist on the wheel. The horn squeaks in response.

"I don't think you're going anywhere tonight. At least not in this car."

"If this engine would start one last time, I swear I'd drive it straight to a dealer and trade it in."

"We could get it towed."

"First thing tomorrow morning," Mckenzie agrees. "But that'll probably cost more money than this piece of junk is worth." She rubs her eyes. "I'm not going to start crying. In case you were wondering…"

"I'm not worried."

"I don't even have money for a taxi." She pulls out her cell phone and glances at the time. "I should let you go. I'll convince one of my friends to come get me. You can go back to the party."

"Get out. I'll give you a ride."

Mckenzie stares up at you for a moment and then climbs out of her car. "I bet you're wishing you hadn't taken a cream puff."

"Are you kidding? Those things were delicious. I could have eaten the whole tray."

Mckenzie opens the passenger door on your car. "Thank you. Tonight would have sucked without Batman."

"Not funny."

"It's a little funny," Mckenzie teases.

You settle into your seat. Mackenzie's already buckled and tapping something into her cell phone.

"Where to?"

"I do like you better without that mask and all those muscles," Mckenzie says. She doesn't look up to meet your gaze. "But that underwear…"

"They're not underwear. They're outer briefs. With a built-in jock strap." You smile. "I really need a shower."

"Me too. I smell like a pastry shell." She sniffs her shirt. "And bacon-wrapped asparagus. My place is on Lexington Avenue."

"By the college?"

She nods.

Of course. She probably lives in a dorm. You curb the hormone-induced thought of asking Mckenzie if she has her own room.

"So, what happened with your last girlfriend?"

"What do you mean?" you ask.

"Why are you single now?"

"I thought it was obvious." You motion down to your outer briefs.

"Costumes weren't her thing?" Mckenzie laughs. "Did you dump her? Or was it the other way around?"

"It was mutual." You drive slow down the wide tree-lined lanes. Maybe it was mutual... You push away the image of Janine in the red dress with the slit up the thigh. Sarah will get to enjoy undressing her later. "Well, technically we haven't broken up. We're taking a week-long break."

You hit traffic as soon as you reach downtown and then slow to stop-and-go as you make your way over to the freeway entrance. Mckenzie shifts in her seat and turns on the radio. You watch her scroll through your preset stations.

"Who decided on the break?"

"Both of us. I'm supposed to meet her tomorrow to talk about our relationship."

Mckenzie clicks her tongue and you notice that she has a tongue ring. Age appropriate. You push away the thought of how nice a tongue rings feel on your clit.

"Do you think it's over?"

"Maybe," you admit. "I don't know. I still think she's hot. I love her accent. Especially when she says sexy things in German. And she's smart. We have a lot in common. Maybe too much." You pull onto the highway and move into the fast lane. "What about you?"

"Me?" Mckenzie sighs. "I was dumped. But not until after I found out she was sleeping with my best friend." She stares out the window. "She said she didn't want to hurt my feelings. We were together for three years. Met in English 101. She writes poetry."

"First girlfriend?"

She nods.

"So now you're out a best friend and a girlfriend."

"Yeah. But it gets worse. My best friend and I share an apartment. So my ex moved from one room to the other. I try not to be home much." Mckenzie glances over at you. "Don't feel sorry for me. I see that look. Don't."

"What look? I'm watching the road," you argue. "This is my *watching the road* look."

"You feel sorry for me. I can tell."

"Okay, maybe a little. Your first girlfriend cheats on you with your best friend and you all still live in the same apartment?"

"Thanks for the recap. Can we move on now? Any of these stations set to classical?" She presses another button on the radio.

"Classical? No."

"Don't judge. I like it." She finally finds a classical station and leans back in her seat. She closes her eyes.

The strings only add to the melancholy mood. You drive in silence for the next several minutes, then hazard a glance at Mckenzie. Her eyes are still closed but her fingers bounce up and down on the center console in rhythm with the concerto. Her skirt has shifted; you can see enough of her thighs to make you swallow hard and quickly glance back at the road. Five minutes later you pull off the freeway and onto Lexington Avenue.

"Want to go for a drink?" Mckenzie asks. "There's a club down the street from my place. Rumors."

"As it turns out, I do know the one gay club in town," you say. "I've been queer for almost as long as you've been alive."

"Don't start with the age thing," Mckenzie complains. "I'm young. I'm inexperienced. I get it. Why hang out with a twenty-one-year-old, right?"

"I didn't mean that. Sorry. But I'm not up for a dance club tonight. Lycra is the wrong dress code. Maybe another time."

"Yeah, sure. Whatever. I'm one block up, on the right. That big apartment building over there." She taps the window. "You can let me out at the intersection."

"Is your roommate home tonight?"

Mckenzie's brow furrows. "Why?"

You pull into a parking spot half a block from the apartment building. "I was thinking…never mind. Forget it."

"Tell me what you were going to say," Mckenzie insists. "This is probably the last time we see each other. Might as well tell me the truth now."

Admitting to yourself that you want to kiss Mckenzie is dangerous enough. But your thoughts don't stop there.

When you don't answer, Mckenzie unbuckles her seat belt. "The light's on in our apartment." She points to a window on the corner of the building two floors up. "So they're probably enjoying a night at home alone. Together. At least we have different rooms. As soon as I walk in, they're going to move apart like they weren't cuddling on the couch and we're all going to pretend like nothing's wrong." She waves her finger at you. "There's that look again. Don't feel sorry for me. I could move out if I cared. But I don't. They can do whatever they want. I'm over both of them. Fuck cuddling." She reaches for the door handle. "Anyway. Thanks for the ride. Hope I didn't ruin your evening completely."

"Wait a minute." You reach for Mckenzie's hand. Your heart thumps in your chest when her eyes lock on yours. It's crazy to think of kissing her. The fact that you want to push her skirt up and run your hand along her legs is worse.

"What?"

"I don't want to go to Rumors. But I still want to hang out with you. I'd ask if I could come up, but I don't really want to meet your roommates." You pause. "How about a drive?"

Mckenzie leans across the console and kisses your lips. She pulls back almost as quick as she moved in, but when you reach for her and pull her into another kiss, her lips open. As the kiss deepens, your hand settles on her thigh. The feel of her smooth skin makes you heady. Her tongue brushes against yours, and you start to imagine what the tongue ring will feel like on your clit.

Reason kicks in slowly. You pull back. She's twenty-one. You shift in your seat. "On second thought, I don't think I'm only suggesting a drive. Maybe you better go home."

"I want a one-night stand as much as you do." Her hand caresses your leg from your knee up to your groin. "I won't even ask your last name. Are we going to your place or mine?"

You drum the steering wheel before chancing a look at Mckenzie. Her skirt is hopelessly short. When she follows your gaze, Mckenzie's lips turn up at the corners.

"Since you're distracted, I'll think for you. Let's go to your place." She reaches for her seat belt and fastens it.

"I can't believe I'm doing this." You glance at your mirrors before pulling out into traffic. Twenty-one. You whistle under your breath.

When you reach the freeway Mckenzie takes your hand and places it on her thigh. "I liked it when you touched me here. I wasn't expecting it." She moves your hand up the inside of her leg. "I was thinking that I was going to have to do more to convince you."

The alarms in your head are firing at full strength. You try to focus on the road. Mckenzie lets go of your hand to unclasp the bow tie on her neck. Then she works loose the buttons on her tuxedo shirt until the fabric gaps and you can make out the edge of a crisp white bra. The shirt slips off her shoulders. Next she takes off her shoes. Short black pumps. And then she takes off her underwear. Black silk. You watch as she slides it down her legs and then drops it on the floorboard.

"Don't get us in an accident," Mckenzie warns. She hitches up her skirt another inch and places your hand on her thigh again.

By the time you pull off the freeway you're hardly noticing the cars. You take a back road up to Park Hill and pull off at the clearing with a view of the city below.

Mckenzie is in your lap as soon as you've parked. You move your seat back as far as it can go and then recline it all the way. Mckenzie pulls off your shirt and then her lips meet yours. You unclasp her bra as she presses hard against your mouth. When she slips off the bra, her breasts fall into your hands. She's petite everywhere except her breasts. You guess those are a C-cup at least, and the rest of her curves match. Soft and full in all the right places.

You inch her skirt up to her hips and slide your hands along the inside of her thighs. She's shaved smooth and you can feel her wet folds as she moves up and down you. Your thumb strums over her wet clit and she arches back. Then she grinds on your hand. She pushes her breast into your mouth and you suck the nipple until it's hard. She moans and rubs against you. Your middle finger sinks in. When you feel her legs part you slip in another finger. Your thumb works over her clit until she's bouncing up and down on your hips. She pushes back against the steering wheel and you follow her, thrusting deep.

"Oh, yes," she moans. "Like that." She grinds down hard. "Oh, God, I'm so close."

Turned on by her speed, you work harder as she leans into you. She's tight, but you shift your position and push in another finger. Her lips part and she moans, gripping the edge of your seat. "Fuck, I'm going to come. Ohhh. Yesss."

She enjoys the climax, holding perfectly still for only a moment before she's bucking up and down on your hips again. Your clit is begging to be touched and every time she bounces against you she nearly hits the right spot on your groin. Nearly. Your fingers drive in and out of her and then your thumb pushes hard on her clit. You wish she'd do the same to yours. Mckenzie's legs clench around you, her eyes squeeze closed, and her head rocks back. She shudders and reaches for your hand. Her fingernails sink into your wrist and she cries out as she clutches you tight against her.

Slowly she relaxes her hold on your wrist. You ease your fingers out, wiping her cum against the inside of her thighs. She finds your lips and the kiss is long and deep. Her teeth tug on your upper lip when she finally pulls back. She looks at you with a half grin as she sits upright in your lap.

"Well, that was fucking good. How's your hand?"

"My wrist's a little sore. But I liked the workout you gave it." You hold up your hand.

Her palm touches yours and your fingers intertwine. "I kind of want you to do that to me all over again." She sighs and drops her head against your chest. She starts to laugh. A moment later, the laughter turns to crying.

You wrap your arms around her and pull her close. "Hey, it's okay," you whisper. "What's wrong? Why are you crying?"

Her body shakes as she tries to stop the tears, catching her breath between sobs. You hold on to her, pulling her body close to yours. Minutes pass before the breathless sobbing finally quiets. You're shaken by her response and more worried by the fact that she won't look at you now. She pushes off of you and reaches for her shirt to wipe her face. Huddled in the passenger seat, the tears still streak her cheeks.

"I can't believe I just did that," she says. Gone is the Valley Girl tone she had at the party. Her voice sounds older, and heavy with regret.

"Usually it isn't until the next morning that I wish I hadn't had sex. If you didn't want—"

"No. Stop." Tears bud in her eyes again, but she wipes them away. "I wanted what happened. That's not what I meant." She stares out the window at the city lights. City lights sparkle in the valley below. The clear night is perfect. She clears her throat. "It's beautiful here. You bring dates here often?"

"First time."

"I'm not going to ask you if you're lying. I want to pretend that you're not a player." Mckenzie wraps her arms across her chest. Her gaze is unfocused, scanning the dark horizon. "I never get off. I mean, not never, you know…It's just really hard. And it's only ever happened when I was alone. It hasn't happened with anyone else. And then you get me off in the front seat of a car in two seconds. Fuck." She starts to laugh again and then covers her face. "And so, of course, I lose my shit and start crying."

"Maybe you should blame it on the cream puffs."

"More likely the wine," she says. "I skipped dinner and ate four cream puffs because my boss said they were shaped funny. Then I downed two glasses of wine that someone was going to toss. Maybe I should get drunk every time I want to have sex."

"Do you want to go get some food?" You glance at the clock in the car. "The diner down the street from my place starts serving breakfast at eleven. We'll be right on time."

"I want you to take me home. Can we go to your place?" She rubs her eyes. "I don't want to sleep alone tonight. Tomorrow I'll go home, and I promise I won't call or stalk you or anything. I just want to sleep next to you tonight."

"Yeah, of course."

She sighs. "What if you're the only person I ever get off with? What if it doesn't happen again?"

"Then we should make sure it happens again tonight."

Mckenzie punches your arm. "I'm serious. You should know that I took a picture of you when you were still in that costume… when you were trying to jump my car. Before you took off the cape and everything. I already posted it online."

"Wait, what? Why'd you do that?"

She grins. "Because you wore a Batman costume to a black-tie dinner. What were you thinking? And then you got stuck trying to jump someone's car. You really should see the picture."

"You're deleting that photo and taking it offline."

"Okay, fine, but I'm going to keep calling you Batman all night." After a beat, her smile fades. "Can we pretend I didn't cry?"

"I didn't see anything."

"Thanks. And I should warn you that I'm not very good in bed. That's probably why I was dumped after three years. Three years of bad sex."

"Sounds like you had the wrong partner. I doubt it was you." You slip on your shirt and start the engine. Fortunately, it's a short drive to your condo. You're uncomfortably wet and in need of a good end to the evening. Even if that end comes in the form of a vibrator. The sooner you can get home, the better.

"I don't think it was my ex," Mckenzie says. "I'm pretty much terrible. If they offered lessons, I'd sign up."

You start to laugh and then see the expression on her face. She's close to tears again.

"You don't know what you've done to me already," you say, reaching for her hand. You grasp her wrist and guide her inside your pants.

"Oh…You're wet. Very wet." Her dimples are back when she looks up at you.

"One finger in the right spot and it'd be all over."

She tries to play with you, murmuring an argument when you stop her.

"I want a shower and a bed first." You put the car in reverse. "Then I want you. And that tongue ring. I'm not settling for only fingers."

Mckenzie shifts back in her seat. "You got it. But you might have to tell me exactly what to do."

"No problem." You feel a throb start between your legs. The thought of ordering Mckenzie down onto her knees and letting her tongue work your clit makes it hard to drive.

Mckenzie pulls her shirt over her shoulders and then hitches her skirt back down on her legs. She buckles the seat belt. "So, did you realize you had signed up to give sex-ed lessons tonight?"

"You know, we all get it wrong before we get it right. It's not just you." You stop at an intersection and look over at her. Without a bra, her breasts peek out of the white shirt. Dark pink nipples tempt you. You try to ignore the continued pulse between your legs. "Whatever happens tonight...Don't worry about screwing up. We'll just have a good time."

Your adventure with Mckenzie doesn't end until daybreak, but you've reached the end of this story. Go to Chapter Fourteen, page 229.

CHAPTER NINE

Leave the party with a wave of your cape and an ounce of dignity

Tomorrow you might regret leaving Janine at the party. But not tonight. The look on her face as you slipped out the door was a mix of anger and frustration. You doubt that you'll ever see her again. Maybe she'll leave an official breakup message on your phone tomorrow. Or maybe you will leave that message on hers. Regardless, she'll never agree to another date with you.

You pass by a fast-food restaurant and your grumbling belly reminds you that you haven't eaten since lunch. So much for the elegant dinner that could have been yours, or the trays of appetizers. Or the sparkling wine. It takes you two seconds to decide on the drive-thru. You order a Coke and fries. The kid at the window laughs out loud when he hands you the soda and then tries to snap a photo with his phone. Clearly a Batman fan.

As you start to pull out of the parking lot the twinkling neon lights of a sex shop catch your eye. The "OPEN" sign above the door flashes as if in some secret code. You chew on a fry wondering if you are desperate enough to hit up a sex shop at seven on a Saturday night. Deciding that you are, you cross the double yellow line and parallel park in the one empty spot in front of the store.

The windows of the store are lined with dark paper so it's impossible to see if anyone is inside. You push open the door, reading the sticker plastered on it: "Bi women, for women. We LOVE women."

Multicolored glass beads hang from a second doorway and separate a short hallway from the main entrance. You push through the beads and then hesitate, blinking in the bright lights. You haven't been in a sex shop in ages. Internet sales are more discreet.

"Don't be shy, Batman." A twenty-something woman with generous curves and lip piercings waves from behind the counter. "Come all the way in and look around. We don't judge." She crosses her forearms and leans forward, giving you a good look at her bosom smack dab between the displays of bullet vibes and flavored lube. When you look up, she meets your gaze and winks. Caught red-handed.

You smile and she chuckles.

"Let me know if there's something you're looking for in particular. I like helping customers find exactly what they want."

From her tone you guess that she's volunteering to be helpful in more ways than one. "Thanks. I'm just browsing tonight."

An hour before closing, the store feels crowded with a half-dozen shoppers. A middle-aged straight couple peruse the video rentals while a young lesbian couple sort through the displays of vibrators. Toward the back a group of three women are laughing and holding up dildos. You wander over to the book section first, not because you are planning on reading tonight but because you feel a sudden awkwardness knowing that the salesclerk is watching you.

The salesclerk comes out from behind the counter and hands you a book. Above the picture of a nurse kissing a doctor are the encouraging words: *Overcoming Inhibitions Through Costume Play.*

"You're a little late for Halloween. Or a little early. But I like the outfit."

"I have a good excuse," you say, flipping the book over and reading the blurb on the back. "*How to pick out the right costume for your mood...*" You read the glowing reviews and then shake your head. "I'm really not into costumes. I'm not even sure what I'm doing here."

The clerk's surprised look makes it clear that she doesn't believe you.

"It's a long story. I've had a crappy night," you add.

This time you get a sympathetic nod. "Shopping always helps my mood too. Usually I go to Macy's, but I get it."

When the clerk walks back to the counter you replace the book on the rack and head over to the video section. The straight couple eye you and move to the far side of the aisle.

After a few minutes of browsing you decide that you aren't in the mood for a video. The rubber mask is making your head itch and your padded chest chafes at the armpits. What you really want is a shower and a vibrator. Despite your collection at home you are always in the market for a new toy, so you decide to check out the towering display of vibrators. A pair of purple rabbit ears attracts your attention and you pick up the vibrator on the display table.

"The 'on' button is tricky to find," a woman says.

You look up to see an Asian woman in her early forties eyeing you from the other side of the display table. You saw her earlier in the group of women browsing through dildos, but you didn't recognize her then. Now your heart pounds in your chest and you can hear your pulse in your ears. Margo Yamada. She works in upper management at your firm—several pay grades above you. Her usually demure pixie cut is spiked with gel tonight. And she's wearing a black leather vest. A red bandana is tied around her bicep, and you see part of a forearm tattoo as she tries to point out the button from three feet away. Distracted, you don't even look in the direction she's pointing.

"I'm just browsing. I wasn't going to turn it on."

"I love browsing. For shoes, not vibrators. But, let me guess, you weren't planning on buying a vibrator at all, right? That's what I always say about shoes just before I take home another pair." She walks around to your side of the table and holds out her hand for the vibrator. You pass it to her and she switches on the power. A second later she hands back the twitching bunny ears. "*Always try before you buy.*" She cocks her head and says, "I know you, don't I?"

You nod. She's still trying to place your face—at least the half of it that she can see below the mask. "We work together."

"Of course." She smiles and says your name. "Second floor. You took on that McDermott case that no one wanted. Congrats. I heard you won."

The compliment would mean a lot, under other circumstances. You look down at the vibrator. "This thing is ridiculous."

"And you're dressed up like Batman. Which isn't ridiculous at all."

She starts to laugh. You can't help but join in. The bunny ears spasm in your hand. You hardly know Margo Yamada. All of the conversations you've had with her before could be summed up in a minute or two. And yet now she'll never forget you. And she's on the board and has hiring and firing power at your firm.

"Just so you know, there's a really good reason why I'm dressed up like this."

"I'm sure there is. But I like the idea that you go to sex shops in costume for no reason at all."

Without waiting for you to explain, Margo spins on her heel and walks off. You watch her rejoin the group of friends she was with earlier. The two other women, seemingly a couple since you'd noticed they've been holding hands all the while, both glance in your direction as soon as Margo says something. All three start to laugh.

You switch off the vibrating bunny and carefully set it back in its holster, then reach for the next vibrator on the table. The teal handle is bedazzled with sparkles and the tip is shaped like a dolphin head. Despite the dolphin's vibrating prowess and the fact that there are a series of oscillating patterns to choose from, you decide that cute animals aren't going to help you get off tonight. You reach for the "Guaranteed WaterProof" black-

and-red vibrator with the nubs along the shaft, and then you feel someone tap your shoulder.

"Hey, I wanted to let you know that I won't mention anything to anyone at work about seeing you here. Dressed up. Like that." Margo gestures to your costume. "But you do pull off a convincing Batman. And if we decide to implement a costume day at work to boost morale, I think you have your outfit ready."

"I'll keep that in mind. But it'll be a tough call choosing between this and the French Maid uniform I have hanging in the back of my closet."

"I didn't need to know that." Margo laughs.

"And you don't have to worry. I won't mention seeing you here either."

"Thank you." Margo glances at her friends and then back at you. "This is probably crazy, but...We're going to get a drink at Rumors and I was wondering if you'd like to join us."

Do you:
A) Keep searching for the perfect vibrator (read on)
B) Accept Margo's invitation and leave the sex shop
(go to Chapter Ten, page 169)

The perfect vibrator

"I don't think I'm up for Rumors tonight." Rumors is the one lesbian bar in town. If there was any doubt about Margo's sexuality, she's confirmed her queer status by the mere mention of a hole-in-the-wall place like Rumors. Ordinarily this alone would be enough for you to agree to almost anything. An interested attractive woman asks you out for a drink? Done. But you've made a fool of yourself in front of enough women for one evening. The last thing you want to face is a crowded bar full of half the eligible lesbians in town dressed in an unfathomable amount of Lycra, rubber, and polyester. "The truth is, I just want to go home, take off this damn costume and take a shower."

Margo reaches for the black-and-red vibrator. "And try out a new waterproof vibrator?"

"That sounds like a perfect end to this evening." Maybe you are throwing away an offer that will never come your way again. The next time she sees you, Margo will likely ignore you. Fraternizing is not only frowned upon, it's specifically a cause for termination—at least according to the employee handbook. "You know, I really would love to have a drink with you sometime. Any chance you'd consider a rain check?"

Margo hesitates. She glances at her friends hovering near the shop's front door. They are close enough to have overheard your conversation, but judging by the way they have their arms wrapped around each other, you doubt they were listening. Finally, Margo looks back at you. "Yeah. Sure. You know where to find me."

As Margo and the other two women leave, you eye the black-and-red vibrator. Shaped like a medium-sized dildo with a slight curve to the shaft and a mushroom tip, its swirl pattern creates an attractive gender-non-conforming image, exactly as advertised on the box. You hold the base in one hand and then run a finger up one of the lines of nubs. The exact purpose of the bumpy shaft is a mystery you find yourself wanting to solve. With a slight rotation of the base, the vibrator begins its show of force, throttling away at the air in front of your chest—Batman's muscle-padded chest. You turn the dial up, feeling a rush with the increased pulsation just as you'd imagine a biker would on revving a motorcycle's engine. When the vibrator reaches maximum speed the rumbling sound is unmistakable. And strangely a turn-on.

"Yep. This is the one," you say out loud.

The clerk grins when you look over at her. "And it's on sale," she adds.

"Perfect."

As you walk out of the store with your purchase carefully concealed in a glossy teal bag, your cell phone rings. You unlock your car and drop the vibrator in the passenger seat, then glance at your phone's caller ID. Maxine. Your best friend has impeccable timing. She always manages to catch you in your low moments.

"Hey, Max."

"Janine texted me. She said you left the party. And she's pissed. Why the hell did you leave? I've had to listen to you whine about wanting to get back with Janine all week and then you just walk out on her?"

"Max, I'm dressed up like Batman."

"Why?"

In the long silence that follows, you stare at the bag in the passenger seat. With any luck the new vibrator will get you out of your funk. But its presence as an alternative to a real date is undeniable. You consider admitting what you've bought to Max. Unfortunately, her laughter will only be icing on the cake.

"Are you okay?" Max asks.

"I totally screwed everything up with Janine. And I'm dressed up like Batman. How the hell do you think I am?"

Max starts to laugh. She doesn't stop until she has to pause for air. Between breaths, she manages, "Come over. I want to see you as Batman."

"No. I'm not giving you that satisfaction."

"Please?"

You glance over at the Hot Vibes bag. "I went to Hot Vibes and bought this big vibrator with all these bumps on it. I'll probably hurt myself trying it out, but I'm also totally turned-on by the sound it makes. I'm going home."

More laughter. You have to wait for Max to suck in a breath and then she manages, "God, I love you." And she's laughing again. "Any crazy shit I do never compares to the crap you pull off."

"I'm hanging up now."

"No, wait. Get your butt over here. Jen and Colby are already here for poker night. I've got box wine I've been wanting to open, and Roger has a college friend coming. We'll get you drunk, and you can forget about the German girl."

"Janine."

"Whatever. Come get drunk with me."

"On box wine?"

"Don't pull that 'I'm a lawyer and too good for box wine' crap, Batman." Max chuckles. "Just because you walked out of a party on Rich People Hill does not mean you are too good for box wine. Besides, I don't want you hurting yourself with that new toy. Imagine the ER visit."

"I thought Roger was a wine connoisseur."

"Yeah. He's not as excited about the box wine as I thought he'd be," Max jokes. "Go figure."

Roger is Maxine's boyfriend. At the moment. He's not smart enough for Max and he never seems to laugh, but you aren't in a position to critique anyone's dating choices. Max never stays with any guy for long, and you figure Roger will be old news in a month.

"Come on, poker and cheap wine—how can you say no?" Max plies. "You always win at poker."

You do play a mean game of poker.

Do you:
A) Drown your sorrows at Max's poker game (read on)
B) Decide on a sure thing and go home with the vibrator (go to Chapter Twelve, page 206)

Go to Max's house for poker

"For what it's worth, that is an awesome Batman costume."

"Don't even start."

Max grins and waves you inside her apartment. She's wearing navy blue sweatpants and a white tank top. Sexy as usual. Her dark brown complexion looks amazing against white. But you've never told her that. With Max, you don't dare slip up and admit how attracted you are to every part of her. A neon orange sports bra peeks out from underneath the tank top. You glance away quickly, trying not to imagine her breasts underneath. She pulls off casual sexy like no other woman you know. But, you remind your hormones, Max is straight. And she's not interested in knowing how attractive you think she is. You stare at Max's feet. Her toenails are painted sparkly blue.

"Roger and his friend are on the balcony smoking. We waited for you to start the first hand. But the wine's already poured. I'm not sure if box wine needs to air or not," Max admits. "You want a change of clothes?"

"I'd love a shower first."

Jen and Colby are already at the kitchen table dealing cards. They look up and say hello in unison.

You follow Max to her bedroom. She pulls a Giants T-shirt and a pair of black shorts out of the top drawer of her dresser—*your* Giants T-shirt and black shorts. "Why do you have these?"

"You don't remember?" Max smiles. "Last New Year's. I thought I was the only one drunk enough to forget what happened that night. I took off my shirt and threw it out the window of your car. Remember? That guy was yelling at you."

"He was yelling because you gave him the finger."

Max laughs. "And then you took me home, and I woke up at your place wearing this."

Max tried to kiss you that night. But she was too drunk to remember that part, and you haven't brought it up since.

"I still don't know what happened to my pants."

"You took a shower in them. And then you told me to throw them out. I didn't. They're on a shelf in my closet. I keep forgetting to give them back to you."

Max covers her face as she laughs. "God, don't ever let me get that drunk again." She glances at you and sighs. "I'm sorry about Janine and the party. But I feel like we never get to hang out anymore, so—lucky me." She points to the bathroom. "Use my shampoo. Roger doesn't like to share his stuff."

Despite one hand with a flush and another with a full house, you don't win the night's poker game. So much for your lucky Giants T-shirt. Roger's college roommate clears everyone out and then leaves as soon as the wine box is empty. Jen and Colby leave a few minutes later. Ever since New Year's you've avoided being alone with Max. But being a third wheel isn't any better. The last thing you want to see is Max and Roger cuddling up together. You search for your cell phone, calculating how much cash you have for a cab ride home.

"Movie? I can make popcorn," Max suggests.

"Not tonight. I've got an early shift tomorrow. Seven a.m." Roger kisses Max's cheek and then picks up his coat. "I'll call you after work?"

Max nods. Roger waves to you and then slips out the front door, already digging in his pocket for a cigarette.

"I thought he was sleeping at your place. All his stuff is in the bathroom."

Max nods. "He was. But he's been under a lot of stress at work and we talked about having some space to figure things out."

"You guys about to break up?"

"Maybe. I don't know." Max starts a bag of microwave popcorn. "I told him that we need to talk. Tonight was bad timing since his college friend was in town and I'd already invited Jen and Colby over for poker."

"But you could have talked after everyone left. I should have left. If I'd known…"

"No. I didn't want you to leave. Besides, you would have had to call a cab. You're a mess." Max chuckles. "I didn't want to have the talk with Roger tonight. I'll break up with him tomorrow. Or the day after. I've been planning out the conversation for the past week. It can wait." She pulls the puffed-up bag of popcorn out of the microwave. "Find us something to watch."

You flip through the television channels until you land on a cable station with a home improvement show.

"Stop there," Max says, plopping down on the sofa next to you. She hands you the bowl of popcorn. "I love this show." It doesn't matter that she lives in an apartment and hasn't yet saved a nickel for a mortgage down payment. Max has had her dream house in the suburbs planned down to the color of the tile in each one of the bathrooms for as long as you've known her. Two kids, two dogs and a blue house with real shutters and a red door.

You take a handful of popcorn and then hand the bowl back to Max. "So, what's wrong with Roger?"

Max studies you with scrunched eyebrows. "Why do you want to know? You never ask about my boyfriends."

"I'm curious this time. Was something wrong with him? He's good looking, he's black like you said your mom wanted, he's got a solid job, sometimes he even makes funny jokes...But you aren't into him. Why not?"

"When am I ever that into any guy I date? And yes, my mom wants me to marry a black man. She also wants me to go to grad school. And she wants grandkids yesterday." She sighs. "Can we talk about something else? I don't want to think about Roger anymore tonight. Or my mom."

"Okay, forget about Roger. What about every other guy you've dated in the past five years? Each one lasts four, maybe five months. No one's lasted six."

"Thank you for that reminder. And now you sound like my mom. Why are you keeping count?"

You shrug. You think Max would be happier dating a woman. But you can't say that. "Why date some guy if you aren't that into him in the first place?"

"What's with the twenty questions?" Max points at the screen. "I don't want to be grilled about failed relationships—by you of all people."

"What's that supposed to mean? If you can't talk to your friend about it, who are you going to talk to?"

"See that hottie there? I'd totally date him. I might even marry him if he asked. You should see him with a skill saw."

"The home improvement guy? He's gay."

"A girl can still have a crush," she argues. "Anyway, how can you tell he's gay? You can't always tell," she adds. Max tries to pass the popcorn bowl back to you.

"I'm not really hungry. I drank too much wine." You pull out the blue-and-white striped blanket that Max keeps tucked under the coffee table. "And I'm tired. Mind if I sleep here?"

"The couch is yours. But you're not tired. You're moping. Stop moping about a girl. You'll have a new one next week." Max punches your shoulder lightly.

"No. I've decided I'm taking a break."

"Yeah, right. And because you screwed up with the German chick, you're giving me a hard time about the guys I date. You are going to be moping around until you find the next girl on tap."

"On tap? What's that supposed to mean?"

"Whoever you meet at the bar. Whoever gives you a second glance online. Whoever's easiest." Max arches her eyebrows. "You give me a hard time about dating men that I'm not really into, but you do the same thing all the time. In fact, you're worse than me. All it takes is one spark and you fall head over heels. Then a month later you realize that you have nothing in common with them, but you keep dating because you don't want to be single. Tell me I'm wrong."

You pull the blanket up and don't answer.

"At least I'm up front about all of it. I admit that I'm only using them for sex. Maybe I'm not even looking for love."

"Screw you."

Max holds up her middle finger.

"We're both looking for love," you argue. "But we suck at finding it. And I don't date women just to have sex. I want to fall in love every time. Every time I'm hoping it will happen."

Max is your best friend. You've known her since college, and she knows you better than anyone. You look over at her profile—the curve of her jaw, the slope of her cheeks. You'd love to caress her face. Instead, you close your eyes.

"You're right. Sometimes I do use women to pass the time. Just like you use men."

Max doesn't argue. She crunches popcorn and stares at the screen, pretending to ignore you.

"But Roger seems like a nice guy. Maybe you need to give him another chance."

"He is nice," Max says. "And he's not you."

"Thank God for that, right?"

Max throws a popcorn kernel at you. You reach for the bowl and spill half the popcorn when she tugs it back. Max picks up a handful from the bowl and hurls it at you. As the pieces fly past, you reach for the bowl again and wrench it out of her hands. Max moves to the edge of the couch, ready to jump off as you taunt her with the bowl of popcorn. But she's laughing, and you know that she won't be able to move fast enough.

"You are helping me vacuum," she says. "I'm hiding your car keys, and we are going to vacuum tomorrow if you even think of throwing that at me."

You raise the bowl as if about to throw the contents, but before you do, Max tosses a pillow at your head and then jumps. The popcorn bowl clatters to the floor. She lands on your chest, laughing, and then her hands pin your shoulders to the sofa cushion. You try to wrestle away, but she holds you fast. You thrash harder, but Max outweighs you and lifts weights for a hobby. Her legs are between yours, and the more you try to wriggle free, the more uncomfortable your thoughts become. Wrestling is one step away from making love, and you would do anything to kiss Max right now. You hold your breath, wondering if she can possibly feel the mix of chemicals and nerves racing through your body. The familiar rush that comes whenever Max touches you is now amplified by a thousand. Max locks eyes with you. The grin on her face slowly slips away.

"I'm serious," she says.

"Okay, I'll help you vacuum. Now get off me." You try to push Max off you, and she abruptly lets go.

She shifts back on her knees, staring down at you. The air zips out of your chest like an unknotted balloon. You break the staring contest and look down at the mess on the floor. Popcorn is under the coffee table and scattered across the length of the sofa. Of course Max didn't feel anything when she jumped on you. But you can hardly look at her now. You've been trying not to admit it for years, but the truth is you are impossibly in love with your best friend. You swallow hard and close your eyes.

"I'm not talking about vacuuming," Max says. She's suddenly upset, and the volume of her voice has jumped up several notches. "I'm tired of not talking about this. This thing that we don't talk about. It's driving me crazy. And I'm starting to realize that's my problem."

Your pulse is thumping loud in your ears. "What the hell are you talking about?"

"You. You're my problem."

"I'm your problem?"

Max nods.

"Wait a minute. You can't blame me for the fact that you pick up crappy guys. That's not my fault. Or for the fact that when you do find good guys, you make them feel like you don't care about them." You shift on the sofa and rub your eyes. Your head is still buzzing from the cheap wine. "None of that is my fault."

Max squeezes her eyes closed and you realize suddenly that she's holding back tears. One tear escapes and slips down her cheek.

You reach to touch her shoulder and she pushes your hand away.

"Leave me alone," she says through clenched teeth. She scoots back on the couch, a full foot away from you, and then pulls her knees up to her chin. You can hardly hear her crying, but her body trembles.

"Max?"

"Don't."

You take a deep breath and wait. Another tear escapes. You brush it off her cheek and she leans into your hand instead of balking. You shift over to her side of the couch.

"I'm sorry if I said something stupid. I drank too much." You hope she'll say something, but she only starts to cry harder. "Can you tell me what I did?"

She shakes her head.

"Don't close up like you do. I'm not going to let you off easy like your boyfriends always do." You grin. "Come on, tell me all the ways I messed up. I know you want to."

"Sometimes I hate you," she says.

"Sometimes? How do you feel the rest of the time?" you tease.

Max turns and thumps her fist against your chest. She won't look at you. Her head drops to your shoulder. "Screw you," she says. The tears have stopped. Her voice is clear when she continues. "I don't hate you. I just hate that you make me feel this way." She pushes away from you and stands up.

"What way?" It doesn't seem possible, yet suddenly you know. But Max has to tell you. You're done with guessing. "What way do I make you feel?"

Max doesn't look back at you as she walks to the kitchen. She opens a cabinet and stares at the neat row of glasses. Then she sighs. "Vulnerable."

"Vulnerable? Who says that?"

Max laughs, but the sound is hollow. "My shrink." She fills a glass of water. You watch her, waiting for her to come back. She stares at you from across the room, taking slow sips. "Yeah. I started seeing a shrink. After New Year's. Are you going to ask why?"

"Why?"

"Because of you. Because I kissed you and then you never said anything about it. Like it never happened. Or that it didn't matter if it happened. Shit, I can't believe I'm telling you this." She sets down the glass of water and braces her hands on the counter. Her eyes lock on yours. "My shrink told me that I wasn't ready to talk to you. Because I hadn't *accepted* it myself. Oh well. At least now we'll have something new to discuss at my next appointment. I think I was beginning to bore her."

The sarcasm is the old Max. The familiar Max. A minute passes, and then another. You know you should argue that New Year's was only an innocent kiss. That it didn't mean Max wasn't straight. And that friends sometimes kiss. Straight girls even kiss other straight girls. But maybe there wasn't anything innocent about it. Maybe Max felt crazy when she touched you. Just like you felt.

"Can you say something?" Max stares at you. "Tell me I'm being stupid. Tell me you aren't into me 'cause I'm a straight girl. I've heard you say it before—how you hate straight girls flirting with dykes. How straight girls only kiss dykes when they're drunk or when their boyfriends are watching. And how you can't stand all of that. You might as well tell me now. I feel like shit anyway."

It only takes ten steps to be standing in front of her. Doubt fills your thoughts, but you reach for her anyway, wrapping your arms around her body. When she's close to you, everything feels right. It always has. She lets you hold her briefly but then pushes away, wiping at her eyes.

"I'm drunk, and I know what you're thinking," Max says. "That I'm only telling you this because I'm drunk."

"Would you tell me this if you were sober?"

Max holds up her middle finger again. She goes over to the sink and fills the water glass, then looks back at you. "Don't look like you know what's going on. You don't. You're always so damn cocky." She cusses under her breath.

"You know, you're right. I hate it when straight girls lead dykes on," you say. "But it's even worse when it's someone that you are really into. Someone who you've had a crush on for too many years to count. Since maybe the first day you met her." You stop. Max is staring at the dishes in the kitchen sink. Wine glasses. Dinner plates. "And I think you've known how I've felt all this time. But you never say a word. So, stand in my shoes. What if, one night, your straight best friend kisses you? Finally. But you realize even in the moment that it's happening, that they had to be drunk to do it. That they were too scared to do it sober.

"They didn't do it because they really wanted you. They did it to try it out. Maybe so they could say they'd kissed a girl. And tell their friends afterward that it wasn't all that. Bragging rights. Or maybe because kissing feels good but even at the time, they probably wished they were kissing a guy. Whatever the reason, the kiss was only a game to them."

"It's not like that," Max says.

"You don't get to play a game with me," you counter. "Tell me how you really feel. No bullshit."

Max locks her gaze on you. "I'm not playing."

"That kiss made me dizzy and sick in the stomach," you say. "And you were drunk and hardly noticed. And now you're drunk again so we're talking about this, but as soon as you sober up…"

There's too much you want to say. You've been in love with her for so long that you hate even thinking about the word. And you've tried to fall in love with other women, but it never works out. You want a million kisses from her, not one. A million kisses that all mean something.

Max is quiet. You wish you knew what she was thinking. Maybe she wants you to leave but you can't bring yourself to call a cab now. You can't walk out without knowing how she feels.

After a long minute, you continue. "Yeah, we didn't talk about that kiss. Because I couldn't think about it. My best friend turned my world upside down with one kiss, and it probably meant nothing to them. I couldn't talk about it. I didn't want to lose you," you confess. "If it meant nothing to you, I didn't want to take that chance."

You wait for some response but she only closes her eyes. Your thoughts are jumbled and you're done talking. Maybe it's the box wine. You want to kiss her and see if she slaps you or pulls you in for a longer kiss. But instead you only stand there waiting for her to say something and worrying that she'll say nothing at all.

"You might lose your best friend. I'm going crazy wondering how we could end up if one of us just makes a move—one move. But you won't and I can't." Max sets the glass down and looks over at you finally. "Every time I see you, I want to kiss you again so much that I can't think of anything else."

You step forward, closing the distance. Your heart is racing in your chest. Max doesn't wait for you. She leans close and her lips press into yours. The roaring in your ears blanks out all other thoughts. All you can feel is Max. Her lips match yours. She's tentative at first, but then you can feel how hungry she is, how much she wants you, and the kiss deepens. When she starts to pull away, it's your turn. You step forward, pulling her into your arms and finding her lips again. She opens up to let your tongue touch hers. All you can think of is the stupid hope that this moment won't end. That you will stand in Max's kitchen kissing her forever. This woman who you've dreamed of kissing for too many years to admit. When she steps back you worry that her face will show the mistake she's made. Instead you only see longing. She reaches for your hand.

"I want to sleep with you," Max says. "But I don't want to screw it up. What if I'm terrible?"

"It's possible."

Max sticks out her tongue.

"Now that's the Max I know."

You stare down at Max's fingers interlaced with yours and then slowly open her hand, tracing the lines of her palm. Her skin is warm and damp. She really is nervous.

"Do you know how long I've wanted to hold your hand like this?" you ask. "How many times I've thought of you when I was sleeping with someone else?"

You find her lips again. Her hand slips under your shirt. You don't want to just sleep with Max. You want to make love to her. But somehow, tonight, you have to convince your brain that it is only sex. She might change her mind in the morning. Her hand moves up to find your breast and she looks up at you when you gasp.

"I've wanted to do that for a long time," Max admits. She continues a tender massage until you push forward into her hands. Then she nods and says, "But you're going to have to teach me how to do it right."

"I think you'll figure it out."

You pull her to the couch, hitting the light switch as you pass. The lights dim slowly until the apartment is dark. A pale glow from the streetlights outside the window is enough to see Max's face. She's watching you. Waiting. After brushing popcorn off the sofa you slip off your T-shirt and lay down. Max stands there, staring down at you, then slowly reaches out to touch your chest. Her fingertip draws a line between your breasts and past your belly button. She pushes your shorts down until she can feel the start of your trimmed hair. A flood of longing swells over you and you hope that she doesn't change her mind. Her fingers linger for a moment, exploring, but then she pulls back as if she's gone too far.

You slip off the shorts and reach for her hand, placing it in the same spot she'd just left. She doesn't meet your gaze but her hand moves over your middle, down the inside of your thighs, back up along the outside of your legs to your hips and slowly to your chest. You want to pull her on top of you, but she seems frozen in place.

You shift up on your elbows and move so there's room on the couch. "Sit down with me."

She sits on the edge of the cushions and you trace up her arm lightly. Her back stiffens when you move closer to her, making you doubt everything. Curbing your desire, you shift back on the sofa. "We don't have to do anything more than kiss, you know. Maybe we aren't ready for more yet."

"It's not like I'm a virgin," Max says, forcing a smile. "I want to do more than kiss you."

"But?"

When she doesn't answer, you lean forward and the sounds in the room all slip away. Her full lips press against yours. She doesn't pull back when you touch her shoulder and she moves into your hand as you caress the curve of her cheek. As you trace the line of her collarbone she opens up for another kiss. You trail down her back and then slip under her shirt, expecting to feel her tense, but instead she murmurs softly and pushes against your hands. The warmth of her smooth skin brings thoughts no one should have about a best friend. Then she takes off her shirt and her bra and impossible desire blurs any hesitation.

"Can we go to your bedroom?" you say, hoping the huskiness in your voice doesn't make her reach for her shirt again. It's dangerous pushing her—she might change her mind. But you need to know now if sex will scare her off. A make-out session isn't enough. "There's not a lot of room on the sofa for kissing."

"For kissing? Since when do you need a bed for that?" Max winks and pushes your shoulder.

"It's a dyke thing. You probably wouldn't understand."

"Oh, I am so getting you for that." She laughs and presses you back against the cushions. "You better watch it. Not only can I pin you, I know where you're ticklish." She stands up then and your heart skips a beat. Bare chested she's more beautiful than ever and now you don't need to pretend that her sexiness goes unnoticed. She gazes down at you for a moment and then spins on her heel and heads to the bedroom.

A few steps behind her, you reach the bedroom after she's pushed down the covers. She looks over her shoulder. Maybe it's nervous tension that has her stopped at the foot of the bed, or maybe it's second thoughts. She stills when you come up behind her. You touch her arm lightly, hoping that she'll turn to you. All you feel is longing, dry and hot. Max is your drink of water. But if you reach too quickly...

When she doesn't turn around, you start on a massage. You've given her a back rub before. The only difference is that this time you're in her bedroom and she's half-naked. Starting at her shoulders, you knead the sinewy muscles of her arms and back, keeping some distance between her body and yours. Before you've finished, she steps away from your hands. She doesn't look at you as she pulls off her sweats and moves to the bed. Stretched across the mattress, the curves of her naked body are gorgeous even in the weak glow of the streetlights, but you long for the sunrise. Until then you'll lie awake, waiting to see her in the morning light.

You sit down on the edge of the bed and start back at the massage. But the more you rub her back, the more you want to feel other parts of her. You straddle her, still keeping up the pretense of the massage despite the wetness between your legs. If she feels it, Max doesn't say anything. Moving down her body, you knead the pressure points of her lower back, then the muscles of her butt and thighs. When she doesn't tense at this, you move lower still and work down her legs. She shivers and you reach for the blanket to cover her.

Max rolls onto her back and pushes off the blanket. You don't expect her touch, but she goes right for your breasts. She strums your nipple until it hardens and then runs her fingertip over your lips. "I don't want you to cover me up. I want you to see me. I love the way you're looking at me right now."

You can't wait any longer. You lie down on her, feeling the intoxicating rush of her body under yours. Naked skin against skin. She reaches between your legs, moaning softly as she feels your wetness, her fingers slipping inside to find your swollen clit. The next kiss unleashes all the pent-up desire you've been holding back. Your clit is already buzzing; her fingers hardly had to touch you. You try to calm your body down, but Max is strumming faster now. Her fingers don't feel novice. She has you on the edge, and if she went hard with her thumb, you wouldn't be able to stop the climax. But you want more. You reach down to guide her fingers inside. You want to feel her everywhere. Two fingers push in and then her thumb presses once more on your clit. Gasping, you come hard, clutching at her hand. The wave rushes over you and your legs clench tight around her hand, holding her inside.

"God, you feel good," she says. She thrusts in and groans when you contract on her fingers.

After a moment, your body relaxes, and you pull her fingers out. She murmurs an argument and tries to push inside again. You grab her wrist and pin her hand down on the bed, shaking your head.

"That was too fast," she complains, reaching for you again. "I want more."

"You'll get used to it. The novelty wears off."

A smile crosses her lips. "I doubt that. Come on. Just a little." She tries to pull her hand free, but you hold firm.

"It's my turn with you."

You kiss her wrist above where your fingers are wrapped around it and then kiss a pathway up the underside of her arm to her collarbone. Finally you let go of her wrist as you kiss her neck and then find her lips. Before she can touch you, you move down on the mattress. Sucking the dark tip of her nipple into your mouth, you get rewarded with a long, low moan. Shifting lower you lick your fingers and find her center. She's impossibly wet. You encircle her engorged clit over and over until you can't wait any longer to taste her. Tipping your head between her legs, you breathe in deeply of her and then rasp your tongue across her.

"Oh yes," she says, running her fingers through your hair.

Sliding your arms under her legs, you rock her pelvis up into your mouth. She groans as your tongue strokes inside. Fingernails sink into your skin as she grips your shoulders. You stroke faster with your tongue and then suck her clit between your lips. She thrusts her pelvis up off the bed, shoving hard into your mouth and then grinding down as you lick circles around her swollen clit. When she's moaning and tugging on your hair, you slip one finger inside and find her g-spot. She sinks down on your hand and groans. Your tongue laps faster and you lose yourself between her legs, your face covered with her sweet-salty taste, her sultry scent the only thing you want to breathe. Her body quivers under you. She's close. You look up to see her face when you feel the tremor start.

Her head is thrown back on the pillows and her lips are open as if she's about to cry out, but a soundless gasp follows. She squeezes her legs together when the spasm of her climax hits. Moving up to find her lips, you kiss her gently, loving that you've given her this release. Slowly her expression softens and the grip her legs have on your hand relaxes. When you try to pull out she tenses up again as an aftershock races through her body. You wipe your chin, tasting Max on your fingers, lips—everywhere. Maybe you'll only get this one night, but you won't forget any second of it. A minute passes and she reaches down to clasp your hand.

"I love you," Max murmurs.

The same words form on your lips, but you can't say them aloud. Not yet. Max loves easily. And she falls out of love easily. If you say those words, it will change everything. "You know it doesn't count when you say that right after sex."

Max chuckles. "I knew you were going to say that." She sighs and lets go of your hand, then rolls on her side and pulls her knees up to her chest. You straighten the blankets, covering her body and then curl up against her. She pulls your arm over her. "I love being with you like this. And having my fingers inside you. I loved making you come…and your tongue. Mmm. I love all of it."

Max's naked back against your chest reignites your desire, but her breathing has slowed and you wonder if she's falling asleep. Several minutes pass and all you can think of is what you want to do next, where you want to touch her, and when she'll be ready for you again. If she wants you again.

"I've wanted to sleep like this with you...So many nights I've thought about what you'd feel like," Max says. Sleep edges her soft voice. She pulls your arm tighter around her body and then kisses your palm.

"Me too," you say. You embrace her and close your eyes.

Go to bed. This is the end of your adventure.

CHAPTER TEN

Accept Margo's invitation and leave the sex shop

You set the red-and-black vibrator back on the shelf and turn to Margo. Her offer is an interesting one, mainly because by the look in her eyes, you guess that she's open to more than a drink. But you're still dressed as Batman.

"I don't think I'm in the right costume for Rumors. I usually wear my dyke outfit for that place."

"Some sexy tight shirt and your favorite jeans?" She grins. "Maybe tonight you need to go a little out of your comfort zone. Besides, no one will recognize you in that mask."

You smile. "But you recognized me."

Margo tilts her head. "Touché."

Margo's two friends had been hanging back by the dildos, but you notice them now in the vibrator section. The tall one with the pierced eyebrow walks up, eyeing you as if she's sizing up the competition. "We're ready to leave whenever you are," she says to Margo. She motions to your costume. "Great outfit, by the way. Picking out toys for a costume party?"

You wonder how common it is for people to stop in at sex shops on their way to parties. In costume. "Not exactly. I'm looking for a consolation prize."

Pierced eyebrow laughs and then Margo says, "Actually, she's coming out for a drink with us."

Soon Margo is introducing her friends, and you realize that a drink with strangers might be a better way to get over Janine than an inanimate sex toy. The tall white woman with a pierced eyebrow is Frankie. Her dark brown hair is shaved in a buzz cut. Her date, a lithe Asian woman with blue eyeliner and red lipstick, is Liz. You glance away from Liz when you notice Frankie's protective arms circle around her waist.

"Want to drive with us?" Frankie asks.

"I might only stay for one drink. I don't want to give you all a curfew."

Frankie pulls Liz over to the sales counter to buy two packets of flavored lube and a blue double dildo with an extra bullet vibe. No secrets as to how their night is going to end. You listen to Frankie joke with the saleswoman about watermelon gum reminding her of flavored lube. Liz glances over her shoulder at you and Margo.

"Frankie and Liz have been dating for years," Margo volunteers. "But I've known Frankie for even longer. I met her the first time I walked into Rumors. She makes friends with everyone."

Frankie and Liz head for the door and Margo follows. She stops by a display of harnesses with various sizes of strap-ons. She picks up the large dark purple dildo on display and angles it at your crotch. "Batman should be equipped with one of these." Before you can argue, she's picked out a harness and is holding this up to your hips. She notices you squirm at the contact of her hand against your leg and chuckles. With a smirk she pops open one of the packaged purple dildos and slides the tip through the harness's O-ring. You straighten up as she positions the setup right at the center of your briefs. Her touch has your pulse racing. "This will do," she says, barely hiding her enjoyment at making you uncomfortably hot. "Trust me on this. You're going to be happy with the purchase."

With that recommendation, you can't leave the store empty-handed. You follow Margo up to the front counter. She sets the dildo and harness on the counter. "We'll take these."

"Looks like you found what you were looking for," the store clerk says.

In fact, you hadn't come in looking for a date. Or a strap-on. But you hand over your credit card. Tonight is not at all what you expected.

"Come again," the clerk says, handing your bagged items to you. She winks as you reach for the bag.

You step outside the shop and Margo points at your car. "This one's yours, right?" She walks over to the passenger side and waits for you to unlock the door. You wonder what else Margo knows about you. She recognizes your car and she knows you're into women, but she could have guessed both of those facts. Frankie and Liz are parked two spaces up. They're both leaning against their car, waiting. Margo waves to them. "We'll meet you guys there."

You hadn't planned on giving Margo a ride. But now that this has been determined, you wonder if you'll be giving her a ride home as well. Margo Yamada. No way would you ever risk asking her out, but if she's volunteering, you aren't going to turn her down. You've heard she's a formidable lawyer, but fortunately you've never had to face her down in a courtroom. All you know for sure is that she looks good in a black pinstripe dress suit. Since she's one of the execs and you've only been at the firm for a year, you've had little chance to get to know her beyond the monthly meetings. Office gossipers haven't mentioned anything about her, and until a half hour ago, you would have guessed that she was straight.

You slip into the driver's seat and toss the bag from the sex shop in the back. You glance over at her. "Ready?"

"Can I take off your mask?" Without waiting for you to answer, she reaches over and pulls off the cowl. Her fingers ruffle through your hair. "That's better. I like seeing your face. You're cute."

You feel a flush come up your neck and turn on the car. "But how is everyone going to know that I'm Batman now?"

"If there's any doubt, I'll tell them. But I think the bat wings on your chest give you away." A ringtone interrupts and Margo glances down at your cell in the center console. "Is that your girlfriend?"

"I doubt it. I left my girlfriend at the party. We didn't officially break up, but after tonight I have a feeling she'll never want to talk to me again." The phone rings again, but you resist looking at the screen.

"Maybe she wants you to come back to the party," Margo suggests. "Change of heart?"

"I guarantee you that she isn't the one calling. You can check." The ring sounds again.

Margo's eyebrows raise. "Open book, huh?"

You nod and pull onto the freeway.

Margo picks up your cell phone and reads the screen. "Who's Max?"

"My best friend."

"Can I say hello?"

"To Max?" You laugh. "Sure, why not?"

Margo clicks accept on the phone and says, "Hello, Max."

You try to focus on the road as Margo talks to Max. First she introduces herself as the hottie you picked up in the sex shop. Then she admits that she's on the board of directors at your work and if you didn't take her up on a drink offer, your chance at all future promotions would be lost. You hear Max's laughter on the other line and Margo cracks a smile. Then she asks Max if you regularly dress up as a superhero or if it is only for special occasions.

You can only guess at Max's response. Judging by Margo's expression, Max is probably telling her way too much. Margo goes on to claim that she felt sorry for you and is taking you out for a drink since everyone else thought you were a freak. By the end of the conversation Margo is promising to make sure you get home safe.

She hangs up the phone and looks over at you. "I love your best friend. What a kick in the pants. I can't wait to meet her."

"Is she coming to Rumors?"

"No. Something about a boyfriend and a poker party. But if we want to leave the club early, we've got a backup plan."

"Poker night?"

Margo nods. "I count cards. And I wouldn't mind winning tonight."

"I bet you can bluff well, too."

"I don't need to bluff," she argues. "Unless it's strip poker."

Margo's confidence is hard to resist. Soon she's telling a story about playing strip poker with her friends Liz and Frankie and an actual stripper in a back room at the club. Distracted by her story, you don't have a chance to work out the details on what you'll say if anyone at the club recognizes you under the Batman cape before you're parked in the back lot.

"You sure you want to be seen with me here? Like this?"

"Are you kidding? I love costumes. I only wish I had one on tonight." Margo smiles. "I was in a bad mood earlier. My ex stopped by with a box of my stuff from her apartment, and you know how that goes...So Frankie was letting me tag along with her and Liz, but I felt like a third wheel. Then I saw you. And my bad mood went away. Arguably, that was mostly because I was trying not to laugh at you. How can you be in a bad mood when one of the sexy young lawyers at your work shows up in a sex shop looking like she needs to be rescued from the worst day of her life?" She pats your knee. "But now I just want to have a drink and a good time. I want to be clear that I'm not looking for anything more. Not tonight, anyway."

"All clear. As long as you don't put anything in my personnel file about the costume, I think we're both good."

"I'll think about it," she says.

You pick up the cowl and pull it on. Somehow, the mask is more comfortable now. "Ready to go clubbing with me?"

She laughs. "Yes. And I dare you to walk in wearing that mask."

"Oh, I will," you promise.

"You know, I never would have had said hello to you if you weren't wearing that."

"I needed one good thing to happen tonight." You smile. "Let's go have fun and forget about our exes."

"Wait a minute," Margo says, reaching into the back seat. She hands you the bag from the sex shop. "You have to add something to that costume. I'll be in line waiting for you."

The bouncer at Rumors gives you a long once-over as you hold up your ID. When you tug off the mask, he recognizes you and says, "You know it isn't Halloween. What's with the costume?"

Margo steps up next to you and flashes her ID. "She didn't want anyone to know she was coming here with me."

The bouncer starts to laugh, but Margo is already pulling you into the club. The mischievous look in her eyes combines with the loud dance music and the flashing lights. Suddenly you don't care that you are dressed up in a Batman costume. And for the first time all week you aren't wondering about Janine.

Margo orders a beer and you decide on the same thing. You perch on the edge of a barstool and eye the front door. You recognize a woman coming in. She's a friend of Janine's and she's stopped in the doorway, talking to the bouncer. You start to put your mask back on, but Margo stops you. She runs her fingers through your hair and holds your gaze.

"Don't put the mask back on. You look good just like that. Besides, we aren't going to sit at the bar," she says. She looks over at the woman you were staring at. "We've got better places to be. If I stay here at the bar, I'll start to think about Lara."

"Ex?"

Margo nods. "And then I'll think about all of the mistakes I made with her. If we stay right here, there's a good chance I'll start to sulk." She takes a sip of her beer and continues, "Which is why we are going to make friends with the go-go dancers and get up on stage. You're going to be perfect as an amateur drag king."

"Wait, what?" Nothing about getting up on stage with the professional dancers sounds like a good idea.

"It's part of the drag show. Beginners are always encouraged. And the go-go dancers take very good care of you. You're going to love that part."

"Drag show?"

"Yes. Bring your beer." Margo grins and grabs your gloved hand. "You'll thank me later. Come on."

"There you are," Frankie says. Her arm is linked through Liz's. "Where are you two going?"

"I'll get drinks," Liz offers.

Frankie lets go of her arm and turns to Margo. "Did you see the sign? Chris is in the drag show."

Margo nods. She smiles when Frankie whistles. Then Margo turns to you and adds, "Chris is an old friend of mine."

"Old friend? Is that what you're calling Chris these days?" Frankie teases.

"Yes. Friends." Margo's sharp tone stops Frankie's jeering. "We were about to go say hi. I'm signing Batman up for the drag show."

Frankie slaps your shoulder and congratulates you. "That's awesome. You're going to be great on stage. I can't wait to watch the show."

"The go-go dancers are going to have their hands all over this one," Margo says.

Frankie winks at you. "Chris will make sure you get plenty of attention."

You glance from Margo to Frankie. "There's no way I'm getting up on that stage."

"Why not? You've already got the costume and the dancers will take care of the act. What do you have to lose?" Margo reaches up to pat the bat wings on your chest. "What would Batman do?"

"Batman would be all about the go-go dancers," Frankie says.

"Come to the back room with me and meet everyone. Then see how you feel." Margo adds, "The dancers are great with beginners. They do the hard work and make you look good."

Do you:
A) Follow Margo to the back room (read on)
B) Stay at the bar with Frankie and Liz (go to Chapter Eleven, page 189)

Follow Margo to the back room

Maybe a go-go dancer would help you forget your night's mistakes. And chances are no one will recognize you with a Batman mask. "What the hell. Tonight I don't have much to lose."

"Good attitude," Margo says. Before you can change your mind she's pulling you through the crowded dance floor and past the stage to the back room marked Employees Only. Margo knocks on the door and you read the flyers for the night's drag show papered all over the hallway. The drag king in the picture looks like a cross between an Elvis impersonator and a used car salesman. But sexier. You're out of your league.

"I changed my mind. I think I'd rather stay at the bar drinking. This drag show thing looks like the real deal."

Margo ignores you as the door swings open. A forty-something dyke with tanned skin and spiked bleached blond hair leans out. She's wearing a sports bra and fluorescent green bikini bottoms that show off her well-oiled and well-toned body. She wouldn't be out of place on the pool deck of a gay cruise ship, but here…

"Margo!" The woman claps Margo's shoulder and pulls her into a hug. Then she looks over at you, and her brow furrows. "And Batman?"

Margo quickly introduces you. "This is one of my friends from work. She just left a costume party. Somehow I convinced her it would be a good idea to come out with me."

You don't correct Margo's mistake. Chris leans farther out the doorway and shakes your hand. "Any friend of Margo's is a friend of mine." She looks back at Margo. "God, it's been a long time. What, two years now? I thought you'd sworn off the club scene."

"I did," Margo agrees. "But after Lara and I broke up, I needed to get out of the house…It's been a month now."

"You and Lara broke up? We've got to catch up." She glances at her watch. "The first show is at nine. Why don't you two come in and keep me company while I get ready to go on stage?"

Chris pushes the door open all the way and waves for you to come in. The dressing room is small. One red sofa stands in the middle of the space; the fabric is ripped in more than one spot and stains dot the bottom cushion. Two dressing room chairs face two rectangular mirrors edged with bright lights. Chris goes over to the sofa and fishes through a duffel bag. She pulls out a leather harness and a fat beige dildo complete with bulging veins and a bulbous tip. You watch as she steps into the harness and then pulls the straps up to her hips. She tightens the straps and then pushes the dildo through the O-ring in the center. Once everything is snug and in place, she turns to stare at her reflection. The green bikini peeks through the spaces between the leather.

Margo grins at Chris's reflection. "You look hot."

"Thank you," Chris says. She turns around and faces Margo. Then she steps forward and kisses Margo on the lips, the dildo wagging in the space between their bodies.

Margo laughs and pushes Chris back. "Keep getting dressed. You've only got twenty minutes before show time."

You aren't sure what to say, but it's awkward standing around in silence while a stranger gets dressed. Still, every question that comes to mind seems somehow inappropriate. Why the fluorescent green bikini? Ever go for a dildo with a set of balls for authenticity? When propositioned during a show, what are the rules for taking up an offer afterward? "So, Chris, how long have you been doing drag king shows?"

"Three years. You'd think I'd have time to perfect the act, but I still haven't figured out how to dance. I kind of gyrate my hips and strip." She grins and plucks the waistband of her green bikini. "Lucky for me, the regular dancers back me up. They're the ones the crowd's always watching."

"I think you're wrong about that," Margo says.

Chris winks at Margo and then grins at you. "You two would be cute together. Only friends?"

"Friends," Margo says. She doesn't look at you. "I'm not ready to date another lawyer."

Chris goes back to the duffel bag and pulls out a pair of cargo pants. She steps into the pant legs. "But Lara was a bartender."

"Yes," Margo agrees. "And she's going to law school. She graduates in May." Margo looks at you and adds, "My ex and I met here. She was bartending at the time. Then she decided to go to law school. And I wouldn't be surprised if she applied for a job at our firm."

"Would you hire her?"

Margo sighs. "I think she's going to be a good lawyer."

"If you're the one in charge, don't hire her," Chris says. "You never want to work with an ex. Too much baggage." Chris slips a belt through her cargo pants. You can't help but stare at the bulge in her crotch. She rifles through the duffel bag again and pulls out a button-down dark blue shirt. The sports bra disappears as she does up the buttons. Finally, she reaches for a red tie and loops it around her neck.

Margo steps forward and adjusts the knot. After she's snugged the tie up to Chris's collar, Margo leans forward and kisses her lips. Chris slips her hands behind Margo's head. You watch as their kiss deepens. Neither seem to mind the audience, so you don't look away. Chris opens her mouth and Margo's tongue pushes in.

The dressing room door swings open and in walks a woman in a tight black dress. You do a double take at the dress before recognizing the woman. Three weeks ago you pushed a twenty-dollar bill under the band of her thong. She's one of the dancers. The woman eyes Margo and Chris, still lip-locked, and then you. You feel a flush come up your neck hoping she won't recognize you.

"Hi, I'm Courtney," she says. "You must be one of the new drag kings?" She extends her hand. "I like the Batman costume. Is it a superhero theme?"

"Um, no, I'm with them," you say awkwardly. Margo and Chris have stopped kissing but their arms are still linked.

"We're short tonight, Court," Chris says. "I'm the only drag king that's shown up so far. Nash is coming at ten."

"Nash flaked last month. But Tyvonne said she'd be here at ten."

"Good. Let's hope they both show." Chris sighs. "But as a backup plan, want to do your pole routine in drag?"

"Not a chance," Courtney says. "I don't do drag. But we could totally make Batman an act. Batman could try tying me up to the pole, but then I get loose…"

"That's not a bad idea," Chris says. She looks you up and down as if appraising the costume as well as your chances on stage. "What do you think? You really wouldn't need to do much. Want to try your hand at catching a pole-dancing villain?"

"How much of your costume can I strip off?" Courtney asks. "And I like the idea of turning the tables and tying you up after you've tried to catch me."

The thought of Courtney stripping you is uncomfortably arousing. Except when you consider an audience. "I don't think I'm the right Batman. I've never done any acting…"

"Relax. It'll be a breeze." Chris waves off your insecurities and turns to Courtney. "I didn't think you were going to make it tonight. What about that formal dinner party thing you had to go to with Becca?"

"Oh, we went. Becca was hanging all over her ex. When Dana called and said we were shorthanded, I figured I might as well make some money. I'd rather work than watch Becca screw around on me. I'm done with her." Courtney gives Chris a long look. "Anyway, tips are good on drag king nights."

"Becca doesn't know the good thing she has with you."

"Had. Like I said, I'm done…Whatever. Let's get to work. I need a distraction." She motions to you. "I'll work on Batman. Dana and Jenny are already out on the bar. You okay working with them on backup?"

Chris nods. "They know my act. Batman, are you packing?"

"I'm not getting up on stage." You realize that your protests are falling unheard, but that doesn't make you any more willing.

"She's packing," Margo says. "I picked it out for her."

Courtney, Chris and Margo all stare at your crotch. Your hand reflexively drops to the prominent swelling in your outer briefs.

"Perfect. Then we're set." When you shake your head, Chris says, "Courtney, you convince her. It's almost nine."

"I'll only take you down to your underwear," Courtney promises. She walks over, stopping a few inches in front of you. Uncomfortably close. Then she reaches up to pull off your mask. She brushes her hand over your cheek and combs her fingers through your tousled hair. You remember to breathe after a long moment of staring into her blue eyes. Her lips turn up in a coy smile.

"You've got the wrong person for this," you argue. "I can't act."

"Really? Because I think you've been pretending like we haven't met this whole time when in fact I'm pretty sure I've kissed you."

Chris and Margo take an audible breath. You wish you could pull your mask back on.

Courtney smiles. "You don't have to admit anything, but we both know you can act. Anyway, you won't have to do a thing once you get on stage. I'll take off this costume one piece at a time and you can pretend to fend me off. The crowd is going to love every minute."

"I'd love to stay around and hear details," Chris says. "But I think you two need some time to talk. And plan your act." She takes Margo's hand. "I'm stealing you."

Margo glances over her shoulder as she heads for the door. "By the way, Batman broke up with her girlfriend tonight. She might need a little extra encouragement."

"Got it," Courtney says.

And then Margo and Chris are gone. You walk over to the sofa and sink down. "I'm not going on stage."

"You'll change your mind." Courtney follows you to the sofa. She reaches down and pulls the top band of your outer briefs back enough to see the purple dildo. "Too bad it isn't black. It would match the rest of the outfit."

You shift away from her hand. Despite being turned-on by the contact, you know this is only work to her. And now that she remembers the kiss, everything is on the table. "I've never been on stage for anything other than piano recitals. In high school."

"Time to change that." Courtney touches your shoulder. "I really will take care of everything."

You drop your head into your hands. Even piano recitals used to fill you with dread. And your dance moves are limited to hip swaying. "The other thing is that the idea of you stripping me is way too much of a turn-on."

"Too much of a turn-on?" Courtney laughs. "Poor you. I think you'll find a way to suffer through it."

"What if I freeze up?"

"Then we'll make that part of the act," Courtney says. "You walk out there, stand in a superhero pose, and I'll take it from there. Before you know it, you won't be thinking about anyone in the crowd. You'll only be thinking about me." Her hand slips down to stroke the purple dildo. "I think purple will show up better than black under the lights anyway. Do you want to practice?"

You don't move. Courtney tilts your chin up so your eyes meet hers. "You're cute. If I hadn't just broken up with my girlfriend, I'd try to get you to ask me out...You know, we have a lot in common."

"How's that?"

"We both broke up with our girlfriends tonight."

"I haven't told mine yet," you admit. "I just walked out."

"Me too," Courtney says. "So why don't you help me forget about mine and I'll help you forget about yours?"

When you don't answer, Courtney moves forward and straddles your legs. "If I remember right, you're a good kisser."

After you gave Courtney the twenty, she kissed you. So you kissed her back. And then you handed her another twenty. Toward the end of the night she showed up on the dance floor. Janine loved watching Courtney rub up against you; she was so turned on seeing you with someone else that she started slipping Courtney twenties herself. The rest of the night was worth all the money you dropped. And it isn't hard to guess why Courtney remembers you.

Courtney tugs at your chest plate. "This looks complicated. It isn't a one-piece, is it?"

"I'm not going on stage."

"That's too bad. I think you'd enjoy it." Courtney touches your cheek with the back of her hand. "Are you always this difficult?"

"Difficult?" Her caress is hard to ignore, but you try.

"Yes. Difficult." She sighs. "Don't get me wrong, I like a challenge, but long-term, I'd rather have someone chasing me than the other way around."

You smile. "I'd chase you. But you're working at the moment. I know better."

Courtney's lips jut out in a pout. "I'm not working."

"So, I could stand up and walk out of here? What about the act?"

"What about it?" Courtney is defiant. "Look, I'm not working until I go on stage. And I could walk out there and make plenty of money without you. Chris isn't my boss. I don't have to run an act with you. I don't even have to be here tonight."

"Then why don't you leave?"

"Because I don't want to," she answers sharply.

You stare at her for a long moment, acutely aware of an undeniable urge to kiss her pouting lips. But you don't move a muscle.

"Difficult," she says, jabbing her finger at your chest plate.

You smile. "Determined."

Courtney takes your face in both her hands and locks her lips on yours. Your body jolts to attention. Before you can pull away, she has you in another kiss. Her tongue traces your lip and then she opens up, waiting for you. Her dress hikes up when she shifts on your lap, giving you a good feel of her toned thighs. You pull your hand away and try to back up from her lips. She moves with you until she has you pinned against the back of the sofa. Her mouth presses hard against yours. After struggling to remember why you're fighting her, you give in. She murmurs her approval as you slide your hand up her thigh. Your thumb brushes the lace edge of her thong. And then her lips press in again. Her thighs are dangerously smooth and her soft moans encourage you. Abruptly she stops kissing and her hand presses against your Batman insignia, holding you in place.

"We need to focus," she says.

"On what?"

Her hands drop down to the latch on your utility belt. You watch her fingers work. She unhooks the belt and pulls it off. "Our act."

"I thought this wasn't work."

"That kiss wasn't work. But we've only got a half hour." She pulls you up to your feet and kisses you again. Then her hands trail down your body to your briefs. She rubs against the dildo and then looks down at your boot covers. "We can't get too distracted if we're going to make it on stage at nine thirty."

You hear the DJ announce the drag king show and then the sound of the crowd cheering. "Or we could just go back to my place," you say. You wonder how much Courtney usually makes in tips. You'd offer more.

"Most of the drag kings like to do everything themselves." Courtney runs her hand down your chest. "They don't like touching. Unless they're the ones doing it. But tonight you're going to let me be in charge. I guarantee you'll like it. And so will the crowd." She tugs your briefs down a half inch. "Okay, I've got it. What if I pull these down and you swing out the dildo, but we keep your pants and the boots on?"

You pull the briefs back up. "Or I could pay you to go home with me."

"You're not paying me, and don't you dare bring that up again." Her jaw clenches.

You feel a flush come up your neck. "I'm sorry. That was stupid."

"It was." Courtney stares at you for a long moment and then glances at the clock. "When we go out on stage, I'm working. If I kiss you in this room, I'm not working. If you ask me to go home with you and I say yes, I'm not there to work. Clear?"

"Clear."

"And now that we have that settled…" She clears her throat and steps forward to touch your chest plate. "Let's talk about taking off this outfit. I'll start with your gloves," she says, pulling off first one and then the second glove. "Then we take off the armor." She pulls off the chest plate and the fake arm muscles next. Underneath, you're wearing a thin, long-sleeved black shirt. "Take that off. I can't work with that."

Reluctantly, you take off the shirt. Fortunately, you're wearing your sexiest black bra.

Courtney runs her finger under your bra strap, and your nipples harden. Frustrated by your body's response, you close your eyes.

"Drag kings can't wear bras and be taken seriously," Courtney says. She goes over to a rack of costumes on the side wall and begins flipping through the hangers. Most of the outfits are brightly colored and some have feathers. Courtney stops when she comes to a pair of red leather pants. Cussing, she pulls the pants off the hanger and throws them in the trash. Then she goes back to the clothes rack and finds a black tank top off the same hanger and tosses this to you.

"You're a little broader than Becca, but I bet this will fit. And it will look good tight." She waits for you to pull it on and then nods. "You've got nice abs."

"Pilates. The teacher is hot so I show up early."

"Whatever it takes." Courtney runs her hand down the muscles in your arms. "Maybe I should take up Pilates." A round of applause breaks out on the other side of the door, and Courtney glances again at the clock. "We go on in fifteen minutes. Take off the underwear."

"The costume guy called them outer briefs." You slide the underwear down your legs.

"Why is it that all the old school superheroes wear their underwear on the outside?" Courtney asks. "I used to dress up like a cowgirl. I had a whip and everything."

"Cowgirls are hot."

"I was six. I grew out of the costume. But I kept the whip."

"Are you trying to make me feel like an idiot tonight?"

"No, you do that all on your own," Courtney says. She jabs your arm. "But I still think you're cute."

"Maybe you should dig out the whip for tonight." You adjust the straps of the harness, and the dildo waves up and down. You look up and grin. "This is ridiculous. I can't believe I'm going to be on stage like this."

"You're wrong. This isn't ridiculous. And you're going to be so turned-on you won't even notice the crowd."

"I don't like to be told that I'm wrong," you admit.

"I bet you don't like to take orders, either." Courtney cocks her head and smiles. "And now I wish I had that whip." She steps forward and the suggestive look in her eyes make you melt. "From here on out, I tell you exactly what to do. You walk out there and try to stand still." She strokes the length of the dildo, pushing the base against your groin, then her fingers travel along the straps of the harness.

"If you touch me like that out there, standing still is going to be hard."

"Oh, I'm going to do more than that." Courtney slips her hands under the tank top. Her cool fingers move from your belly to your back as she pulls your groin towards hers. Her touch sends a shiver up your spine. The tip of your dildo pushes between her legs and the fabric of her dress presses in exactly where your body suddenly wants to thrust. You hardly know her. Perfect breasts, smooth thighs, full lips, and a siren's smile with half-closed eyes. You can chastise your body all you want for the lust that's taken over your thoughts—or you can accept it and let desire have its way.

"I can't wait to get you up on stage. But what exactly should I do to you…" Courtney's hands massage up and down your back. Her eyes drop to the dildo pressing against her dress. "Giving Batman a blow job could be fun."

"Are you serious?"

"Why wouldn't I be?" Her fingers tiptoe up the shaft of the dildo. "Maybe we should practice."

Courtney drops to her knees, and you feel your groin clench. Your throat is dry and you can hardly swallow. Before you can think of something to say, her lips circle around the tip of your dildo and the shaft slides inside her mouth. Arms wrap behind your legs and your clit spasms. She pulls you toward her and you can't help but thrust. The surge of adrenaline has your knees weak. As she takes the shaft deeper into her mouth, her eyes close. The base of the dildo rubs the seam of your Lycra pants right over your clit and there is suddenly no line between where your body ends and her lips begin. The strap-on is only an extension of you. Purple, engorged, hard you.

She doesn't let up, sliding you in and out of her lips. One well-placed finger and you'd come in a perfect climax, but she doesn't touch anything except the strap-on, and that only makes you want more.

Courtney stands abruptly. You try not to show your disappointment. "Think that would work on stage for you?" she asks.

"Yeah, sure." The last thing on your mind is going on stage.

"Good. Then I want something from you before we go out there." She pushes you down on the couch. "We don't have time..." She glances at the clock. "But I want it anyway."

Her lips part as she touches your strap-on. Then she slips out of the black dress. She's wearing a strapless bra and a black lacy thong. Without thinking, you reach out to touch the thong. Your fingers slip under the cloth. She's shaved clean and impossibly smooth. She pushes away your fingers and then pulls off the underwear. The next thing you know, she's pushed you back on the couch and is climbing onto your strap-on.

"I don't have any lube," Courtney says. "But you've got me so wet I won't need it." She straddles your legs and the tip of the dildo edges her center.

With one thrust, you push it into her. She gasps and then grinds down on you. "Oh, that's what I wanted," she says. "You've got ten minutes to get me off."

She leans forward and the dildo moves deeper into her. You push your hips against hers as you thrust the shaft again. She moans and clutches at your arms. You give her a ride that has her mouth open and her fingernails digging into your skin. Your underwear is wet; you wish you were naked so you could feel the base of the dildo right up against your clit. But somehow the layer of Lycra is making the sensation all the more enticing. The more she grinds down, the more she rubs you in exactly the right spot. The first hint of a climax has your clit buzzing. You clench, trying to slow it. You want more.

"I'm getting close," she says, bouncing up and down on you. "Don't stop."

You pump your hips, matching her rhythm, and then lick your finger. She moans as you draw a wet circle around the edge of her clit, shoving her hips hard and smashing your hand between your hips and hers. When she rises up again, you pull the dildo all the way out. Her chin juts up and she grabs your butt cheeks, trying to pull you toward her again. You shift back, resisting.

"What are you doing? I want more of your cock," she complains.

"I'm about to come," you promise. "I wanted to make sure you were ready." Your clit is pulsing now.

"I'll come when you do. Make a little noise and you'll push me over the edge." She spreads her knees, waiting to take you in. Her glistening lips and swollen clit tempt you. With a slow stroke over the nub, you position the head of your cock at her wet hole. You grip the shaft as you enter her, feeling her muscles quiver as she takes you in. Then you let go of the shaft and thrust. When she moans, you echo her. You're so close it's impossible to slow down now.

"Give it to me hard."

You don't hold back, giving her all of your cock, hard and fast. Moaning as your climax starts, you try to pump through it, ignoring the clenching muscles and the pulse at your clit. She leans down to kiss you and then is riding you again. You clench your jaw and try to keep up.

Finally she cries out and squeezes her legs tight around you. You're sweaty and breathless. And you're wearing a stranger's tank top and a brand new strap-on. It was brand new, anyway. But now it's officially broken in. Courtney lays down on you, her chest pressed against yours and the dildo still inside her. When her eyes open she looks first at the clock, then at you. She sits up slowly.

"We're two minutes late," she says. "But I needed that." She maneuvers the dildo out of her.

"I don't think anyone will notice the time."

The door opens and Chris comes in. Fortunately, she's alone. She seems to take in the scene in one glance. "Looks like you two are practicing."

Courtney stands up. "Yes. And I think we have the kinks worked out." She walks past Chris and over to the rack of clothes. She doesn't try to cover her nakedness. You can't help but stare at her butt. You wonder if she'd let you slide into her from behind. Your groin aches at the thought of pushing in again. You imagine how she'd brace her body, hands on the wall, legs parted, as you thrust into her. Once wasn't enough. You want more. She sorts through the outfits until she finds a black leotard, a cat tail, and a pair of black cat ears. She looks over her shoulder at you and smiles. Of course she knows how she's left you still wanting more. That's her job. Then she turns to Chris.

"We've just got to get our costumes on."

"I'll tell Mac you'll be on stage in five." Chris nods at you. "Showtime."

If that was enough of the club scene, your story ends here.
If you are wondering what would have happened if you'd stayed at the bar to finish your drink, read on to Chapter Eleven.

CHAPTER ELEVEN

Stay at the bar with Frankie and Liz

"I don't think I'm up for go-go dancers tonight," you admit.

"You're welcome to stay with me and Liz," Frankie says. "Chris can entertain Margo."

Margo turns to you. "But you'd be perfect in the drag show. And this might be your one chance."

"Maybe I'd consider it if I had an act or if I was wearing something else." That excuse may only be partially true. "I can't even believe I'm here in Lycra."

"But you don't need an act. Chris will have one of the dancers take care of everything. Besides, you're already Batman. What more of an act do you need?"

Liz walks back from the bar with two cocktails. She hands one glass to Frankie and then looks over at you and Margo. "Everything okay?"

Frankie nods. "Margo's trying to convince Batman to sign up for the drag show. I told her she was welcome to stay at the bar with us if she wanted an excuse to avoid getting felt up by the go-go dancers"

"If you're scared to get up on stage, I don't blame you. Stay and have a drink with us," Liz says.

"I'm not scared, I'm overdressed," you argue.

"That's the excuse you're going with?" Liz grins and whispers something to Frankie.

"Yes." You look back at Margo. "I'm sitting this one out."

"Final answer?"

You nod.

"Okay. You're missing out," Margo says. "But don't think I won't ask you again."

The thought of Margo walking into your office and asking you to go to a club to meet go-go dancers is something to look forward to. Maybe you could even convince her to go on a real date with you. Someday.

Liz links her arm through yours. "Don't worry, Margo, we'll make sure she has fun with us."

Frankie glances down at Liz's arm and then looks over at you. You're ready for her to be upset. Instead she only sips her drink and holds your gaze.

"I'll call a cab or catch a ride home with Chris. Don't worry about waiting for me," Margo says.

"Oh, we won't," Frankie says. "I know how you get when Chris is around. And I also know Chris won't let you call a cab."

Margo cuts a path through the dance floor to the back hall. Meetings in the boardroom are going to be more interesting from now on. You take a sip of your beer. Liz's arm is still linked in yours. When you look up, she smiles and then reaches for Frankie's hand.

"So, you and Margo work together?" Liz asks.

Before you can answer, Frankie says, "You don't seem like a lawyer."

"Is it the outfit?" You take another sip of your beer while they laugh. At least you can enjoy your beer in good company. The night's not a total loss yet.

"The important question is, can Batman loosen up and dance?" Frankie asks. "Or is your lawyer side too tight-laced for that?"

"You can tell me how I do."

Frankie takes another sip of her drink and tugs on Liz's hand. Liz pointedly brushes past you as she sets her empty glass down at the nearest table. The pair step out onto the crowded dance floor and move to the middle. The spotlights rotate in a circle, catching the swinging mirror ball overhead. The dancers are swathed in flashes of shimmering light. Liz looks back at you and Frankie leans close to say something in her ear.

A woman passes you, bumping your elbow. She glances over her shoulder, apologizing, and then weaves through the dance floor. You recognize her. She's one of the go-go dancers you tipped the last time you came to the club. Janine had convinced you to slip money under her waistband. Now you watch her until she disappears to the back hall. The memory of slipping money under her waistband and the kiss she gave you in return feels distant and surreal. But you acutely remember Janine's jealous energy. She loved watching you kiss another woman, loved watching you bump against her body on the dance floor, and she quizzed you afterward about the night as if she were cataloging all the details to add to her own fantasy. That night you'd had the best sex you'd ever had with Janine. And before you fell asleep you had the only clear thought of the night—that you might be falling in love. You look over at the dance floor and Frankie waves, beckoning you to join them.

The crowd pushes and sways against your body, butches argue as you squeeze past, hands touch your butt and fingers tug at your belt. Someone asks if you brought Robin. You spin around, the blinking strobe lights and the shifting crowd disorienting you. Then you see Liz. Frankie is grinding against her backside. Liz reaches out and grabs your gloved hand, pulling you in front of her. She rests her hands on your shoulders. She's singing along with the song, but you can hardly hear her voice above the bass.

Liz's hands have now started to explore the rippled muscles of your arms and chest. Frankie moves her hands down to Liz's hips, eyeing you as she does. The challenge is obvious in her gaze. Frankie's cute in that tattooed and trying a little too hard to be butch way. Although she's not someone you'd usually go for, you find yourself wanting to kiss her just the same. You wonder if she'd let some of her butch control go for a night.

Liz opens the snaps on the tiny pockets of your utility belt, finding your keys, your cellphone, and your wallet. Then she closes each pocket and brushes her hand over the obvious bulge between your legs. She slides her body up against yours.

"You've got an awfully big hard-on," Liz says, rubbing the bulge against her crotch. "I have this fantasy of making out on a crowded dance floor. Would you mind if I grabbed your cock?"

"Frankie might not like that idea."

Liz laughs. The idea of her touching your strap-on is a complete turn-on, but you wouldn't mind if she did more than grab it.

Frankie moves closer. She cups her hand over her ear. "What?"

Liz leans back and says something to Frankie. By the look in Frankie's eyes, you guess that she's relayed the conversation verbatim. No secrets with these two. You can't help wondering about the double dildo they bought at the sex shop. As much as you'd like to fuck Liz, you'd also love to see them go at it together. Their naked bodies tied together by the same blue dildo.

The song changes and more dancers squeeze onto the floor. Liz rocks her hips against yours with the beat of the music. She reaches again to the bulge under your briefs. Slowly she slides her hand under the waistband to stroke the shaft. The head is turned down and pinned against your groin by the trusty jock strap. Liz's hand lingers long enough for you to forget about the music, forget to move your feet to the song. You're already wet. When she pulls her hand back, she turns to face Frankie as if nothing had happened. Frankie's lips press into Liz. You watch the kiss, enjoying it nearly as much as you would if you were somehow involved. The kiss deepens and you feel Liz's hand at your crotch again.

She doesn't touch the dildo this time. Instead her hand travels under it, following along the seam of your Lycra. Her index finger sinks down on your clit, and you jerk at the probing. Her fingers continue to feel up and down your seam all while her lips are locked on Frankie's. You press into her hand, enjoying her sly attention. Just when you have a rhythm and think you might actually come on the dance floor, Liz pulls her hand away. She says something into Frankie's ear.

Frankie looks over at you. "We want you to come home with us. We're leaving now."

Of course you wouldn't say no. You hardly had a choice anyway. Liz took your keys out of the utility belt and slipped them into her pocket. You'd left your car at the club.

An old Chinese rug warms the entryway but the apartment is otherwise filled with IKEA furniture. The living room looks like a picture straight out of the catalog with a bookcase matching the end tables and the coffee table. You even recognize the pattern on the sofa cushion. And the whole place is meticulous. You take off your mask and ask if you can shower. Liz goes to the kitchen for water, but Frankie walks you straight upstairs. Framed photographs of Frankie and Liz kayaking, climbing Mayan ruins, and skiing line the stairway up to the bedroom.

"How long have you two been together?"

Frankie looks down the stairs to where you've paused by the kayaking picture. "Ten years."

"You two look good together."

Frankie nods. "I think so."

The longest relationship you've been in lasted ten months. You haven't celebrated an anniversary with anyone. Yet. Frankie points out the bathroom and asks if you've been tested. You nod. Before Janine. After Claire. Five months ago.

"After you shower, put the costume back on, okay?" Frankie says.

You don't ask why. Clearly you've been brought here for a reason, and the costume must be part of it. You've already decided to go along with the ride, and it's too late to wonder if you've made a bad choice. You pee and then strip down. After a quick rinse in the shower, you dry off on a towel embroidered with the initials *F* and *L* and then piece your costume back together again until Batman is your reflection.

Frankie is leaning against the doorway when you come out of the bathroom. She gives you an approaching once-over. "Liz is really into costumes. I've always thought it was kind of ridiculous to dress up for sex, but she has a bunch of costumes and is always trying to get me to try it. The thing is, I've been wanting to try a threesome. It's just hard to find the right person. So you're kind of perfect for both of us." Frankie points to the bulge in your briefs. "Liz told me you were packing."

You pull down your outer briefs enough to show the shaft of your purple cock.

"Do you have to put a condom on that?"

"I just bought it tonight. Never been used."

Frankie watches as you tuck it back in and pull the briefs back up. The base of the cock presses against your groin. You adjust yourself, noticing that Frankie licked her lips. You don't have to wonder what part you'll play in their threesome.

"You like strap-ons?"

Frankie blushes. "I like them all right, you know." She continues, "Mostly Liz is into oral sex. We don't use toys much. But we've been talking about it. That's one of the reasons why we were at Hot Vibes tonight. Looking for toys." Her gaze drops to your outer briefs again. "How would you feel if I took pictures?"

"Are you serious?"

Frankie nods. "No one will see your face. You've got the mask."

"I don't think so."

"Why not?" Frankie asks.

The challenge is back in her voice. You grin. "How about this: you let me fuck you first and then you can take a picture after."

Frankie chuckles. "Liz is the one who's into costumes. She's the one you're supposed to be thinking about fucking."

"What if I want to fuck both of you?"

Frankie laughs again.

"So, you're not saying no?"

"I'm not answering the question," Frankie says.

"I noticed."

Frankie reaches up and adjusts your mask. "You have to keep the mask on for the pictures. It's perfect."

"I thought you didn't like costumes."

"I mean, I think it's ridiculous, but...I know Liz is going to like it. That's all."

"That's all, huh? So, you're not even a little bit into the idea of Batman fucking you?"

Before Frankie can answer, you step forward and touch her chest. You can feel her breath against your skin, smell her cologne. She straightens up so she's nearly your height. You brush your gloved hand against her cheek and then slip it behind her head. She tenses up and leans her head back. You wait for a moment, your lips inches from hers.

"I think you want to do more than watch."

"Maybe I do." Frankie closes her eyes and tips her chin up. You move in, covering her lips with a hard kiss. Your desire for Frankie isn't something you could easily explain. But the more you kiss her, the more you want her. You pull back when you hear a door creak.

Liz is standing in the doorway to the bedroom. She's Wonder Woman. A short red skirt and knee-length tights show off her thighs while a tight blue bodice hugs her chest and highlights her shoulders and slender neck. She adjusts the headband and then puts her hands on her hips.

"Hands off, Batman. That one's mine," she says. Her voice is serious but she can't hide her grin. "She's my imprisoned lover."

"Wonder Woman. I didn't hear you slip past," you say, rubbing your lips.

"Well, clearly you were distracted."

You do your best to not crack a smile. In fact, Liz's commanding tone and her sexy outfit has you reconsidering costume play after all. "Maybe you'd consider sharing your imprisoned lover with me."

"Whoa, imprisoned lover? How'd I get that role?" Frankie holds up her hands and steps back from you. She laughs, but you can hear the nervous edge to it. "I'm only the audience tonight."

"There's no audience," Liz says. "Now step away from Batman and come here, lover."

Frankie goes for the stairs. "I'll be right back. I'm going downstairs to get my camera. You two can keep playing."

"Stop right there," Wonder Woman says.

Frankie looks first at you and then at Liz. Wonder Woman. "You're serious?"

"Yes, come on, you promised you'd play along." Liz continues in her Wonder Woman voice, "And in case you weren't listening, you happen to be my imprisoned lover. Batman here thinks she can break you loose from my lasso and have you for her own. But she's wrong."

Frankie laughs.

You touch Frankie's cheek with your glove. "In fact, I know I can steal her away from you. One kiss from me, and she's already thinking of an escape."

"Wait a minute. That's not true," Frankie says, her eyes darting over to Liz.

Liz smiles. "That's why I have handcuffs." She holds up rubber handcuffs and walks over to Frankie. Liz takes Frankie's hand and pushes the first cuff on her wrist. Frankie doesn't resist. She only shakes her head.

"Since when do we have handcuffs?" Frankie asks.

"Since I bought them tonight," Liz says. "You didn't notice because you were busy checking out Batman over here. Meanwhile, I was busy thinking of ways to suitably punish you."

Frankie blushes. "This is crazy," she says. "You two can tie each other up and I'll take pictures. How's that sound?"

Frankie backs away from Liz and tries to pull off the handcuff. Liz grabs Frankie's hand. "We're trying to make sex more interesting. Remember? And weren't you the one who said you wanted to try out bondage?" Liz guides Frankie's hand toward her body and then pushes it up under her skirt. Frankie draws in a quick breath and Liz smiles. As the fabric pulls back, you realize she isn't wearing anything under the skirt. "You wanted this. And now you're scared?"

"I'm not scared," Frankie says. "But I like to be in charge." Her hand is still under Liz's skirt. "God, you're already so wet."

"Mmmhmm." Liz moves forward, rubbing herself on Frankie's hand. She murmurs her enjoyment as Frankie's fingers work under the cloth. "What if I want one night where I'm in charge?" Liz asks. When Frankie doesn't argue, Liz continues, "For one night, I want a love prisoner. And I guarantee you that I will be very wet." Liz pulls Frankie's hand out from under her skirt and then kisses her fingertips. "All you have to do is play along."

Frankie stares at Liz. You know that she wants to say no. She wants out of the handcuffs. But you can also see that part of her wants to say yes. Finally, she nods.

"I want to make a deal with you, Wonder Woman," you say.

"I like deals," Wonder Woman says. "Tell me more."

"Tonight we join forces. We share this prisoner and give her more pleasure than she's ever known. Then I agree to never kiss her again. By morning, neither of you will ever see me again."

"I like your plan, Batman. But how can I trust you won't go back on your promise and try to steal her away?"

"You'll have my word."

Wonder Woman points to Frankie. "Help me get the prisoner to the bedroom. We can strip her there."

"Strip me?" Frankie laughs. "Okay, maybe this won't be so bad. Is the prisoner allowed to enjoy this?"

Wonder Woman smiles. "Only a little."

You step forward and Frankie holds up her handcuffed hands. You grab the rubber links binding the handcuffs together. Of course she could slip out of the cuffs if she tried. But she isn't trying. Instead, she's grinning.

"I wish I could take a picture of you two," Frankie says, following you down the hall to the bedroom. "Love prisoner… Thank God I don't have to wear a costume."

"Too much talking, prisoner," Liz says. She spanks Frankie's butt as she enters the bedroom. They both grin at each other.

The lights are off in the bedroom, but candles fill the room with a soft orange glow. The blankets and top sheet have been stripped from the bed, and only the fitted sheet and two pillows remain. You walk Frankie over to the bed and say, "Shoes off first."

Frankie shakes her head at you but kicks off her shoes and then tries to undo the zipper on her jeans. You pull her cuffed hands away from the zipper, then unzip the jeans and yank them down her legs. She's wearing boxers under the jeans, and you pull these down, too. You have to slip off one of her handcuffs to get her T-shirt off. Her small breasts hardly need a bra, and she isn't wearing one. Her flat belly is covered in a tattoo of a two tigers circling each other, and she has another tattoo of a grapevine that reaches up nearly to her armpit. A snake is crawling in the vines. You touch the top of the grapevine and she shudders. "That had to sting."

"It didn't," Frankie says. Her voice is defiant. She's holding on to the tough butch attitude. For now.

"No more talking, Prisoner," Wonder Woman says. "Unless I ask you a question."

Frankie smiles again. "Yes, ma'am."

Wonder Woman shakes her head. "You are a naughty prisoner. We're going to have to teach you a lesson."

"Please do," Frankie says. She turns and presents her backside to Liz. Frankie looks over her shoulder at Liz, her eyes taunting.

Wonder Woman cocks her head to the side and wags her finger at Frankie like a schoolteacher. When Frankie shakes her butt, Wonder Woman spanks her butt cheeks hard enough to turn them pink.

Frankie straightens up, laughing. "Shit, that felt good. Want more?" She sticks her butt out again.

"No talking and no swearing," Wonder Woman admonishes. She walks past Frankie to the nightstand and picks up the bag from Hot Vibes. She pulls out the flavored lube and the blue double dildo. Wonder Woman turns to Frankie, waving the dildo. "If you're good, I'll give you this present later. But if you're bad, you'll be sleeping alone in the guest room." She tosses the double dildo back on the nightstand but keeps the bottle of watermelon lube. "Now lay down and don't say another word."

Frankie murmurs an argument, but she can't hold back her smile. She stretches across the bed, belly up, and then throws her cuffed hands up over her head on the pillows. Her feet reach the foot of the bed.

Liz squirts lube into her palm and then reaches between Frankie's legs. She smears the lube inside as Frankie squirms.

"Damn, that's cold," Frankie says, wiggling her legs.

Liz walks to the end of the bed and tickles Frankie's bare feet. Frankie reflexively pulls back, laughing.

"And no laughing, either," Wonder Woman adds. She smiles down at Frankie. "I do love to see you like that. Wet and spread. Open your legs a little for me." When Frankie complies, Liz nods her approval and then walks over to you. "Now, Batman." She touches your chest and slides down to your belt. "We have some things to discuss."

"I'm all ears."

"My prisoner needs something from you," Wonder Woman says. She squirts more lube into her hand. "Take off the underwear."

You drop your briefs, and your strap-on springs out. You turn the shaft in the O-ring until the tip is pointing up. Fully erect. Wonder Woman steps forward and grabs hold. Her hand strokes up and down your cock until it's glistening with lube, then she pushes the base against your clit. You squeeze your muscles, enjoying the pulsing sensation.

"My prisoner is going to enjoy this. But you're going to have to go slow. I don't know if she can take something this big."

"I know what I'm doing."

"Good." Wonder Woman continues, "You're exactly what I was looking for," she says. "You see, my prisoner needs a little attention. A little of this," she adds. "But she won't let me use a strap-on. I know that she wants it. We've talked about it in counseling. She keeps bringing it up. And I've watched her with a dildo. She jams it between the sofa cushions and then—"

"Oh, God, Liz, I can't believe you're telling her all of this." Frankie rolls over, burying her face in the pillows as she laughs. "I'm telling Batman how you masturbate next."

"Quiet, Prisoner," Wonder Woman says. "Remember, I can decide to punish you at any time."

"I'm counting on it." Frankie's voice is muffled by the pillows.

Wonder Woman smiles and pulls her hand off your cock. She goes over to the bed and braces her hands on her hips as she stares down Frankie. Frankie reaches up and touches her skirt. "You can pretend that you don't want that cock, but I know you do," Wonder Woman says. "You can't ask for it, but you want it bad. So I'm asking for you."

"I can say it," Frankie argues. She moans and rolls over onto her back again. "And maybe I do want it. But it's ridiculous with you two in costume. I can't keep a straight face." She grins and rocks her hips up, her knees dropping to the side. Her pelvis pumps the air. "Do you want to see me beg? How's this?"

"Don't tempt me." Wonder Woman slaps Frankie's thigh lightly. She shakes her head and smiles. "Now stop distracting me." Wonder Woman looks back at you. "After you fuck her, she'll realize how good it feels, how much she likes it, and then maybe she'll let me pleasure her the same way."

Frankie covers her face with her cuffed hands and laughs again. "I can't believe we're doing this. This is crazy."

"Maybe you need crazy," you suggest. "To help you get over it." And what a burden it will be to help. Your groin is already aching to push Frankie's knees further apart. You walk over to the bed. Frankie's cuffed hands fall back on the pillows and she looks up at you.

You glance at Wonder Woman. "What are you going to do while I'm keeping her busy?"

"I have a few things planned out," she says. "Don't worry, I won't feel left out."

Wonder Woman touches your cheek and then pulls you into a kiss. You hear Frankie groaning but you let Wonder Woman have another kiss. You grope up and down her body. The costume crinkles as you push up her skirt. You feel her naked thighs and then the trimmed hair. The tip of your cock pushes toward her as she opens up her lips. Then abruptly she steps back and wipes her mouth.

"You should get to work," Wonder Woman says.

You look down at Frankie and kick off your boots. She watches you climb onto the bed. She's nervous and shifts on the pillows. You touch her thigh and she quivers.

"Relax. I'm not going to do anything until you're ready." You move between her legs, watching her chest rise and fall. Your mouth waters as you brush your hand over her triangle of trimmed hair. You eye the slit, your body begging to push her apart and drive in hard. "We'll go slow. Like it's your first time."

"I want you to just push it in," Frankie says. "I don't want you to go easy."

"Have you ever had something this big?"

Frankie shakes her head.

Wonder Woman sits down on the far side of the bed. She moves up to the pillows and kisses Frankie. Then she licks her fingers and strokes wet fingertips over Frankie's slit. She shifts up to kiss your lips and then leans back down to kiss Frankie as her fingers work inside.

You watch as the kiss deepens. As soon as Wonder Woman pulls her fingers out, you move forward between Frankie's legs. When you push her knees apart, Frankie looks up at you. The bulged tip nudges her. Liz turns Frankie's face toward her lips and kisses her again.

You press into Frankie. It's a tight fit and Frankie groans as you rock from side to side trying to get the head inside. Liz holds Frankie's hand, kissing her chest, her breasts, her neck and then her lips all while Frankie moans. Once you're inside, you know it won't hurt her, but she's tense. You ease the lubed shaft slowly forward until it slides inside.

Liz pulls away and watches you. Frankie tries to reach for her, but she climbs out of bed and starts to undress. Frankie eyes you. She pushes up into you.

"You like this big one, don't you?"

Frankie groans. "Yeah, I like it," she says. She closes her eyes. "I like big cocks." She laughs. "But I don't think you're going to get me off with only that."

"We'll see." You start to thrust.

As you go faster, Frankie fights your rhythm, wriggling back against the pillow when you rise up and then surging up when you try to push down on her. She still hasn't let go of her control. You pull back, and she groans when the head pops out.

"What are you doing?" She catches her breath and sits up, trying to grab your cock. "Come on, put it back inside me."

"You need to let me do this."

You shift forward and press her shoulders back on the pillows. Then you kiss her lips hard. She surprises you, opening up for your tongue. You reach down and maneuver the tip of your cock so the head is at her opening. Then you kiss her again and rock your hips forward, driving your erection inside. She grips your shoulders and moans.

"That's what I wanted," she says. "Fast and hard. God, that felt good."

You pull all the way out and give it to her again. She moans louder. Then you get to work. You ride her hard until your clit is pulsing and you're dripping wet. The rubbing alone will get you off in no time.

The sound of Velcro splitting apart breaks your concentration. Wonder Woman is pulling off her skirt. Next she takes off the bodice. She smiles when she realizes you're watching and she reaches down to fondle her own breasts. She pinches her nipples until they are two dark, hard buds. She still has her knee-high tights on. Red, white, and blue with yellow tassels.

Liz saddles up to Frankie and pushes you back. You shift off of Frankie's chest and squat between her legs, working to keep the cock from slipping all the way out. You hold the shaft so the bulged head catches on the rim and wait as Liz straddles Frankie's face. Her hands grip the headboard.

"I know you want a taste," Liz says. "Greedy prisoner."

"Your greedy prisoner. You smell so good," Frankie says.

"Start licking," Liz says as she lowers her pussy onto Frankie's waiting tongue. Liz bounces up and down on Frankie's mouth. All you can see of Frankie is her belly under you and the curve of her breasts. Her face is hidden under Liz.

Liz's taut arms grip the headboard and the toned muscles of her back work until a sheen of sweat starts at the dimples of her butt cheeks. When she pushes her clit into Frankie's mouth, she sticks out her butt and her puckered asshole peeks at you. You wonder if you could finish with Frankie and then slide into Wonder Woman next. The thought of entering Wonder Woman there while Frankie eats her out has your clit throbbing. You start thrusting in Frankie again, keeping your eyes on Wonder Woman's bottom and hoping for another flash of her hole. Soon you feel your own climax pushing up.

Wonder Woman is moaning and rocking the headboard against the wall as she humps Frankie's face. You know that she's close to coming with Frankie's tongue rasping her clit, but you can't tell how close Frankie is. You try to slow down your own climax, but the pressure is getting higher. You clench your teeth and pump harder.

Wonder Woman pulls her pussy off Frankie. She rolls onto her back and stretches out on the bed. She spreads her legs and dips her finger inside. She watches you for a moment, eyeing the purple cock that slides in and out of her girlfriend, before closing her eyes. Her hips rock up and down as her index finger beckons her clit to come. You continue your thrusts as Frankie writhes under you, her fists gripping the sheet. Frankie looks up at your cock every once in a while, but then her head drops back on the pillows. You steal glances at Liz and listen to her panting. She's close.

Frankie's cries break loose and you focus on her. The sound of her moans and the look on her face, so close to coming, push you over the edge. You bear down on her, the base of the dildo pressing hard on your swollen clit, and you come in a sudden spasm. You stop thrusting long enough to ride out your climax. Frankie tries to rock her hips enough to get you to start pumping her again, but you hold tight, your cock deep inside her and an orgasm still rippling through your body.

"More," Frankie moans. "Don't stop, I'm almost there. Don't stop." She juts her pelvis up into you and then rocks from side to side, murmuring, "Come on."

Somehow, you convince your spent body to give her what she's asking for. You grit your teeth and start thrusting again. Frankie's knees splay out as she rises up into you. "Oh, God, yes," Frankie moans again. You drop deep into her, and as you start to slide back, she reaches for you. She grabs your forearms and pulls you down on her body. You sink your weight onto her. The Batman plate smashes against her bare chest. Your utility belt chafes the soft swell above her pussy. You know that you'll leave marks on her, but she won't release her grip on your arms and she bucks up into you again and again. "More," she demands. She's worked over but still filled with need.

You lick your finger and reach down to find her wet and swollen trigger. You pump her with your cock, as your thumb encircles the engorged clit until she groans and folds up on you, pinching your hand between her legs. You pull your hand free as she tightens on you, her fist rapping your upper arm as she hurls cuss words. When she falls back on the pillows, you start to slide out.

"No," she says, reaching for you. She holds you tight. Slowly, her knees draw up. You drop deep into her once more and feel her body clench as if she's actually tightening around you instead of the store-bought cock. You watch with satisfaction as a tremor races through her body and then finally her legs gape. You pull out gently and sit back on your heels.

"That felt so damn good," Frankie says. She's slack-jawed and her arms are at her sides, palms up and open. Her fingers twitch, and you wonder if you gave her an orgasm that reached all the way to her fingertips and toes. Maybe she'll remember the sensation of tingling nerves tomorrow. You know she'll be sore and thinking of your cock.

You glance over at Liz. Her face is relaxed. You didn't notice her climax, but now she's lying limp next to Frankie, one hand still between her legs and a sly grin on her lips. She touches your gloved hand and then pulls it toward her exposed belly, positioning it just above her belly button.

"Do I get you next?" you ask. You'd like to fuck her in the Wonder Woman costume, pushing up her short blue skirt just far enough to see her slit and then giving her enough of your cock to make her moan with pleasure. Just enough so that she misses it when you pull out. And begs to have you back inside her. You move your hand to brush down the inside of her leg. She looks up at you, and her knees part. Forget the costume, you think. It's too tempting to simply slide over to her side of the bed. She's naked and asking. You could slip inside her with your cock still wet from Frankie.

"You don't get to fuck her," Frankie says. "I get to do that."

Liz curls up against Frankie's side and whispers something into her ear. Frankie sighs. Liz wraps her arm around Frankie's middle, hugging her body tight. She kisses Frankie's cheek and then looks up at you.

"I told her that it's fun to watch," Liz says. "And you promised her a picture."

"Did I?"

Liz nods. "Wonder Woman and Batman together. Where are the handcuffs? Wonder Woman gets to catch Batman this time." She climbs out of bed and picks up the pieces of her costume she discarded on the floor.

Frankie sits up. She holds up the handcuffs that she managed to slip out of without any help. Liz snags them from her, shaking her head. Frankie slowly climbs out of bed. "If we're all going another round, I need a glass of water. And don't do anything until I get my camera." She steps gingerly, holding her pussy as she walks. She stops in front of Liz, who's now halfway to Wonder Woman. She's got the bodice on, and the thigh-high tights, but her butt is bare. "I think I might be into costumes after all," Frankie says. She rubs her crotch. "And big dicks."

"I told you this was going to be fun," Liz says.

Frankie smiles. "You're always right."

This is the end of your night's adventure.

CHAPTER TWELVE

Go home with the vibrator

"You're home early," Angie says. She's sitting on her front steps. Her legs dangle over the stairs, ankles crossed. "And since when are you alone? Where's your girlfriend?"

"Janine and I broke up." You stop on the sidewalk, eyeing your neighbor. "And I come home alone all the time."

"No, you don't. You've always got a date on the weekends."

"Always?"

Angie nods. "I've been keeping track." She flips a pack of cigarettes upside down and taps the base. She doesn't smoke, or at least you've never seen her light up. "What happened?"

You shrug.

Derek and Angie own a third-floor condo in the brownstone next to yours. You've got a third-floor condo as well, but you have the added draw of a private roof patio with a view of the park. Derek and Angie routinely invite themselves over to your place for barbeques on the roof. They bring the food and you love the arrangement. In fact, they're perfect neighbors. The one downside to the situation is that only a narrow alleyway separates your two buildings and you have to keep your blinds drawn at night or Derek and Angie can see right into your kitchen from their bedroom. This also means you have accidentally seen Derek and Angie in bed on hot summer nights when you've gone for a midnight snack.

"Did you break up with Janine? Or did she break up with you?"

"I don't know," you admit. "Maybe I liked her too much. I walked out on her tonight."

"That was dumb," Angie says. "Janine was hot."

"Thanks for that reminder. I doubt she ever wants to see me again." Maybe it's not too late to change and go back to the party. But Janine is probably already with someone new. And she probably wouldn't want to talk to you now.

"Don't worry. You'll find someone new in a week or two."

"Are you calling me a player?"

Angie grins. "I didn't say that." She spins the pack of cigarettes.

"Everything okay with you and Derek?"

"Everything's good." She pulls a cigarette out halfway and then pushes it back inside the pack. "But sometimes I want more. Know what I mean?"

Angie moved in with Derek two years ago. She's an artist. He's an accountant. After two years, Derek still acts as if coming home to Angie is the best part of his day. You've seen his face light up when she looks at him, and you know he's in love. But you've wondered if Angie feels the same.

"Can we go back to talking about you? Are you always an asshole to the women you date?"

"Not always." You walk up the first two steps of Angie's stairs and then lean against the railing. "And I do feel terrible about what happened."

"Call and apologize."

You shake your head.

"Then you don't feel that bad." Angie runs her fingers through her auburn hair, changing the part from the left to the right side with a flip of her wrist and showing off her tattoo in the process. She's got a busty mermaid swimming up the underside of her forearm. The mermaid isn't as full-chested as Angie, and you have to catch yourself from glancing at the line of cleavage that her scoop-neck tank top reveals. "I thought the two of you were going to move in together."

"She's probably already hooked up with someone else."

"Well, I'll miss seeing Janine around here," Angie says.

"That doesn't make me feel better."

"Good. You screwed up. I don't want to make you feel better." She motions to the Hot Vibes bag. "I recognize that bag. Tell me you didn't drive straight to the sex shop after you broke up with Janine."

"I don't have to tell you anything. Besides, what's wrong with going to a sex shop after you break up with someone?"

"I can just picture you walking in to Hot Vibes. Batman, fresh from a breakup, rushes in for a late-night emergency vibrator… God, what are we going to do with you?" She slaps her leg as she laughs. "But you do make a good Batman. I have to admit that I jumped when I first saw you coming up the street. Whose costume party anyway?"

"No costume party. I just get dressed up like this to go to Hot Vibes."

"Shit, that's kinky." Angie grins. "I wish I could have seen you wandering around the sex shop like that. People must have thought you were totally crazy."

You can't stop yourself from laughing along. Angie has an easy laugh that spills out often, and she laughs at herself as much as she laughs at anything else. Finally she stops laughing and pats the stair next to her.

"Sit down. Now I want the real story. What happened with Janine?"

You drop your bag from Hot Vibes on the top step and then peel off your gloves and your mask. "I'm an asshole. Let's just leave it at that." You sit down next to Angie and exhale. "Are we going to smoke?"

She holds a cigarette up to her lips. "You want to smoke?"

"Yeah. I've had a crappy night."

"In that case, no. Derek told me you quit."

You glance down at the Lucky Strikes. "Why'd you buy them?"

"I've always thought it looked sexy seeing someone smoking outside a dance club."

"You're going dancing?"

She shrugs. "Maybe. Or else I'll pretend that I did and just sit right here smoking. Fantasies are usually better than the real thing."

"Not always." You reach for the pack, but Angie swipes it away.

"You've got no restraint. I know you. All or nothing." Angie wags her cigarette at you, scolding. "One smoke, and you'll be back at the habit."

"After tonight, maybe that wouldn't be such a bad thing. It might distract me from women."

"Has that worked before?"

"Not yet."

"Tell me about the costume party." She waits for you to answer. When you don't, she slips the cigarette between her lips. After one feigned inhale, she takes the cigarette out. "Think I look sexy?"

"Yes. But not because of the cigarette. You look sexier without it, in fact."

Angie narrows her eyes. "Are you flirting with me?"

"With my luck tonight, no." You have to cover with a lie before the flirting leads to any assumptions on your part or hers. "I'm only trying to bum a cigarette off you."

"My loss." Angie smiles. "You know, I quit smoking five years ago. It was right after I broke up with my girlfriend. But I still think about it sometimes. I've only dated guys since."

"Is that your way of telling me you're bi? I already guessed."

She blushes. "How'd you guess? We've never talked about it before."

"Sometimes you look at me a certain way."

Angie claps her hands over her face. She peeks out from between her fingers. "You're not supposed to notice."

"It took me a while to realize what was going on. At first I thought you were only being nice. Then it occurred to me that you were probably curious. Since you and Derek are great together, I never asked."

Angie nods. "Derek is great. But sometimes…"

"Why'd you stop dating women?"

"It wasn't intentional. I couldn't find a woman that I wanted to date. But there were plenty of guys who asked."

You wait for Angie to continue, but she only stares down at the cigarette. "I forgot to buy a lighter and I can't find a match. Got a light?"

"Upstairs."

Angie glances over at your front door. "Are you inviting me up to your place?"

"No. I think we'd both get in trouble with Derek if you came over tonight. I'm not going to be the one that gets you back on old bad habits." You couldn't look at Derek in the morning if anything happened. And you don't trust Angie or yourself tonight. You stretch out your legs and tap your black Batman boot against her sandal. She's wearing tight blue jeans. As much as you'd love to run your hand up the length of her leg, you know you can't touch her.

"As soon as I met you, I started thinking about my old bad habits," Angie admits. "You are a bad influence."

You move over a half foot, leaving a gap between her spot and yours. "Is that better? Or am I still a bad influence?"

Angie scoots to fill in the space you just left. Her hip is now sandwiched against yours—even closer than before. Close enough to get too many ideas racing through your mind. She sets her hand on your leg. "Turns out I like bad influences."

"I like Derek. I'm not coming between you two," you say. Angie settles her hand on yours. Your fingers interlace. An uncomfortable urge to kiss her makes you quickly stand up. "We shouldn't go there."

"You're right. No hand holding. It's a gateway drug." Angie sighs. "Anyway Derek already knows."

"What does he know?"

She doesn't answer until you tap your boot against her sandal. Then she looks up and says, "He said he didn't blame me for liking you. He likes you, too."

"That doesn't mean he'd be okay with me kissing you. And since when are you two talking about me?"

"Oh, you've come up more than once." Angie stands up as well. She catches your hand. "Will you invite me over if I promise not to kiss you?"

You shake your head.

"You have me over at your place all the time, you know."

"With Derek."

"And when he's in the kitchen and we're up on the patio talking, nothing happens," she argues. "It's not like I have no self-control. I only want to come up to talk."

"What if I don't want to talk?" Her grip on your hand isn't unwelcome. In fact, the touch sends a surge through your body that you have a hard time dismissing. And the longer you stare at her, the more you know that you'd go along with any of her suggestions. But Derek... "Anyway, I don't think you want to talk either."

She lets go of your hand and leans back against the stair railing. "You really are a bad influence, you know that? Even if I don't go up to your place I'm going to be thinking about what we could have done together."

"The only thing I'm going to do is take a shower and find a bed."

"That sounds like a good start." Angie touches your chest. A warm thrill races through your body; her magnetic pull is hard to resist. She laughs and then steps back from you. "Relax, I'm only teasing."

"I don't believe you." You've never wanted to kiss her more than now—if only to prove your point. But the kiss would change everything.

Angie glances back at the door behind her. "What if Derek was part of the package? Ever have a threesome with a guy?"

"No."

"Maybe you'd like it," Angie tempts.

"Thanks, but I prefer fake dicks." She laughs as you add, "They're always hard, you can pick the right size and if you add in a bullet vibe…"

Angie holds up her hands. "Okay, you win that argument." She motions to the bag from Hot Vibes. "Is that what you're hiding in there?" When you don't answer, she adds, "Can I peek?"

Do you:
A) Say good night to Angie (read on)
B) Show off your new toy (go to Chapter Thirteen, page 218)

Say good night to Angie

You pick up the bag from Hot Vibes and swing it on your wrist. "I would show you. But I think we've already crossed a few lines tonight that maybe we shouldn't have crossed."

"Whatever. We both wanted to cross those lines," Angie argues. "You know, Derek would love if I brought you upstairs to test out a new toy. He has a thing for you as much as I do, but don't tell him I told you that."

"I won't."

Angie sighs. "Don't tell me that you haven't considered the possibility."

"Maybe I've considered it," you admit.

"Then what's holding you back?"

Angie holds your gaze long enough to make you question your resolve. A one-night stand with Derek and Angie could be fun. Or it could change everything. The truth is you're too attracted to Angie to risk sleeping with her. Derek would be on the sidelines. "I need to say good night."

"Fine. Good night, you." Angie picks up the pack of cigarettes. "Tomorrow, I'm going to go back to pretending that I don't think you're hot. So, don't expect me to flirt with you."

"I won't." You smile and head down her stairs. When you reach the sidewalk, you hesitate. You know Angie's waiting for you to look back.

"Enjoy your new toy."
You hold up the bag. "I plan to."

With the lights off in your place you can clearly see across the alley to Angie and Derek's place. Their windows are open, and with their lights on you can't help but see everything. From your kitchen window you spot Angie in the bedroom. Derek is on the couch in the living room. The television screen casts his face in blue. You glance from the living room back to the bedroom and watch Angie open the drawer to her nightstand. She tosses the pack of cigarettes into the drawer and then kicks off her sandals.

As an excuse to stay in the kitchen, you go to the refrigerator and pull out a beer. Before you've even taken a sip, your gaze is focused on the bedroom again. Angie is turning down the sheets on the bed and you feel a rustling in your chest. Your desire for Angie hasn't come out of nowhere. But you've taken pains to avoid her noticing the attraction. No touching. No hugs after a shared meal. You won't even stand too close to her and you're careful not to have any conversations with her without Derek being around. No chance for any spark. And yet the attraction kept growing despite your best attempts. Tonight it's at a fever pitch. And knowing that she wants to have sex with you only makes it worse.

Guilt makes you want to look away, but still you watch her. Angie and Derek could close their blinds if they didn't want an audience. If anyone asked, your excuse would be that the window view works both ways. They know how easy it is to see into your kitchen.

The first time you met Derek was in the alley between your two buildings. After you'd introduced yourself, you'd mentioned that you could see his bedroom from your kitchen window—in case he hadn't noticed that he could count the number of beer bottles in your fridge while he was taking off his clothes. To stop him from wondering if you were a Peeping Tom, you said that you hadn't wanted to stare so you'd pulled the blinds closed whenever his light was on. He said he'd try to close his drapes if there was a reason to be discreet but that never seemed to happen.

You sip your beer and steal another glance next door. Angie's gone to the living room. Derek is still watching TV. He's got his shirt off, showing off his six pack and chiseled pecs. Derek is as meticulous about his workouts as he is about his account books. You train at the same gym, and he often spots you on weights. His shoulder-length hair falls loose about his neck and he's got a light shadowing of a beard as if he's missed his morning shave. He hardly fits the typical nine-to-five accountant image. But he does look good in a suit, and he wears glasses when he's working on the computer.

Derek's condo noticeably improved when Angie moved in. Within a few weeks of dating she'd brought some of her art collection to Derek's place, replacing the white walls with nude paintings of men and women. She specializes in oil and most of her paintings are dark, brooding figures, but your favorite is a simple charcoal sketch of a cat hanging over the dining table in the kitchen. The cat is stretched out on her back licking her paw. Aside from this piece, your other favorite is the brown-and-orange swirl of naked embracing women above the couch in the living room. In the bedroom there's another painting that often catches your eyes. Dark red-and-black lines form a naked man with an oversized, fully erect cock. In front of him, another man on his knees, bare butt to the viewer, waits with his mouth agape. Both figures are clay red on a stark black background. Angie's paintings are usually solitary figures in different poses, but the lovers are Derek's favorite.

Angie walks over to where Derek's sitting and starts to rub his shoulders. He glances up from the screen, and she leans down to kiss him. You guess that you have some time to kill, so you go to your bedroom and strip off the Batman costume. The shower steams away the day's disappointments and after five minutes you emerge hot, wet and wondering if you have enough time to wash your new toy before the first use.

After toweling off, you slip on a pair of loose boxer shorts and a black T-shirt and then head back to your dark kitchen. You unwrap your vibrator and take another sip of your beer.

The television is off across the way, but you can still clearly see Derek and Angie. They're both on the couch now, and you wonder what they're talking about. Maybe you. You watch them kiss knowing you should probably close your blinds or at least switch on your light so they could see that you are in the kitchen. But then they would know that you could see them.

Angie stands up and walks in front of Derek. He leans back on the cushions as she pulls off her shirt. Her red bra cups her ample breasts. She unhooks the bra and her breasts hang out for Derek. He reaches up to fondle the nipples and Angie leans into his touch, enjoying his hands. She pulls away to shimmy out of her tight jeans. Her red underwear is gone a moment later. Naked, she straddles Derek's lap and unzips his pants.

You feel a sudden pulse between your legs and reach inside your boxers to feel yourself. You're already wet. Probably you could get off with a little finger on your clit, but you decide to wash the vibrator anyway.

By the time your toy is scrubbed with scalding hot water, Angie is on her knees in front of Derek. Her head is bent over his lap, cock in her mouth. Derek pumps his hips up rhythmically, pushing deep with every thrust. Then when you think she's going to get him off with the blow job alone, she stops abruptly. She wipes her lips and stands up, brushing a fingertip up the length of Derek's erection before heading to the bedroom.

Derek stands up and pulls up his pants, but the erection sticks out so he keeps a hold of his belt as he shuffles to the bedroom. Angie has disappeared to the bathroom. You sit down at the kitchen table with your vibrator and your beer.

In the bedroom, Derek drops his pants and slips out of his shirt. He walks over to the dresser and finds a condom. You watch as he unwraps it. Angie comes out of the bathroom, glances at Derek and then without saying anything goes over to the bed. She stretches out on her belly and looks over her shoulder to watch Derek.

The anticipation of what's coming has your body tense. You sip the beer and part the slit of your boxers to touch yourself, enjoying the slickness that quickly coats your hand.

Once the condom's on, Derek goes over to dim the lights. You can still make out Angie's figure on the bed, but the details are blurred. Derek's at the edge of the bed now. He rubs Angie's back and then pushes her legs apart. Angie goes up on her elbows. She says something, and Derek looks down at the crevice between her legs. Then he pulls her body roughly toward his cock and nudges her with the tip. She rubs her pussy back and forth on him until he climbs into bed behind her. He keeps his grip on her hips and bounces his erection against her a few times until she parts her legs further. Her butt juts up in the air as she leans all the way forward. Her chest is on the pillows, and she grips the wrought-iron bedframe. Her back arches when he pushes into her.

You switch on the vibrator and tug down your boxers. Derek's backside bounces up and down on the bed and Angie holds tight to the bedframe, her face turned away from you and Derek's cock deep inside her. Parting your knees, you pick the low setting and brush the head over your clit. Angie's body rocks forward with every thrust from Derek, and the bedframe knocks against the wall. You turn the vibrator up a notch and feel a warm buzz start.

Derek's working faster now, near his own climax. With the vibrator on high you feel your own climax close. Every few thrusts you slip the tip inside, the nubbed shaft adding an arousing texture. Even without the image across the alleyway your nerves are at full attention. You slide your middle finger inside and hold the vibrator on your clit to bring you to the edge. The climax races through you as you squeeze your legs tight on the vibrator. Your jaw clenches and you close your eyes.

When you open your eyes, you immediately look to Angie and Derek's room. Derek is lying on Angie's back. It looks as if he's got her pinned in a wrestling match. Naked wrestling. The sheets are bunched down at the foot of the bed and both pillows are on the floor now. You imagine the smell in their room, the sweaty, musky scent of sex. When Derek sits up, you can see that they're still tied together, and he takes his time sliding out. He goes to the bathroom, probably to take off his condom, and

Angie rolls over. She lies on her side for a moment, staring at the bathroom door, then rolls over onto her back and starts to finger her clit.

Derek comes out of the bathroom. His dick flops down between his legs. The erection is gone, exhausted in a climax inside Angie. He looks down at his spent cock and then lays down on his back next to Angie. She runs her hand up and down his chest and his lips curve up in a soft smile as his face relaxes. Wholly satisfied. Angie gets up after a few minutes and switches off the lights.

You set your new toy down on the kitchen table and slip your hand under your boxers to press your index finger on your clit, enjoying an aftershock. Your phone beeps with a text. You glance at the screen and Angie's message: "Did you enjoy the show?"

You swallow hard, feeling your heart thump in your throat. Somehow, she knew you'd watch.

This is the end of your adventure.

CHAPTER THIRTEEN

Show Angie your toy

"Showing off sex toys is weird," you say.

"You have no grounds to say what is weird, Batman," Angie contends. "Come on, show me."

Why Hot Vibes picked bright teal to discreetly package purchases is a mystery. If they'd gone with a simple brown paper bag you could pretend you'd brought home takeout or a bottle of wine. But there's no hiding the truth with teal. Angie picks up the bag and looks inside. "Don't worry, I've bought my share of toys. I won't judge. I just want to know what you like." She pulls the vibrator out of the bag and reads the bright red lettering on the package: "Orgasmic Pleasure Nubs. Fully Waterproof in all Seven Modes. Well, damn, you had me at nubs. But seven modes?"

If Derek suddenly appears, you're going to have to explain your taste in vibrators along with why you're dressed up like Batman. And Derek would never let you live down your costume gaffe. You start to pull the package out of her hands, but she tugs it back. She spins away from you and opens the plastic wrapping. Soon she's holding out the toy and running her fingers over the nubs.

"Who needs seven modes?" She switches on the power, and when nothing happens, she looks over at you. "Tell me you bought batteries."

You reach into the bag and hand over the batteries. Angie doesn't take long to have the vibrator assembled. The low hum is unmistakable. She presses the button again and grins as the speed increases. She holds it up in the air. "God, this thing has a lot of power." She hits the button again. "Oh, look, now it's pulsing. I wonder what the seventh mode is. Maybe I do want all seven modes. Think we should try it out together?"

"I think you're dangerous."

Angie grins and points the vibrator at you. She presses the button again, and the speed of the vibrations increases. "Scared?"

You grab the shaft, trying to turn off the power. She fights off your fingers and the vibrator hums on. Angie laughs. "How about we count to ten and whoever's holding this decides what we do next. One, two, three..."

"Four, five, six," you continue the count, bracing your stance. Laughing, Angie falls against you, but she keeps her hold on the toy. The tug-of-war game is on. You hear a car door slam and then footsteps coming up the sidewalk. One of the college kids who lives in your building is probably coming home. You imagine their face when they spot you and Angie—head scratching as they try to figure out the object in the center of the game. But you won't give up your hold on the vibrator.

"Seven, eight," Angie says, stepping back to gain a stronghold.

"No way," you say. "Nine, ten." You jerk quickly, and the vibrator slips out of Angie's hands.

"Maybe I wanted you to win." She steps forward and kisses you.

Her lips are hot against yours. You know full well how dangerous kissing her is, especially with the strong scent of alcohol on her breath, but you lean in, wanting more. You slip your hand behind her neck as she moves closer. Her lips part, and your tongue brushes against hers. The desire in her kiss has you floating.

Angie pulls back suddenly as someone coughs. She glances down the stairs, and her hand swings up to cover her mouth.

You follow her gaze. Standing in the middle of the sidewalk is Janine. She's still in the red dress. Her eyes are locked on you. Your heart pounds. "Janine."

"I don't know what I was thinking," Janine says. She turns around, heading back to her car.

Running has never been your sport but you bolt down the sidewalk and catch up to Janine before she can unlock her car. "Wait. Don't leave. That was a stupid mistake. We were only messing around."

Janine's gaze drops to the humming vibrator. You switch off the power in a hurry, feeling a flush race up your neck and face.

"Messing around?" She glances back at Angie and turns to you. "What the hell? You think I'm going to believe that?"

"There's no good way to explain it but I promise that kiss didn't mean anything."

"Really? I'm certain there's some good explanation." Janine's smile is tight-lipped. "I don't know why I'm here. I had this thought that maybe you'd gone home sulking and were already in bed. Alone. What was I thinking?"

"Well, I was sulking," you admit. "So I went to the sex shop." You hold up the vibrator. "Waterproof in seven modes."

"And Angie?"

"That was…nothing. She wants a one-night stand. I already told her that it wasn't going to be me."

"And now you're going to tell me that was your first kiss?"

"Well, yeah…Nothing's going on with Angie. I promise. I know what it looked like, but it was nothing. I'm not getting between her and Derek." You pause. "Look, I'm sorry about tonight. I shouldn't have left. But I couldn't imagine walking in to that party like this. Like Batman."

"How long have you and Angie…" Janine stops. She shakes her head. "I knew she had a thing for you, but I didn't think you'd go there."

"That was the first time we kissed, I promise. And the last," you add. You feel sick and hope that Janine will believe you.

"She's only looking to hook up with someone tonight. With a woman. She and Derek talked about it and everything."

"I guess I'm the dummy who told you to make me jealous." She glances at the stairs. Angie is gone, but the pack of Lucky Strikes is still on the top step. "Honestly I'm surprised something hasn't happened between you two earlier. I've seen the way you look at each other…But you have terrible timing."

"I'm sorry."

"I don't think sorry is enough tonight." Janine sighs.

"That's it? You want to break up?"

Janine doesn't answer. After a moment she reaches for your utility belt and traces the outline of bat wings. "Why Batman?"

"Trust me, I wish I could go back in time and pick out a different costume. I really am sorry. For everything."

"I know you're sorry. But tonight I needed to know if you were serious—if we were serious—before this got any further. And I got my answer." Janine's green eyes glisten. "I wish it was a different answer, but now at least we both know."

"We can work through all of this."

"I can't." She steps forward as if she's about to kiss you but only caresses your cheek. The feel of her hand on your skin makes your heart drop. You want so much more. "Don't call me," she says. "I'm going to need some time to get over you."

And then she's gone. The tires screech as she pulls away from the curb and guns it down the block. Unable to move, you stare at your black boots. Minutes pass and the street is still quiet. She isn't coming back, and you don't blame her.

"I already know what you're going to say," Angie starts.

When you heard the knock on your front door, you didn't wonder who would be on the other side. You knew it'd be Angie. Now you lean against the doorframe hoping that she won't ask to come in. If she asks, you'll say yes. But if she doesn't ask, what happens next won't be your fault. "What am I going to say?"

"First you'll say that you don't want company. Then you'll tell me that you're going to bed."

Confirming her guesses won't help your case. She'll only gloat. "So why'd you come over?"

"Because you're wrong. You do want company." Angie hands you a bottle of whiskey. "And I like you in pajamas. You're less intimidating in pajamas."

"When am I intimidating?"

"In those suits you wear." Angie runs her hand down the front of your chest. Too late, you step back and she strides past you with a smug look. She knows exactly what her touch does to you—your brain cuts off and your body goes on autopilot. "But you look hot in a suit."

Ignoring a compliment is easy. Ignoring your body's response to Angie is more difficult. Everything about her is complicated: how she *accidentally* brushes against you, how she stares too long, even how she smells. Her perfume mixes with the musky scent of her body just enough to make you want to lean close to decipher the blend.

"You shouldn't be here."

"Are you asking me to leave?" Angie sinks down on the sofa and kicks off her sandals. She tucks her feet up underneath her and leans back.

It isn't too late to send her home to Derek. But you want company. Her company. You hold up the bottle of whiskey. "Am I getting us shot glasses or are we drinking this on the rocks?"

"On the rocks. I want to go slow and enjoy it."

Reluctantly you close the front door and head to the kitchen for two glasses. The lights are off in Derek and Angie's place. Maybe Derek knows that Angie's here. Of course, she could have come up with a good story—you just got dumped and needed comforting. If so, he's gone to bed blissfully ignorant. Or maybe Angie told him about the kiss and he went out to a bar to find his own company. The ice clinks against the glass as you pour the whiskey. What Angie's said and what Derek knows is none of your business. She's making her own decisions. But if you kiss her again...

You hand Angie a glass and sit down. The sofa is short—only a few inches longer than a love seat—to make room for the piano. Unfortunately, that means Angie's legs are much too close to yours. Despite your best intentions to only look at her face, your mind's already undressing her, and you blame the furniture.

"I could tell Janine that I kissed you, that it was all my fault," Angie muses. "Do you think she'd come back?"

"No."

"I'm sorry," Angie says. But you know that she isn't. "But since she's out, now I can tell you that I liked your last girlfriend better anyway."

"Zombie girl? Are you kidding?" You lean back on the sofa and take a sip. "Did she ever tell you her theory about how zombies had taken over City Hall?"

"Oh, I forgot about her. She was weird but sweet—in that smoked too much weed way. And you never know about zombies. Anyway, I wasn't talking about her. I meant Max. You two used to be inseparable. What happened between you two?"

"Max was never my girlfriend. We're friends. That's it." But she's right that something happened. Things have been awkward with Max since New Year's, but you don't want to admit why. You take another sip of the whiskey, knowing that you're drinking too fast.

"Only friends...I don't believe that." Angie sets her glass down on the coffee table and shifts back on the sofa. "Truth or Dare?"

"We're not in middle school. And I know better than to play games with you."

"Just pick." When you don't answer, Angie continues, "Look, I didn't tell Derek the real reason I wanted to come here tonight. I'm not saying that I—"

"Dare," you interrupt.

"I knew you'd pick dare. You're scared of admitting things." Angie leans forward and presses her lips against yours. The kiss deepens and you forget about the look in Janine's eyes as she got in her car. You forget about the party at Katherine's house and you forget about running into Margo at the sex shop. The night's been a blur of bad decisions that you wish you could erase all memory of, and Angie's lips are helping to do just that. When you pull back, you notice her eyes are open. She's wagering everything. And she has more to lose.

"I could get used to that." She reaches for her tumbler and takes a sip. "I have to tell you that I already had two shots before I came over. So if I get too drunk..."

"What's my dare?"

"Threesome. You, Derek, me."

"No."

"You didn't even consider it," Angie complains. "Why are you against a threesome? I know you want to sleep with me."

"I didn't say that."

Angie tilts her head. "You didn't have to. Your body's been saying it all night."

You could argue, but anything you'd say would be a lie. "I don't want you to get in trouble with Derek."

"Maybe I want to get in a little trouble." Angie rests her hand on your thigh. The pajama pants are only a thin barrier as she inches her fingers toward your middle. She grabs the dangling ends of your tied waistband and tugs until the bow loosens. Slowly, she pulls the edge of your pants down far enough to see the start of your closely trimmed hair. "Are you going to stop me?"

"Not yet."

"Good."

Her hands settle on your hips, and she leans forward to kiss you again. Her mouth covers yours and she doesn't let you come up for air. Soon you stop fighting her and she pushes you back on the couch for another calculated kiss. Maybe she's taking advantage of you. Or maybe she's comforting you in exactly the right way. Guilt slips in and you shift away from Angie and stand up. "I think you should go."

Angie sighs and leans back against the sofa. You go over to the piano and sit down on the bench. The music sheets on the stand are from a German song that you wanted to play for Janine. Now you crumple the pages and toss them across the floor. Without looking at the notes, you can play the first few stanzas of several classical pieces, but you're in the mood for something else. Frank Sinatra. "That's Life." As you play, you feel Angie's hands settle on your shoulders. Her touch is light, somewhere between tickling and caressing, and she makes her way down your back and then up again before leaning close to kiss the side of your neck. Her lips send a shiver down your spine. Concentrating on the notes isn't easy. When you finish the song, you start another while pretending that Angie's lips on your neck aren't a distraction. But it's impossible to ignore the effect she has on your body.

"Threesome," Angie repeats. "I dare you."

"I've never slept with anyone on a dare."

"First time for everything. And if anyone asks, I'll say we were only playing a middle-schooler's game."

When you don't answer, Angie continues her massage. Her hands slip under your shirt. She strums over your nipples and circles around your breasts, then moves down your belly. You try to keep playing, but her hands are distracting. Her body is pressed right up against your back and the warmth of her is as arousing as her touch. She tugs your tank top up and you pause only long enough to let her undress you before going back to the music. Half-naked, you're aware that you aren't stopping her, even if you aren't helping. She slips out of her clothes and you hazard a sideways glimpse of her body. Your throat tightens and desire fills you. Her curves are gorgeous and her naked body is too tempting. When you miss a note, she notices. "Don't let me distract you."

"Too late."

She comes back to the piano bench and kisses your cheek. "I love hearing you play. Some nights you leave your window open and I can lay in bed listening to you. It's like we're in the same room." Instead of straightening up after the kiss, she lingers close so you can feel her breath against your ear.

Her hands explore you, slipping along the underside of your arms and down your ribs as slow as dripping honey. The mismatch of your fingers on the piano keys and her fingers on your body is only in the tempo. Otherwise you're playing the same song and the discord of it all makes you reckless for more of her touch. Soon she's pushing the waistband down on your pajama pants and her warm hands dip between your legs as she saddles up behind you on the bench. You scoot forward so there's enough room for her, aware that still you aren't stopping her. Her naked chest rubs against your back, causing you to miss another note. You cuss softly and she chuckles. Clearly she likes the effect she's having on you.

"How long can you keep playing?" she asks. "If I touch you here..." Her fingers find your wet slit and she unabashedly thrusts a finger inside. You squeeze your legs together at the sudden entry. What she lacks in skill, she's making up for in bravado. Yes, she has you dripping, but you'd like a little finesse in your fuck buddy if that's what she's auditioning for. You stop playing and turn to find her lips. There's a limit to your self-control, and she's found it.

When she pulls you to the bedroom, you don't argue. The lights are off. You stumble, kiss her again, and then she's lying on your bed and you're tumbling on top of her. There's no time to push down the sheets. The comforter wrinkles up around her body as she pulls you into another kiss. Her lips are greedy, asking for more every time you start to pull away. She manages to get your pajama pants off and her fingers plunge between your legs again. Skin against skin, you lose yourself in her curves, kissing nipples, thighs, and belly indiscriminately while she drives inside you hard enough to make your eyes water. You wish she had better skill, or accidentally bumped your begging clit, but despite her novice moves she's getting you close.

Close, but not all the way. You take a risk and spin on her body so your crotch is in her face. Without checking in on her, you dip your head between her legs. If she doesn't like the position, she'll let you know as soon as your tongue tests her. A long, low moan is confirmation enough, but she juts up her hips, asking for more. Her tongue rasps over your clit. She could be anyone tonight. You only need to get off. Tomorrow you can figure out the consequences.

You suck her clit between your lips and savor the taste. The musky scent of her sex has your senses in overdrive. Turning circles into sideways swipes on her clit, you lick faster, gaining intensity as she bounces her pussy off the mattress and into your waiting lips. As her groans increase, you grind down on her mouth. She drives her tongue inside your wet hole and then holds steady pressure on your clit. Your orgasm comes in an impulsive spasm. You moan, letting her know that she's got you good, before thrusting your tongue down hard on her clit. She squeezes her legs around your face, murmuring her satisfaction as her climax hits a moment later.

You stay on her, holding steady on her clit until her legs relax. Wiping your lips, you roll off and settle back on the pillows. Angie pulls the comforter over your body and then curls up against you. It was over so quick you could almost pretend nothing happened. But you both got off and now you're wondering if she'd stay for another round.

"I'm not sleeping here. I'm going home to Derek."

"Okay." You aren't certain how you'll face Derek. Maybe Angie will lie about everything, and maybe you'll never have to admit it either. But there's no denying that you screwed him over.

"So when are we going to have a threesome with Derek?"

"I never agreed to that dare."

"It was implied." Angie kisses your cheek. "We had sex. It's only fair that he's included next time. I'm not going to have an affair with you and not tell him. I can't lie to him. And I don't want it to be a one-time thing with you."

"You don't have to lie. Tell him we screwed up. And it won't happen again."

"Is that what you want?" Angie shifts onto her elbow and looks down on you.

"No."

"Me neither." She smiles and touches your cheek. "But tell me that you don't like him—that you haven't thought about a threesome before—and I'll consider that. Just tell me the truth."

You open your mouth and then quickly close it. Yes, a lie is the first thing that came to mind. More than once you've thought about having a threesome with Derek and Angie but you hate admitting it. "Okay, yeah, maybe I've thought about it...but it was only a fantasy."

"Want to hear my fantasy? You fucking me with Derek watching. And in my fantasy, we let him play on the sidelines but he doesn't get to touch until you get me off. What happens in your fantasy?"

"I'm not telling you."

"Fine. But I know you want a threesome and this is our best way out of what happened tonight." Angie wraps her arms around you for a quick hug and then climbs out of bed. "Sleep on it. And then say yes."

Go to bed before you get into any more trouble. This is the end of your adventure.

CHAPTER FOURTEEN

The morning after

From your condo to the café is a short ten-minute walk, but your old umbrella didn't keep out the sideways rain. Soaked from the knees down, your pants cling to your legs and drip onto the black-and-white tile. You cradle your cup of tea and watch each passerby, hoping that the next black umbrella will be Janine's.

"Is that seat free?"

You look up at the man asking and shake your head. Window seats are at a premium on Sunday mornings, but you aren't going to move your book bag. He scowls and walks off.

The wind picks up, and the old single pane window rattles against its frame. Cars slow in front of the café, their windshield wipers spitting back against the gusts. Still no sign of Janine. She's ten minutes late and last night was the first time she'd been late to anything since you started dating. Maybe she won't show. There's been no text and no missed call—you've checked your phone every thirty seconds to be certain. A bell chimes and you glance at the door. An older couple hurries in, shaking off raindrops.

Hands cover your eyes and you smell Janine's eucalyptus lotion. She leans over your shoulder and kisses your cheek. "I hope you were waiting for me." She uncovers your eyes. "Because if you were expecting some other woman, this would be awkward."

You stand up. Janine's eyelashes are wet, along with her hair, and her green eyes shine. She smiles as your hands find her hips and your heart skips a beat when she cups your chin. You lean forward to kiss her, but Janine stops you.

"I told myself that I wouldn't let you kiss me," she says. "Last night I got over being mad at you, but I'm not ready for kissing."

"Okay. No kissing." In fact, she's in a better mood than you expected. But knowing she's happy brings up questions you don't want to ask. She's always in a good mood after sex.

She steps back from you and hangs her coat over the back of the chair. "Sorry I'm late. Traffic was terrible." She moves your book bag and then looks over at you. "That's my excuse. How'd it sound?"

"Believable."

"The truth is I was nervous about seeing you and changed three times."

You smile. She's wearing a loose gray T-shirt and jeans—her usual Sunday-morning attire. The rain-splashed denim hugs her curves and the loose shirt makes you long to slip your hand under the thin material.

She sits down in the chair. "And I didn't get much sleep last night. I drove and parked in the back lot. Walking seemed like a lot of work." Her lips curve with the hint of a smile.

"That explains why I didn't see you walk in, but now I'm admittedly a little jealous wondering about your sleepless night." But you resist asking for details and hand her the cup of coffee. "One sugar, no cream."

"Thank you." She takes a sip. "Perfect. I love that you know my coffee order. Remember the first time we came here?"

"When your freezer exploded?" You grin. You'd met on the sidewalk outside her apartment. Not only were you neighbors, but you had too many friends in common not to know each other better. She invited you over the next day for brunch.

"I was so distracted by you that first day…I still can't believe I put a six-pack of soda in the freezer instead of the fridge. My freezer was so full, I don't know how it even fit in there…Then the next morning, boom! And I wanted to impress you. God, that was such a mess."

"Who knew that freezers could explode?" You repeat the line Janine had said that morning.

Janine punches your arm and laughs. "I blame you entirely. You were such a flirt that day. I fell hard. Anyway, you didn't seem to mind helping me clean."

You'd crawled around on the floor with Janine, mopping up the soda with towels. And then you'd taken a shower together. By the time you decided on skipping brunch, it was after lunch.

"So, how does this go?" When you hesitate, Janine continues, "You don't have to tell me who you slept with. Word travels fast. The hardest part was when I realized you'd slipped out of the party. I wasn't sure I was going to go through with our little dare until that moment. You gave me the push I needed."

Now you want details, but you'd probably regret hearing about her tryst. "Did you have a good time?"

"I'd do it again. If you wanted to, that is." She smiles and sips her coffee. "What about you? Was she a good kisser?"

"Do I have to answer that question?"

"I did dare you to make me jealous."

"But I didn't want to," you admit. "I only wanted you."

"Me, too," Janine says.

"Wait, does that mean we aren't breaking up?"

"I made you sweat that one a little, didn't I? I never wanted to break up. I was mad. And maybe I was a little too rough on you. But I let you in and when you pulled back, I got scared. And angry."

"I'm sorry."

She nods. "I know you are…But what do we do now? I don't think we can pretend this past week didn't happen. Or that last night didn't happen. I can't go back to how things were. I want more."

"More than fancy parties with beautiful women? More than one-night stands?" You pause. "I want more, too. I want lazy

Sunday mornings in bed. I want anniversaries. I want to plan a vacation. And I want those things with you." You meet Janine's gaze. The memory of the party, of how far you'd gone, flashes in your mind. You'd only planned on kissing someone else with Janine watching—never sex. But you don't regret anything. And yet you want Janine more. "I had a good time last night. But not good enough for that to be all there is."

"There you go being sexy and charming as usual." Janine runs her fingers through your hair. "God, I loved you as Batman. Will you dress up for me later?"

You cover your face. "Don't remind me."

"Why not?" She laughs. "That costume was one of the night's highlights. Katherine wouldn't stop talking about it. She's already planning another party. A real costume party this time."

You groan as Janine laughs again. Finally, you reach for Janine's hand. Her fingers interlace with yours.

"So how much fun did you have last night without me?"

"A lot," she admits. "And, no, I'm not telling you anything more."

She pulls away and shifts back in her seat, sipping her coffee. When her hand brushes your thigh, the touch ignites your body. You keep your gaze focused on your cup of tea as her hand moves down to your knee and then up your thigh again.

"The truth is, I woke up this morning and wished I was snuggled up against you instead of sleeping next to someone I hardly knew. Yeah, I had a good time. But after flirting with everyone else, I realized you were the one I wanted. I don't need to diversify my assets."

You grin. "I like it when you talk shop. Maybe you should give me some more financial advice."

"If you take me home now, I'll guarantee your investment will pay off." Janine winks.

"Oh, really?" You laugh and lean over and pull her chair closer to yours. "I want to kiss you."

She nods. "I know you do. You've had that look in your eyes since I sat down. It's driving you crazy that I won't let you, isn't it?"

"Maybe."

"Good." She stands up. "Let's go to your place."

Before you can argue, she's halfway to the door. You find your umbrella and hurry outside. As many times as you've kissed her, now you want her more than ever.

"I'm changing out of these wet clothes," Janine says. She sheds her coat in the front hall, hangs it on her usual hook, and passes through the living room to the kitchen. After dropping off her coffee cup on the kitchen counter, she heads to the bedroom. You follow her with your eyes, watching as she strips off her T-shirt and jeans. Her socks come off next. She keeps her red silk underwear on and glances over her shoulder knowingly. Of course she expected that you'd be watching. Maybe she even wants that.

Janine doesn't have any clothes at your house—she's always careful not to leave anything. But that won't stop her from wearing your clothes. You sit down at the piano bench, waiting and wondering what she'll come out with. The nervous energy you woke with that morning hasn't dissipated. And the song that has been running through your head all morning begins a new loop. One of Janine's German songs. It took you months to track down sheet music, and you've only played it through a handful of times. You stretch your fingers before you test the keys. By the fifth time through, the familiar melody takes hold.

Janine sits down next to you on the narrow bench. She's wearing one of your button-down shirts with the buttons all undone and her red underwear. Nothing else.

"When did you learn this song?"

"I found the sheet music last week. Turns out I couldn't really take a break from you." You smile and start to play again. "Do you want to move in?" She doesn't answer. You continue playing until you reach the last stanza. "I like breakup sex, but... I'd rather have we're-moving-in-together sex."

"Who said we were having sex?" Janine taps the sheet music. "You didn't play the last few notes."

You sigh and shift back on the bench. Your hands are folded in your lap.

"How can you not play the last bit of the song?"

"Maybe I will when you finally kiss me."

"Do you know what this song is about?" Janine asks.

"No clue." You struggle to pronounce the title, as it's all in German and much too long. Janine presses her fingertip to your lips, laughing.

"It's a love song," Janine says. "But it's supposed to be funny." She points to one of the lines, but then her finger drops off the page. "Some things don't translate."

"Try."

Janine stares at you for a moment and then looks back at the sheet music. "She's saying that her lover is all that she needs. That she doesn't need to breathe or sleep."

"That's obsession. Not love."

"But then she admits that she also loves Spätzle. German noodles. And she couldn't live without Spätzle. Or beer. Here in the chorus, she says, 'I love you. I'd rather kiss you than breathe.'"

"But don't ask me to choose you over beer—don't ask me to up my Spätzle."

Janine glances at you quickly. "*Verstehst du*? You understand?"

"Not at all. How could she compare love to noodles?"

Janine laughs. "But she has a point."

"Noodles? Are you serious?"

"Not just any noodles. Spätzle." Janine wraps her arm around your waist. "Play it again."

This time, Janine sings along. She keeps her arm wrapped around you until the end. Then she lets go of you and says, "I like you more than Spätzle."

"Thank you, I think."

"Part of me was hoping that you wouldn't follow through last night," she says. "That you wouldn't sleep with someone else. Maybe a couple kisses and then you'd find me."

"Now you tell me."

You shift back on the bench, and she stands up and walks over to the window. She leans against the windowsill, and you can't help but eye the length of her legs up to where her skin disappears under the shirt hem.

"I wanted to make you jealous," Janine says. "But I didn't want you to go all the way with someone."

"You dared me."

"Knowing that you were going to beat me at my game made me want you even more. But I was pissed."

"Until you found your own lover."

Janine smiles. "I didn't say it was all bad."

You stand up from the piano bench and walk over to the window. The rain has stopped and rays of sunlight filter through the trees. The wet pavement gleams. Janine's car is parked behind yours. You touch Janine's back and she looks over her shoulder at you. "I'm in love with you."

"After last week...I want you to show me."

You feel a rush at her words. At the challenge. One step and your hands slip under the shirt to settle on her hips. Warm, smooth skin. She meets your lips when you lean in for a long kiss. Then she opens up and you feel dizzy as the kiss deepens. As she pulls away, she nips at your lip and you follow her for another kiss. Her hands are full of desire, running up and down your arms and then gripping your shoulders. She holds you tight against her, not wanting the kiss to end, claiming you. Last night was lust. But this is different.

You push the shirt off her shoulders and run your hand down the curve of her slender neck and then over to her full breasts. She pushes against you, moaning with pleasure. Her nipples harden with your touch. All of her is familiar, but something's changed, and you want to please her more than ever.

You pull her to the bedroom, but she stops in the doorway. "Before this happens, I want to tell you something." The shirt gapes open, giving you a good look at all the curves you long to touch. With effort, you look up to her face. She rolls her eyes. "Can you concentrate on something besides sex?"

"Do I have to?"

"Why did I even ask?" She crosses her arms, deliberately taking away your view of her breasts. She knows you too well. "What happened last night, I don't think it was a mistake. But I think we both need to promise that it won't happen again unless we talk about it beforehand…and we agree it's something we both want."

You nod.

"I'm not sure that I want to share you again," Janine continues. "I might want you all to myself every night."

"Every night—but the days are free?"

Janine swats at your chest. "You're lucky I know that you're joking."

"Who said I was joking?"

Janine walks over to your dresser. She pulls open a drawer and begins rifling through your underwear. "Where are those handcuffs?"

When you come up behind her, she laughs and tries to slip away. You catch her hand and pull her toward you. "Come here."

She lets you have another kiss and then pulls away. "Make me a bath."

"What? Why?"

"Because I want a bath."

Waiting for sex isn't something you've ever been good at, but when you try to change Janine's mind about the bath, she only crosses her arms. Stubborn. And sexy as hell.

The water rumbles in the pipes and you stick your toe in the stream to test the temperature. Through the open door you can make out the curve of Janine's back down to the middle of her thigh. She's still wearing the red underwear, but she's hung your shirt back in the closet. Always neat. She turns around and notices you staring. Somehow, the familiarity of her body makes it even more arousing. You know exactly which places to lick to make her moan. And it's been too long since you last pressed your body against hers. You add bubbles to the water and watch the tub fill.

Janine's hand brushes your shoulder. Before you have a chance to appreciate the length of her naked body, she's slipping into the bubbles.

"Join me," she insists.

It doesn't take you long to strip and Janine watches your every move. Once you're naked, she reaches up with a wet finger to slide along the inside of your leg. You settle in at Janine's feet, feeling her toes wiggle against your thigh. The hot water steams the bathroom and clouds the mirror. Janine leans her head back against the edge of the tub.

"Isn't this nice?"

"So is sex," you argue.

She splashes water at your chest and then sinks lower in the water. You find her feet and begin a massage, working up from her heels to her calves. She closes her eyes. The red streak of hair is tucked behind one ear and she's still wearing the earrings from last night. You wonder again who she slept with, who enjoyed her body. But she came back to you. If last night didn't change your mind about wanting Janine, maybe it didn't change her mind either. But still you have doubts. Why did she dare you in the first place?

When you've finished the leg massage, you lean back against the tub, studying Janine's face. Her eyes are closed and her expression is soft. Last night plays in your mind. Maybe you won't be the same again after what you did.

Janine splashes water at you. "Why are you so serious all of a sudden?"

"How do you know I'm serious? Your eyes are closed," you argue.

"I know you." She laughs and leans forward to find your lips. After a long kiss she stands and reaches for her towel. "I hope you aren't having second thoughts, because I want a whole body massage now. I'll be waiting in bed for you."

By the time you've dried off, Janine is stretched out on your bed. The soft curves and hard angles of her body fill you with familiar want. You sit down on the edge of the bed and run your hand over the length of her leg. She looks up and smiles.

"No second thoughts."

"Good." Janine pulls you toward her. The length of her body fits perfectly under yours. You move into her lips and her breasts press against your chest. One kiss follows another as you move between her legs. She's freshly waxed and her slick pussy grinds your thigh until you're drunk on the thought of pushing into her with your fingers. But you won't give yourself that pleasure yet. Instead you lean down and stroke her nipple with your tongue. She moans and pulls you up to her lips.

After a long kiss she pushes you roughly away from her and takes your hand down to her groin. "Now I want this inside," she says. Her passive bedroom personality is gone. And the new Janine is a complete turn-on.

She parts her legs, waiting for you. Glistening wet, her pussy is impossibly ready. But you don't give her what she wants yet. As you slip along the edge of her slit, she closes her eyes and thrusts her hips off the mattress. Still you avoid her clit and keep your fingers from dipping into her.

"I want it inside," she complains.

"I thought you liked waiting."

"Fuck you," she says. She grabs your wrist and tries to push your fingers.

You pull your hand away from her groin and bring your fingertip up to her lips. She licks the length of your middle finger. With no encouragement, she sucks two more fingers into her mouth. Watching her lick your fingers has your clit pulsing in rapid fire. You pull your hand away from her lips and then move between her legs again. She pushes back against the pillows when you shove three fingers in at once.

"Oh..." she moans. "I like that."

You thrust deeper and push your hips forward. Her body is pressed tightly against yours. Bracing one hand on your shoulder and the other on the bedframe, she bucks on the bed, surging into you. You keep pace with her, stroking in and out until your own clit is pulsing. Your knuckles hit her pelvic bone and you know she can't take all of you. But then she cocks up one knee and when you thrust your hand again, four fingers slide in. She cries out and bites your shoulder. Her muscles clench up on you and you hold your position as she cusses. Then you hear her husky whisper of, "Give me a little more."

You work her until your arm aches. She's panting and thrusting her hips up and down, timed with the thrust of your hand. You've never fisted her before, but you know that's what she needs.

Her chest rises and falls with her breath, breasts waiting for your touch and nipples perked with the cool draft in the room. You trace the line of her jaw and then turn her face to yours and kiss her. Her familiar taste is everything you've wanted for the past week. And you can't seem to get enough. You shift between her legs and run your free hand along the inside of her thigh and back to her middle.

She shoves her hips up. "God, I want to come."

"We'll get to that."

"I want to get to that now." She grabs your wrist. "All the way…"

"Not until you're ready."

Janine lifts her hips up, but you only kiss her. She huffs and drops back. "I want more." She narrows her eyes. "You have me wet enough to do anything for it."

"Anything?" You try to inch your hand forward again, but you bump against the rim and she cries out and quickly shifts her hips back.

A moment later, she moves into you again. "More," she says, biting her lower lip.

You change the angle so your thumb can slide in when she's ready and then find her lips. Gripping your arms, her nails dig into your skin. One kiss after another, you keep pace with her rocking, nudging her but not all the way inside yet. Her muscles clench and release rhythmically, trying to draw you in. She shifts her hips up, and finally you shove your knuckles in. She holds onto you, groaning as your hand disappears into her, enveloped in a velvet glove. You turn your wrist and she gasps.

"I've got you," you say, slipping your free hand under her backside and tilting her hips up to you. She moans with the slight turn of your wrist. Then, as her body relaxes more, you thrust deeper. Her hands clutch at your arm and her breathing is ragged as you make short strokes in her. She rocks her hips, bearing down and moaning with pleasure. Every few thrusts she tries to sit up, eyeing your hand buried deep before she sinks back again.

"Oh, God, that feels good."

Collapsed back against the mattress, she's finally given up trying to control you. Her muscles are quivering. You know she's about to come. Her head tilts back and you watch her mouth open as she moans.

You reach down with your other hand to find her clit. In a few strokes she comes hard. Her legs squeeze tight around your wrist. You hold her body against yours as the climax courses through her, your hand still deep inside, and then a moment later she's limp in your arms. Several minutes pass before she opens her eyes.

"God, that felt good." Her voice is quiet and the words slurred. "Why haven't you done that before?"

"I didn't know you could take it."

"No one's fisted me before. You're my first." Her eyes are closed and her face is relaxed. Golden afternoon light seeps in through the bedroom window and plays on her skin.

"I love fucking you." She's yours now more than ever before. "You're beautiful."

You kiss her lips. Lazy, long kisses until she's distracted and you can slowly inch your hand out. Her muscles tense, and you have to wait for a release. Once your knuckles slip free she moans and squeezes her legs together. You wrap your arms around her.

"I want to fall asleep and wake up and have you do that all over again."

You kiss her shoulder and then the side of her neck. "You're going to be sore."

"I don't care. I want to be too sore to move," she says. "I'll call in sick tomorrow. Then I can stay in bed all day. And you'll have to stay home to take care of my needs." She smiles. "You can fist me whenever you want. Before breakfast. After coffee. Before lunch. I'll spread my legs every time you walk by, hoping that you'll stop what you're doing and walk over and fuck me. Maybe you'll run errands, get groceries, and you'll come home to find me laying on your bed naked. Waiting for you. I'll sleep for a few hours and wake up to your hand pushing inside me."

"Damn, now I want to fuck you all over again."

"Good. That was my plan." She reaches for your hand and kisses your palm. "And then later I get you. I know exactly where to touch you," she promises. "I can't wait to return the favor. Unfortunately, I can't move at the moment." Her fingers play up and down your arm. "You know, I don't want anyone else. Only you." She kisses your cheek and whispers, "I love you."

"I love you, too." And you know that the words count this time.

Bella Books, Inc.
Happy Endings Live Here
P.O. Box 10543
Tallahassee, FL 32302
Phone: (800) 729-4992
www.bellabooks.com

More Titles from Bella Books

Hunter's Revenge – Gerri Hill
978-1-64247-447-3 | 276 pgs | paperback: $18.95 | eBook: $9.99
Tori Hunter is back! Don't miss this final chapter in the acclaimed
Tori Hunter series.

Integrity – E. J. Noyes
978-1-64247-465-7 | 28 pgs | paperback: $19.95 | eBook: $9.99
It was supposed to be an ordinary workday...

The Order – TJ O'Shea
978-1-64247-378-0 | 396 pgs | paperback: $19.95 | eBook: $9.99
For two women the battle between new love and old loyalty may prove
more dangerous than the war they're trying to survive.

Under the Stars with You – Jaime Clevenger
978-1-64247-439-8 | 302 pgs | paperback: $19.95 | eBook: $9.99
Sometimes believing in love is the first step. And sometimes it's all
about trusting the stars.

The Missing Piece – Kat Jackson
978-1-64247-445-9 | 250 pgs | paperback: $18.95 | eBook: $9.99
Renee's world collides with possibility and the past, setting off a tidal
wave of changes she could have never predicted.

An Acquired Taste – Cheri Ritz
978-1-64247-462-6 | 206 pgs | paperback: $17.95 | eBook: $9.99
Can Elle and Ashley stand the heat in the *Celebrity Cook Off* kitchen?